L

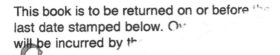

Reviewing Sex

Gender and the Reception of Victorian Novels

Nicola Diane Thompson
Senior Lecturer in the Department of English
Kingston University

MACMILLAN

First published 1996 by
MACMILLAN PRESS LTD
Houndmills, Basingstoke, Hampshire RG21 6XS
and London
Companies and representatives
throughout the world

ISBN 0–333–62216–2 hardcover
ISBN 0–333–62217–0 paperback

A catalogue record for this book is available
from the British Library.

10   9   8   7   6   5   4   3   2   1
05 04 03 02 01 00 99 98 97 96

Printed and bound in Great Britain by
Antony Rowe Ltd
Chippenham, Wiltshire

To Caroline and Georgina

Contents

List of Plates

1 Charles Reade, "Something Like a Novelist", from *Once a Week*, 20 January 1872.
2 Charles Reade at his writing table, by Charles Mercier (reproduced courtesy National Portrait Gallery).
3 Charlotte Yonge's writing desk in her room at Elderfield (reproduced courtesy W. T. Greene).
4 Charlotte Yonge aged 20, by George Richmond, R.A. (reproduced courtesy National Portrait Gallery).
5 Group of contemporary writers: George MacDonald, J. A. Froude, Wilkie Collins, Anthony Trollope, W. M. Thackeray, Lord Macaulay, Edward Bulwer Lytton, Thomas Carlyle and Charles Dickens.

Acknowledgements

I would like to thank my family, colleagues, former teachers, and friends – all of whom, in different ways, have made this book possible.

Two of my former teachers, R. T. Jones of the University of York and Jim Cogan of Westminster School, are principally responsible for my decision to pursue literary studies in general and Victorian literature in particular. I am grateful to each of them as well as to subsequent teachers and colleagues for providing me with inspirational role models.

Many people have read and commented on numerous drafts and revisions of this book over the last few years, and I don't think I could have written it without them. Walter Reed's support and intellectual engagement from the project's inception have been invaluable. Elizabeth Fox-Genovese's faith in the potential of this work sustained me at some difficult moments; I'm grateful for her intellectual support throughout, and in particular for her suggestions on the Introduction. Thanks also to Jerome Beaty for advice on planning the research, parameters, and methodology of the book. The following people have made the last few years much easier with their encouragement and their helpful comments on final drafts: Martin Danahay, Tim Thompson, Tim Raylor, Ellen Gainor, David Faulkner, and, most of all, Thom Bunting. And I would also like to thank John Sitter for his inspirational wit at the 1993 Convention of the Modern Language Association.

A grant from the English-Speaking Union allowed me to conduct research at the British Museum Library and the London Library, and I am grateful for their assistance. I am also indebted to Marie Nitschke of Emory University Library for her generous help with literary detective work at the early stages of this project, when I was feeling overwhelmed by the task of identifying and collecting so many Victorian book reviews and articles.

I would like to thank Tim Farmiloe and Charmian Hearne of Macmillan, as well as Niko Pfund of New York University Press, for their faith in the book project.

A version of Chapter 3 appeared in *Women's Studies: An Interdisciplinary Journal*, vol. 24, no. 4 (1995), and a version of Chapter 4 appeared in *Victorian Literature and Culture*, 22 (1995). I thank the publishers of these journals for permission to reprint.

THE
ATHENÆUM

JOURNAL OF ENGLISH AND FOREIGN

Literature, Science, and Fine Arts.

PART CCCLXXXV.

FOR THE MONTH OF JANUARY,

1860.

LONDON:

PRINTED BY J. HOLMES, 4, TOOK'S COURT, CHANCERY LANE.

PUBLISHED BY J. FRANCIS,

AT THE OFFICE, 14, WELLINGTON STREET NORTH, STRAND;

AND SOLD BY

ALL BOOKSELLERS AND NEWSMEN IN TOWN AND COUNTRY.

AGENTS: FOR SCOTLAND, BELL & BRADFUTE, EDINBURGH; FOR IRELAND, MR. JOHN ROBERTSON, DUBLIN.

PRICE 1s. 4d.

The Athenæum, January 1860 (the British Library)

JANUARY MDCCCLXX.

BLACKWOOD'S
Edinburgh
MAGAZINE.

Nº. DCLI.

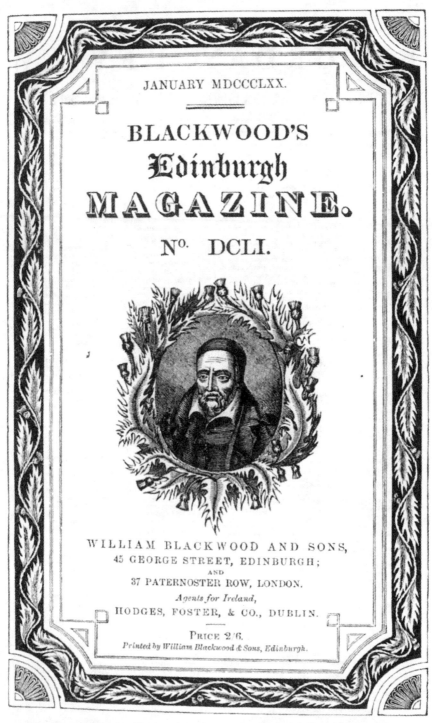

WILLIAM BLACKWOOD AND SONS,
45 GEORGE STREET, EDINBURGH;
AND
37 PATERNOSTER ROW, LONDON.

Agents for Ireland,
HODGES, FOSTER, & CO., DUBLIN.

PRICE 2/6.
Printed by William Blackwood & Sons, Edinburgh.

Blackwood's Edinburgh Magazine, January 1870 (the British Library)

THE
SATURDAY REVIEW
OF
POLITICS, LITERATURE, SCIENCE, AND ART.

No. 1,785, Vol. 69.   January 11, 1890.   [Registered for Transmission abroad.]   Price 6d.

CHRONICLE.

Home Politics. IN home politics there is even less to record this week than there was last, no event corresponding to Mr. GLADSTONE's birthday having occurred. Perhaps the most noteworthy incidents in this division during, at least, the earlier part of the week, were two speeches delivered, in the one case by a member, in the other by an independent supporter, of the Government, which show evidence of somewhat unsound politics in the speakers. Sir EDWARD CLARKE, at Plymouth, besides indulging in some rather claptrap, though not absolutely heretical, remarks concerning prizefighting peers and superannuated bishops, is reported (but not in all the reports) to have made the singular observation that the quarter of a million just given by Sir EDWARD GUINNESS for the benefit of the working classes would be better in the pockets of the working classes themselves. Looked at in one light, this remark is a truism, or even a platitude ; looked at in another, it would seem to be one of those unwise attempts at outbidding Radicals which Tories of the unsounder kind sometimes make. Lord DUNRAVEN, at Liverpool, appears to have exhibited a similar unwisdom by advocating the Eight Hours movement ; but Lord DUNRAVEN, though by no means wanting in ability, has never been particula..ly noted for political judgment. On the other side Mr. ASQUITH, whose capacity ought not to miss recognition on account of the exaggerations of it by his friends, has repeated that demand for some explanation of Mr. GLADSTONE's present attitude to Home Rule which has so much annoyed Gladstonian wirepullers. Were the Gladstonian championship of Home Rule honest, it would be, of course, impossible to refuse this demand. If it is still refused, the inference is too clear to need drawing.

Affairs Abroad. Very important, if true, intelligence was received on Monday from South Africa, the good news that Consul JOHNSTON has succeeded in restoring order on the "Stevenson road," or line of communication between Lakes Nyassa and Tanganyika, to the north of the former lake, being tempered by the still more detailed intelligence of the violence put upon the Makololo by the Portuguese in order to make them discard the English flag. It has also been rumoured, with great probability, that LOBENGULA and other powerful native chiefs of Matabeleland and its neighbourhood are arming, with views that would appear by no means friendly to either of the rival claimants to "influence" in their districts. Some important contributions have been made to the discussion as well as to the knowledge of the subject, the chief of these being a long letter from the well-known and accomplished traveller and hunter, Mr. SELOUS, which deals with the Portuguese pretensions historically as well as actually. But the hearts of the Portuguese are said to be hardened. Meanwhile, that "union of hearts" of which Mr. GLADSTONE's followers prattle so prettily has been illustrated by the fact that the principal Irish Parnellite newspaper speaks of "piratical English Companies," and chuckles over the *canard* that German officers have been torpedoing the Tagus. A real "German officer" could have told these good persons that England is not likely to strike at Lisbon. In Portugal itself attention has been much occupied by the funeral of the Empress of BRAZIL ; but the sister country has experienced a Ministerial crisis which might have been taken more seriously abroad if the opinion that Spanish Ministerial crises are a kind of periodical necessity were not so well established. Much more attention has been paid to the serious illness of the youthful King of SPAIN. Russia has, it appears, taken the new financial arrangements of Bulgaria in serious dudgeon, the ostensible cause of protest being that the pledging of the railway revenues is *ultra*

vires according to the Berlin Treaty, the real, no doubt, being dislike at the assistance rendered to the obnoxious *de facto* Government of the Principality. A very similar spirit still delays French assent to the Conversion of the Egyptian Debt, the demands of the French Government being apparently thought excessive by England. An old wound appears to have been re-opened by the dissensions of the German and Czech parties in Bohemia ; but probably little would have been heard of this in a busier state of politics.

England and Turkey. Strong efforts continue to be made by the representatives of the Atrocity-mongers of thirteen years ago to excite public feeling against the Turks in respect of the alleged condition of Crete, Armenia, and other parts of the SULTAN's dominions, the chief allegation being, apparently, that the recent Cretan amnesty does not give a free pardon, retrospective and prospective, to offenders against the ordinary law. These efforts have received from the Earl of CARNARVON countenance which is more curious than surprising. Lord CARNARVON, who (chivalrously neglecting the unkind attacks recently made on him in Gladstonian quarters as an editor) has written to the *Times* asking whether, "by conniving at the acts" of the Porte, there is not "a danger of setting aside one of the "eternal laws of right and justice," is one of the most estimable of English noblemen ; but, setting aside other considerations, he does not appear to have appreciated the proverb that a door must be open or shut. If England is to dictate peremptorily to the SULTAN how his laws are to be administered, what his amnesties are to include, and so forth, England must be ready to expend her last soldier, her last ship, and her last shilling in defending the Porte against enemies all and sundry. Is Lord CARNARVON prepared to do that ? He was not, if we remember rightly, a few years ago.

The Colonies and India. In Australian affairs the Colonial public has been most occupied by the arrival of Lord HOPETOUN at his Government, to be received with a most loyal and friendly welcome, and a demand note for rather more than a thousand pounds of Customs' duties. Hostilities are still going on in India with the wilder tribes on different parts of the frontier, but nothing of much importance has occurred. The complete pacification of Burmah is apparently still a long way off ; and it may be surmised without injustice that as yet not exactly the right man has been found for the right place there.

Mr. Stanley. Yet another letter has been received from Mr. STANLEY. Mr. STANLEY's industrious pen containing some picturesque, but not uninteresting, remarks on the various native powers surrounding the Nyanzas, on missionaries, and on the virtues of Scotchmen. At the same time, and from the same neighbourhood of Zanzibar, news has been received of severe fighting between the Germans and the natives, in which the success of Major WISSMANN would appear to have been chequered and indecisive. All sorts of rumours have been set flying as to the safety or overthrow of Dr. PETERS, but some of these are demonstrably false, and others are too uncertain in date to be of much importance.

The Influenza. The influenza still continues to be a subject of great interest and of still greater apparent attention both abroad and at home. While Lord SALISBURY's attack was announced as abating, news was brought from Germany of the seizure of the aged Empress-Dowager AUGUSTA, and as the disease has been more severe hitherto on the Continent than with us, and is said to be peculiarly dangerous to persons advanced in years, great apprehension was entertained. This apprehension was justified by the death of the EMPRESS on Wednesday. Her name

Introduction

When *Scenes of Clerical Life* appeared anonymously in 1853, the *Saturday Review* pictured its author, George Eliot, as a bearded Cambridge clergyman and, moreover, the revered father of at least several children. When *Wuthering Heights*, written by Ellis Bell, was published in 1847, critics remarked the "rough, shaggy, uncouth power" (*Literary World*, p. 243)[1] of the book and claimed the author was a man. However, as one reviewer put it, he was "not a gentleman" but probably a "rough sailor" and one who would never be able to "understand women" (quoted in Ohmann, 1971, p. 908). Trollope's *Barchester Towers* was praised by the *Westminster Review*[2] in 1857 as "decidedly the cleverest novel of the season, and one of the most masculine delineations of modern life . . . that we have seen for many a day". When ten years later Trollope published two novels anonymously, *Nina Balatka* and *Linda Tressel*, the *London Review* argued that internal "evidence" required the author to be female: "Linda Tressel seems to us altogether a woman's woman" (quoted in Smalley, 1969, p. 20). By 1884 *The Literary World*[3] stated a commonly held view that "Thackeray was written for men and women, and Trollope for women" ("About Novels", p. 275).

As Hans Jauss reminds us, the reception and evaluation of a literary work necessarily occurs within an "horizon of expectations". There exists, that is, an "objectifiable system of expectations that arises for each work in the historical moment of its appearance" ("Literary History", p. 166). This book examines a particular interpretive horizon – gender – as it operated in the "historical moment" of mid-century Victorian England, within the Victorian institution of the literary review. Gender was not only an analytical category used by Victorian reviewers to conceptualize, interpret, and evaluate novels, but in some cases the primary category. Focusing upon the assumptions about sexual identity and writing that structured the fictional contract between mid-nineteenth-century authors, readers, and literary reviewers, I analyse the role of the Victorian literary review (and of fiction) in confirming and complicating gender conventions and preconceptions.

Many critics speculate in general and theoretical terms about the role of gender in reading, in creating literary reputations, and in canon formation. I have tried in this book to bring a precision to the debate by providing concrete examples of mid-Victorian book reviewers attempting to guide the general reading public according to gendered codes and hierarchies. The book also shows how cultural technologies of control in the Victorian period operated in the construction of authorship and the fabrication, naturalization, and maintenance of Victorian gender norms. Nineteenth-century periodicals, too often neglected, shed light on a particular segment of the historical and aesthetic context in which novels were written and received.

This study analyses over 100 nineteenth-century reviews of four novels, canonical and non-canonical, published between 1847 and 1857, chosen for the ways in which they conformed to and deviated from conventional gender stereotypes: Charles Reade's *It Is Never Too Late To Mend*, Emily Brontë's *Wuthering Heights*, Anthony Trollope's *Barchester Towers*, and Charlotte Yonge's *The Heir of Redclyffe*. All four novelists were popular or controversial in mid-Victorian England and each caused high cultural commotions by epitomizing and/or subverting contemporary definitions of masculinity or femininity. Charles Reade's writing was seen as a clear example of idealized masculinity; my examination of the reception of *It Is Never Too Late To Mend* explores how such conformity to gendered expectations shaped Reade's reception and reputation. In contrast, the roughness and power of Emily Brontë's *Wuthering Heights* served to complicate the novel's reception; reviewers struggled with cognitive dissonance as they sought to reconcile *Wuthering Heights* with beliefs about female authorship. Trollope also troubles the stability of reviewers' gendered categories and constructs of authorship and readership in the way his fiction diverges from preconceptions about masculinity and writing. Charlotte Yonge on the other hand, like Reade, replicates reviewers' gender schema, conforming, in her case, to idealizations about women writers. The juxtaposition of the critical reception of Reade, Brontë, Trollope, and Yonge makes the patterns of evaluative gender hierarchies informing Victorian literary reception stand out in relief.

By 1852 the literacy rate in England stood at over 60 per cent, and the reading public desired entertainment and instruction, desired to participate in the increasingly vigorous production and consumption of information provided by the nineteenth-century periodical. Victorian periodicals, taking it upon themselves to satisfy the needs of the "multitude" for entertainment and education, became by the mid-nineteenth century one of the most influential and culturally significant forms of popular entertainment and instruction.

The mid-nineteenth century was, in fact, a particularly vibrant period for the literary periodical. The Newspaper Press Directory for 1865 lists 544 UK periodicals; 105 new journals were started in 1844 and 126 in 1864 (Ellegard, 1957, p 4; North, 1978, p. 5). Historians place the total number of periodicals published in the Victorian period at between 25,000 (Houghton, "Periodical Literature", p. 3) and 50,000 (North, 1978, p. 4). Over one thousand journals in the mid-nineteenth century concentrated in some way on literature.

The extraordinary rise and dominance of periodicals in this period can be attributed in part to increasing literacy and a growing middle class, whose new prosperity was accompanied by a corresponding desire for education. Other factors behind the multiplication of periodicals include the price of books and the technological developments which allowed the provision of cheap reading material.[4] New inventions in communications (the telegraph in the mid-1840s) and transportation (the steam-engine at the turn of the century) increased the availability of periodicals, and the repeal of stamp duty after 1836 and paper duty in 1861 made journals more viable economically. The popularity of Dickens's serial novels in the 1830s and 1840s helped increase the vogue for all kinds of literary magazines, and many famous Victorian novelists first became known through Victorian periodicals.

The new importance of reviews coincided, predictably, with a rise in the number of novels published. By the late 1840s, the novel was universally acknowledged to be the representative artistic form of the period. Half of the books that Mudie[5] bought for his Library during this period were novels. By the 1850s, critics and the reading public had developed critical standards and vocabulary for discussing the novel, and a coherent discourse had emerged. The literary review and literary article became important mediators between literature and the reading public.

Despite the fact that Victorian periodicals were, to a great extent, responsible for the rise of literature to professional status; despite the fact that these journals, "because of their influence, . . . are indispensable for an understanding of mid-nineteenth century literature" (Dawson, 1979, p. 11), Victorian periodicals have not been thoroughly investigated.[6]

The literary magazine and the genre of the literary review served, under the aegis of the print media as a whole, as educational institutions whose larger role in Victorian society was the cultivation and transmission of Victorian culture. George Henry Lewes, in an 1856 article entitled "Criticism in Relation to Novels", presents the literary critics as cultural police responsible for protecting public standards and taste: "[T]he vast increase of novels, mostly worthless, is a serious danger to public culture . . . and can only be arrested by an energetic resolution on the part of critics to do their duty with conscientious rigour" (Nadel, *Victorian Fiction*, 1980, p. 354). Walter Bagehot also believed that periodicals had a crucial didactic role for the vast reading public, estimated at between five and six million in 1852: "It is indeed a peculiarity of our times that we must instruct so many persons" (quoted in Houghton, "Periodical Literature", p. 5).

Since reviewers were usually anonymous and often used the pronoun "we", the individuality of particular critics was suppressed. It was replaced by anonymous, oracular voices which seemed to speak with the authority of Culture behind them. John Woolford describes the pervasive first person plural thus:

> the editorial 'we' expanded to allow the critic to assume his role as delegate of the public and custodian of the criteria of artistic language. And hence . . . that odd combination of assertive language with anonymous format in Victorian reviews. The anonymity, with its overweening 'we', represents the extent to which the critic has dissolved his individual identity into the collectivity of a wider consensus; his virulence of language stems from the enormous and overbearing authority he derives from this centrality.   (Woolford, "Periodicals", p. 115)

The extent to which the individual perspective of the reviewer or critic became submerged by the journal's persona is evident in a remark by Victorian critic Leslie Stephen, who, going through the *Saturday Review* file years later, is unable to identify his own work: "I had . . . unconsciously adopted the tone of my colleagues, and like some inferior organism, taken the colouring of my 'environment'" (quoted in Smalley, 1969, p. 21). This assumption of the editorial "we", combined with the fact that the Victorian theory of the novel (and of literature in general) valued didactic fiction, rendered literary critics guardians and inculcators of artistic, ethical, and cultural standards, thus confirming and perpetuating the unconscious assumption that the Victorian views of gender, class, and morality were not ideological, but natural, not relative to nineteenth-century England, but transhistorical.

If we combine the power of this collective "we" with the tendency of a periodical to create, as Margaret Beetham puts it, "a dominant position from which to read" (Beetham, "Open and Close", p. 99), the potential influence of a review on the Victorian reader assumes an even more significant role. It is not difficult to see how readers' expectations and judgements about fiction might be shaped by the reviewers' promotion of gendered hierarchies of authorship and of male/female distinctions. Beetham, writing of periodicals in general, suggests that we should not overlook the tendency of a journal to dictate a reading position, nor the desire of many readers to "be confirmed in the generally accepted or dominant discourse" (p. 99).

The Victorian reviewer, therefore, consciously sought to educate the "multitudes" and instill in them the values of Victorian culture. The institutional context and the social and intellectual prestige wielded by respected periodicals authorized the review to prescribe and regulate critical value. The review thereby functioned as a social structure which reproduced and naturalized the dominant ideologies of the period. And the "right" representation of gender was a central concern for the culture-transmitting institutions of Victorian England. Questions of class and its intersections with gender, along with the role of gender in the growing split between popular and "high" art from the 1860s onwards, are important areas that deserve investigation but are beyond the scope of the present work.

This study is both related and indebted to general theoretical attention in recent years to the role of the reader in literary interpretation.[7] Reception, reader-response and feminist literary theories inform the work's conceptual framework and shape the questions I wish to address. Reader-response critics, whether they believe that the text, the reader, or the reader's interpretive community plays the largest part in the production of literary meaning and value, all agree that the reader's cultural and social "background" influence the individual interpretation and evaluation of a literary work. But as Jauss has argued,

> the question of the subjectivity of the interpretation and of the taste of different readers or levels of readers can be asked meaningfully only when one has first clarified which transsubjective horizon of understanding conditions the influence of the text. ("Literary History", p. 167)

As feminist criticism has demonstrated, a large portion of the "transsubjective horizon of understanding" operating in a given historical period is constituted by culturally contingent beliefs about sexual identity and sex roles. According to Mary Crawford and Roger Chaffin, recent experiments suggest our assumptions about appropriate gender roles, or our gender "schema", are likely to be activated, probably unconsciously, when we read, providing a framework through which we perceive the text.

Concentrating on critical reaction from 1847 to 1867, I analyze how expectations about the sex of the writer in particular, and about the role of women in general, create what Elizabeth Flynn describes as "dominant" readers ("Gender and Reading", pp. 267–88), readers whose rigid preconceptions inhibit and often prevent the inter-active, self-revising process which Wolfgang Iser in *The Act of Reading* identifies as crucial in making sense of a book's material.

My work also builds upon existing historical studies of Victorian reading and publishing.[8] Of the many analyses of the intersections between gender and Victorian literature, two stand out as most clearly related to the present work in their discussion of reception issues: Elaine Showalter's pioneering *A Literature of their Own*, and Gaye Tuchman's *Edging Women Out: Victorian Novelists, Publishers, and Social Change*.[9] Showalter focuses on women writers, covers a broad historical span (Victorian to contemporary), and draws conclusions about the sexual double standard. Tuchman's analysis of Victorian publishing makes similar arguments about the discrimination against female authors. This book differs from these valuable contributions to the field in several ways: in its historically focused concentration on the cultural institution of Victorian reviewing and in its argument that it is gender, sometimes more than sex, that determines the shifting politics and standards of reception. Male writers, such as Trollope, were in fact also constrained by the masculine/feminine hierarchies of Victorian literary criticism, and women writers, such as Charlotte Yonge, could actually benefit from gendered evaluations. Yonge, for instance, conformed so closely to the ideal and idealized view of feminine writing that she is chivalrously exempted from more critical examinations of intellectual content. Hence my findings argue against the familiar sexual double standard and suggest the existence of a more complicated and multi-layered gender code.

Barbara Herrnstein Smith, in her discussion of canon-formation, argues that interpretation and value are products of classification: "In perceiving an object or artifact in terms of some category, as, for example, 'a clock,' 'a dictionary' . . . we implicitly isolate and foreground certain of its possible functions and typically refer its value to the extent to which it performs those functions more or less effectively" ("Contingencies of Value", p.17). I aim to show that both the "categories" Victorian critics used to critique novels and the "functions" of the novel they foregrounded and evaluated were informed by a poetics of sexual identity, a rhetoric that betrayed the ideological premises underlying both specific critical analyses and the Victorian literary review as a social institution. Of course these gendered classes and functions are not objective, transcultural entities or processes; rather, as Jane Tompkins and others have argued, they are contingent upon the "changing currents of social . . . life" (*Sensational Designs*, p. 192), currents which themselves affect the "gender-schema", the perceptual frames, the horizon of expectations through which individual reviewers read and evaluate texts (Crawford and Chaffin, "The Reader's Construction").

Chapter 1 explores the literary and social background of the Victorian literary review and situates the critical reading of sex and gender within its ideological framework.

1
Reviewing and Writing: Sex and Gender

Victorian periodicals came out at quarterly, monthly, and weekly intervals. The four main quarterlies, in order of importance, were the *Quarterly Review*, the *Edinburgh Review*, the *Westminster Review* and the *North British Review*.[1] The first three of these prestigious periodicals pre-date many Victorian journals: their respective starting dates were 1809, 1803 and 1824. In general, as Houghton states (1957), quarterlies were considered "weightier and more authoritative" than monthlies ("Periodical literature", p. 17). All four of these journals could be classified as literary and general; Kathleen Tillotson singles out the *Westminster Review* and the *North British Review* as vehicles for serious novel criticism, but all four periodicals contained reviews and/or articles on the state of contemporary literature. They were also four of the twenty-three periodicals stocked by Mudie's Circulating Library. The seriousness with which these quarterlies assumed their responsibility as shapers of public opinion can be seen in Walter Bagehot's remark about the *Edinburgh*: "The modern man must be told what to think – shortly no doubt, but he *must* be told" (quoted in Houghton, "Periodical literature", p. 7).

Monthly magazines were a more diverse group. The most popular ones include *Bentley's Miscellany* (1837–1868), *Blackwood's Edinburgh Magazine* (1817–1980), *Cornhill* (1860–1975), *Fraser's Magazine* (1830–1882), *Macmillan's Magazine* (1859–1907), *St. James's Magazine* (established 1861), and *Victoria Magazine* (1863–80). Mudie carried *Cornhill*, *Fraser's*, *Macmillan's*, *St. James's* and *Victoria*. Both *Blackwood's* and *Fraser's* contained reputable novel criticism, and Ellegård identifies *Fraser's* and *Macmillan's* as two of the more important contemporary journals. *Cornhill*, with Thackeray as its editor from its inception in 1860 until 1862, quickly established a reputation as one of the most brilliant and popular of the literary journals, and was an important influence, spawning imitators such as the *St. James's Magazine*. It declared itself to be non-partisan in its literary criticism, and its early contributors included Anthony Trollope and Charles Reade.

The *Athenaeum*, established in 1828, was undoubtedly the most prestigious weekly journal, and is often claimed to be the single most important literary periodical of Victorian times. In *The Athenaeum: A Mirror of Victorian Culture*, Leslie A. Marchand describes this journal as the most influential and respected literary journal in England. Ellegard believes it to have been "regarded as almost indispensable among literary and scientific men. Its coverage of events in the literary world was much fuller than that provided by any other periodical" (1957, p. 22). Part of the journal's reputation stemmed from its claim to be rigorously fair and independent in literary criticism at a time when many journals succumbed to the practice of "puffery", producing flattering reviews that pandered slavishly to publishing houses or friends. The *Athenaeum* devoted regular and generous space to articles on literature and reviews of specific books: in 1850 it carried 55 reviews, and in 1860 133 (Casey, "Weekly Reviews", p. 8). It did, however, tend to be somewhat conservative when it came to literature, though it had a reputation for being radical in political matters.

Other weekly journals include *All The Year Round* (1859–1895), *Chambers's Journal* (1832–1956), whose manifesto was to include the poor in its educating mission, the *London Journal* (1845–1912), the literary and philosophical *London Review* (1860–69), the influential *Saturday Review* (1855–1938), and the political and literary *Spectator* from 1828. The *Examiner*, the *Spectator* and *All The Year Round* were family journals, and selected excerpts were often read out loud to the family. The most important of these journals in terms of literary criticism was the intellectually oriented *Saturday Review*. It was successful, influential, and poisonous in its position of intellectual condescension. E. E. Kellett calls it "a new phenomenon . . . [which] represents. . . revolt of the intelligentsia against the bourgeoisie" ("The Press", p. 56). Later in the same essay he refers to its "obnoxious brilliance" (p. 57). Ellegard claims that the *Saturday Review* was partly responsible for the rise of literary reviewing in weeklies (though the *Athenaeum* was of course already famous for its reviews) and that "it was far above all other political–literary Reviews of the time, both in terms of quality of writing and importance as an organ of opinion" (1957, p. 24). But while Merle Bevington, in her book on the *Saturday Review*, argues that it "did not play favourites" (1941, p. 202), her earlier description of reviews would seem to contradict this, and J. W.

Robertson Scott quotes a contemporary critic who claimed that the
Review had " 'too much gall' ": " '. . . it could never review Trollope
or Mrs. Gaskell fairly – was she not a Nonconformist minister's wife?' "
(1950, p. 124).

The review, as a genre, has to place the literary work in a certain framework in order to come to terms with it; it has to label, name, and put
the work in context before it can proceed to analyze and evaluate it.
One of the ways in which this naming takes place is through definition of the "type" of work it is; another way is through comparison
or juxtaposition of the reviewed work with other works. Analysis of
these classifications and rhetorical modes helps reveal the reviewer's
own aesthetic and ideological preconceptions, and provides insight
into how both the individual critic and contemporary literary conventions process a new work. Since gender roles were thoroughly
patriarchal and sharply polarized in nineteenth-century England,
especially in the middle class at mid-century, it is not surprising that
a distinctly gendered aesthetics of reception surfaces in Victorian literary criticism. This chapter provides historical contexts for the intersections between sex, gender, reviewing, writing, and reading.
   There was often a high degree of consensus between critic and general reader about literary criteria and values. Andrew Blake believes
that ordinary readers and literary reviewers had similar reactions to
books because of their similarity in background and culture: "Readers
and writers from the same class backgrounds with the same domes-
tically-taught literacy, shared common reactions: they were members
of . . . the same literary culture" (1989, p. 70). Thus, he believes that
there was no clear separation between readers and writers. Houghton
states that the most influential critics "may be said to represent the
best thought of the age" ("Periodical literature", p. 9). Back in 1865, a
writer called E. S. Dallas had a similar viewpoint: "no critic worth his
salt . . . does not feel with the many" (quoted in Woolford,
"Periodicals", p. 115).
   Clearly both male and female reviewers were part of the same literary culture. Did female critics "feel with the many", as Dallas put
it? Might we expect differences in content and tone based on differences in sex? As Jonathan Culler puts it, "Suppose the informed reader of a work of literature is a woman. Might not this make a difference
. . . to 'the reader's experience'?" (p. 43).

Until the 1860s, Victorian periodical articles were anonymous and it is often necessary to speculate about the reviewer's sex. Historical studies of individual periodicals, along with works such as the *Wellesley Index*, have now made it possible to reconstruct at least a partial cast of Victorian reviewers and to come up with some preliminary conclusions about sex, gender, and Victorian reviewing.

Probably the most famous female reviewer and publisher's reader to be re-discovered is Geraldine Jewsbury. She reviewed around 1600 novels for the *Athenaeum* over a thirty-year period from 1849, and she was also a reader for the publishing house of Bentley and Sons from 1858 to 1880. Royal Gettmann describes her as "[t]he advisor [to Bentley] who was most trusted and whose reports were sent out as models for other readers to emulate" (1965, p. 194). Although Jewsbury's own novel *Zoe* was perceived as shocking when it appeared in 1845 (see Tillotson, *Novels*, 1954, pp. 60–1), Jewsbury as a reviewer for Bentley (from 1858 until her death in 1880) adopted conventional Victorian moral standards. Monica Fryckstedt views Jewsbury as the quintessential reflection of mid-Victorian literary convention, sharing the taste of Mudie and his all-important reading public: "her reviews reflect a woman reader's view of fiction at a time when a large portion of it was written by and for women. The principal value of Geraldine Jewsbury's reviews, however, lies in the fact that they mirror the preferences and prejudices of a middlebrow reader endowed with unusual expertise" ("Geraldine Jewsbury's *Athenaeum* Reviews", p. 14). Bentley employed other women readers, although some other publishing houses, such as Macmillan, avoided this practice. Women who reviewed for the *Athenaeum* included Christina Rossetti, Mrs Gaskell and Julia Kavanagh. Harriet Martineau and Elizabeth Rigby reviewed for other journals.

If we examine the reviews of women such as Geraldine Jewsbury, Mrs Oliphant, and Elizabeth Rigby, among others, we see that they are often harsher on women novelists who deviate from gender stereotypes than are many of the male reviewers.[2] Henry Fothergill Chorley, for example, one of the most frequent and influential literary reviewers of the mid-nineteenth century, had, according to Leslie Marchand

a particular fondness (or weakness) for literary ladies and became something of a specialist in reviewing books by women writers, which he usually praised with a generous hand guided by a forlorn bachelor's chivalry toward "the sex." Almost every flattering

review in The *Athenaeum* of Lady Blessington, Miss Mitford, Mrs.
Hemans, Elizabeth Barrett, Geraldine Jewsbury, and many
others may be traced to the pen of Chorley.   (1941, p. 185)

It is perhaps not surprising that female critics' voices might be often
indistinguishable from those of their male peers, particularly if we
remember Leslie Stephen's comment cited earlier, about the
chameleon-like merging of his style with the normalizing, generic
quality of the other anonymous *Saturday Review* articles. The anonymi-
ty of the reviewer, the use of the pronoun "we", and the "dominant
discourse" tendency inherent in the periodical and the review might
well cause female reviewers to internalize the patriarchal voice of
Victorian literary culture, erasing or minimizing any differences in
reaction or interpretation that might have otherwise been supposed
to exist. Then too, it is understandable that female reviewers would
want to consolidate their precarious hold on literary authority and
respectability, and would desire to be taken seriously and accepted
as part of the patriarchal establishment.

George Eliot's literary criticism, for example, aligns her with the literary establishment's attitude towards Victorian women writers in
mid- to late nineteenth-century England. Eliot's ambivalence about
the "Woman Question" had an apocalyptic ring of anxiety to it: "[T]here
is no subject on which I am more inclined to hold my peace and learn,
than on the Woman Question. It seems to me to overhang abysses, of
which even prostitution is not the worst . . ." (quoted in Byatt and
Warren, 1990, p. xiii).

In a review of Geraldine Jewsbury's novel *Constance Herbert*, Eliot
criticizes the "standard of ordinary feminine novelists" (Byatt and
Warren, p. 320) and states that Jewsbury deserves to be measured
instead by a higher standard. Clearly Eliot's own decision to adopt a
masculine pseudonym reveals her desire to be perceived as distinctly separate from "ordinary feminine novelists", a conscious and delib-
erate alignment with the apparently more "serious" and authoritative
world of masculine authorship. And Eliot's own writing style was
often considered, as we saw in the *Saturday Review*'s comments on
Scenes of Clerical Life, and as Margaret Oliphant later remarked, much
more "masculine" than "feminine".

As a critic, however, Eliot criticizes women writers' attempts to imitate or exaggerate masculine style. Throughout Eliot's criticism we
find the idea that women have the potential to equal men in their writing but that they retain an essential difference and that this difference

is a precious addition. In "Woman in France", for example, she argues that sex is inevitably involved in literature:

> in art and literature, which imply the action of the entire being, in which every fibre of the nature is engaged, in which every peculiar modification of the individual makes itself felt, woman has something specific to contribute. Under every imaginable social condition, she will necessarily have a class of sensations and emotions – the maternal ones – which must remain unknown to man; and the fact of her comparative physical weakness, which, however it may have been exaggerated by a vicious civilization, can never be cancelled, introduces a distinctively feminine condition into the wondrous chemistry of the affections and sentiments, which inevitably gives rise to distinctive forms and combinations. A certain amount of psychological difference between man and woman necessarily arises out of the difference of sex, and instead of being destined to vanish before a complete development of woman's intellectual and moral nature, will be a permanent source of variety and beauty, as long as the tender light and dewy freshness of morning affect us differently from the strength and brilliancy of the mid-day sun. (Byatt and Warren, 1990, pp. 8–9)

In such remarks (and in her choice of gendered adjectives), Eliot's perspective is extremely close to that of the reviewers of *Wuthering Heights* and *The Heir of Redclyffe* who were, respectively, horrified or delighted at the woman writer's deviance from or conformity with conventional ideas about psychological and moral aspects of women's "natures".

George Eliot is an important test case for this study in that she demonstrates in her fictional writing and in her criticism that it is reductive to try to distinguish between male and female critics' perspectives on the relation between gender and writing. It seems more productive to examine the operations of reviewers' preconceptions about gender in literary reviewing than to focus (or speculate, in the case of the numerous anonymous articles) on the sex of the individual reviewer.

Victorian women novelists operated under several crucial constraints which complicated their access to critical approval, not least of which was their idealized role as pure, domestic angel of the house. According to the *Quarterly Review* in 1869, women had " 'sprightly intuition' ", and should not strain themselves trying to achieve the male "reasoning faculty" (quoted in David, 1987, p. 19). Men were thought to be obviously superior in intellectual activities, while women excelled in emotional matters. Men could thus create artistic masterpieces, whereas it was futile for women to compete in such unnatural areas; moreover, such attempts threatened women's moral/spiritual effectiveness in domestic areas. Mary Poovey claims convincingly that the idealization of women "was also critical to the image of the English national character, which helped legitimize both England's sense of moral superiority and the imperial ambitions this superiority underwrote" (1988, p. 9); she argues, therefore, that the Victorian habit of establishing binary divisions between the sexes was a crucial part of "the consolidation of bourgeois power" (p. 10).

When women writers transgressed from the standard of idealized purity, reactions were likely to be extreme, as we see in Mrs Oliphant's semi-hysterical critique of female wickedness in Rhoda Broughton's novel:

> Nasty thoughts, ugly suggestions, an imagination which prefers the unclean, is almost more appalling than the facts of actual depravity, because it has no excuse of sudden passion or temptation, and no visible boundary. It is a shame to women so to write; and it is a shame to the women who read and accept as a true representation of themselves and their ways the equivocal talk and fleshly inclinations herein attributed to them ... a woman has one duty of invaluable importance to her country and her race which cannot be over-estimated, and that is the duty of being pure. There is perhaps nothing of such vital consequence to a nation ... there can be no possible doubt that the wickedness of man is less ruinous, less disastrous to the world in general, than the wickedness of woman. That is the climax of all misfortunes to the race.   (Quoted in Helsinger, et al., 1983, vol. 3, p. 143)

Women's symbolically crucial "purity" was associated with female ignorance for mid-century Victorians – an ignorance that was both intellectual and sexual. Being a conventionally successful "good woman" entailed being ignorant in certain ways; when women writers display these types of "ignorance", however, they are criticized for their superficiality and faulted for their inability to stretch beyond limited domestic knowledge. The following quotations from Mrs Oliphant are characteristic of the kinds of remarks both male and female critics sometimes made about "ignorant" women writers. Writing about the Brontë sisters, Oliphant states that "their philosophy of life is that of a schoolgirl, their knowledge of the world almost nil" (*Women Novelists*, 1987, p. 5). Elsewhere, Oliphant blames the scandalous tone of the conversations between Jane and Rochester on Brontë's mixture of "overboldness" and "ignorance": "There are some conversations between Rochester and Jane Eyre which no man could have dared to give – which only could have been given by the overboldness of innocence and ignorance trying to imagine what it never could understand, and which are as womanish as they are unwomanly" (Nadel, *Victorian Fiction*, 1980, p. 558). The "damned if you do, damned if you don't" kind of criticism often levelled at women is evident here – Brontë's discussions of sexual matters are unwomanly because good women are not supposed to acknowledge such things, but their ignorance also betrays a typically "womanish" quality of stupidity. Thus there are many different variations on the term "woman" when it is being used as a critical insult.

This double-bind type of an argument can be summarized as follows: a truly pure woman is too ignorant to be a good novelist, and conversely, any insightful female novelist is morally suspect. W. R. Greg encapsulates this brand of argument beautifully in his 1859 *National Review* article:

> whole spheres of observation, whole branches of character and conduct are almost inevitably closed to her [the female novelist] . . . many of the saddest and deepest truths in the strange science of sexual affection are to her mysteriously and mercifully veiled . . . The inevitable consequence, however, is, that in treating of that science she labours under all the disadvantages of partial study and superficial insight.   (Quoted in Helsinger et. al., 1983, vol. 3, p. 3)

Other critics, including George Eliot, attack women writers because of their educational limitations, which seems ungenerous, considering that Victorian society did not encourage serious education for women.[3] In 1856, a *Westminster Review* essay by Eliot, "Silly Novels by Lady Novelists", criticizes the quality of women's writing. Eliot ridicules the intellectual pretensions of so many "silly" novels by women. She justifies her attack in a curious manner: "If, as the world has long agreed, a very great amount of instruction will not make a wise man, still less will a very mediocre amount of instruction make a wise woman. And the most mischievous form of feminine silliness is the literary form, because it tends to confirm the popular prejudice against the more solid education of women" (Nadel, *Victorian Fiction*, 1980, p. 454). Her first sentence balances "a very great amount of instruction" with "a very mediocre amount of instruction", and balances man against woman in the same pattern, thereby implying that men are more likely to be wise than women. She then implies that "feminine silliness" exists in several forms, and concludes the sentence by claiming a solicitous concern for women's education, a concern that strikes one as somewhat suspect given the context of the rest of the sentence and the rest of the essay. The argument is circular: most women do not deserve education because they are silly and ignorant; most women's writing is silly and ignorant because women have not had the benefit of a serious education.

For the most part, literary critics admired and endorsed writing by women that formed an extension of their domestic role. Women were expected to preach morally improving lessons that featured self-sacrificing female characters in happy domestic settings and that contained idealized views of family sanctity and domestic harmony; such writing created minimal conflict between accepted notions of women as receptive and passive and women's role as writers. Conventionally acceptable fiction by women had the added advantage of being unthreateningly "second-class". An 1860 *London Review* article describes the situation thus: "The female novelist who keeps strictly to the region within which she acquired her knowledge may never produce a fiction of the highest order, but she will be in the right path to produce the best fiction of the class in which she is most likely to excel" (quoted in Helsinger et al., 1983, vol. 3, p. 53).

When women stepped outside their "natural" region by displaying "unbecoming" knowledge, or by attempting to write something that clearly transcended the second-rate, they were sometimes accused of betraying woman's true role. Ambitious writing demonstrates self-assertion and self-confidence, and betrays an absence of "diffident, feminine and submissive" behaviour, the qualities that Sara Coleridge identifies in an 1849 journal entry, "Strong-Minded Women", as characteristic of true feminine genius (1874, p. 375). Serious writing, like serious education, was regarded as a masculine activity that threatened to divert women's energy from their reproductive organs to their brains. Literary women, therefore, "were ridiculed in caricatures and admonished in conduct manuals and major periodicals" (Helsinger et al., 1983, vol. 3, p. 4). Since women novelists were regarded primarily as women, it is not surprising that, regardless of their merit, they tended to be grouped together and evaluated in terms of each other. Many women novelists protested strongly at this treatment, as we shall see later.

One of the worst crimes that women writers could commit, for critics ranging from Eliot to writers from the *Saturday Review*, was to attempt to mask their ignorance by a pretentious show of knowledge. In "Silly Novels", Eliot mocks women writers whose heroines casually learn Greek and Sanskrit, for example. In 1858 the *Review* criticized religious novels for the ignorance of their authors, "more commonly ... females", who tried to "[make] a show of learning" (quoted in Bevington, 1941, p. 200). By "making a show of learning", pretending to knowledge that they do not have, given the limitations of their education, women are thought to step out of their proper roles and attempt to obtain the status of a man.

If critics did not attack women writers for their presumptuous ambition, they often criticized their "inevitably feminine" creative limitations. R. H. Hutton, in an 1858 essay for the *North British Review*, attributes women's supposed inability to depict men as evidence of their lack of creative power:

> It may seem a harsh and arbitrary dictum that our lady novelists do not usually succeed in the field of imagination ... Yet we are fully convinced that this is the main deficiency of feminine genius. It can observe, it can recombine, it can delineate, but it cannot trust itself further; it cannot leave the world of characteristic traits and expressive manner ... Thus no woman, we believe, has ever painted men as they are amongst men. Their imagination takes no grasp of a masculine character that is sufficiently strong to enable them to follow it in imagination into the society of men. (Quoted in Helsinger et al., 1983, vol. 3, p. 52)

An 1864 review of the anonymously published *Hazel Combe* in the *Saturday Review*, believes that the novel's limitations are typically feminine: "Every allowance made for the distinctive peculiarities of female authorship, and all deference paid to the claims of mere politeness in our criticism of feminine labours, we feel bound to protest against the weakness ... which could prompt the publication of a book so devoid of purpose, so inconsecutive in plan ... and so insipid in style" (quoted in Bevington, 1941, p. 201).

"Insipid" and "weak" are terms typically used to criticize women's writing, along with "feeble", as we see in Eliot's "Silly Novels" essay: "In the majority of women's books you see that kind of facility which springs from the absence of any high standard . . . that fertility in imbecile combination or feeble imitation which a little self-criticism would check and reduce to barrenness" (Nadel, *Victorian Fiction*, 1980, p. 400). Eliot mirrors the popular association of women with lack of creativity in her emphasis on "combination" and "imitation". Her use of "fertility" versus "barrenness" is interesting: she uses "fertility" in a negative sense to describe women's inability to discriminate, whereas "barrenness" is the desired result of self-criticism. Such language, along with the distinctly vitriolic tone of the article, leads one to speculate on whether Eliot felt (consciously or not) that women had to "unsex" themselves, disassociate themselves from the rest of their sex, as she does in this article, in order to be serious writers.[4]

Obviously intellectual women writers, Eliot included, were censored for precisely this apparent tendency to "unsex" themselves, as Deirdre David argues in her discussion of Harriet Martineau, George Eliot, and Elizabeth Barrett Browning:

> these three writers struggled against an authority which defended itself against an unsettling conjunction of powerful intellect and female sex and gender they embodied by labelling Martineau "strong-minded" for her forthright ambition, Barrett Browning "unchaste" for her choice of eroticized female imagery, and Eliot "masculine" for her putative affectation of "male" modes of thought. (David, 1987, p. viii)

If women writers separated themselves from the predictable but acceptable second-rate didactic and domestic novels, they were criticized for being masculine; if they consciously chose to distinguish themselves from routine and approved "feminine" fiction, they might well have deliberately adopted so-called masculine styles and subject-matter.

The *Saturday Review* is often a helpful source for the most outspoken and forthright voicings of Victorian gender stereotypes, though it is unusually harsh at times in its criticism of women writers and readers and its dismissal of all qualities they associated with the female sex. Male novelists are sometimes castigated by the *Saturday Review* for catering to women readers and for being too feminine in their treatment of emotions. Dickens, for example, receives criticism for trying to make women cry and "send[ing] half the women in London with tears in their eyes, to Mr. Mudie's or Mr. Booth's" (quoted in Bevington, 1941, p. 162), and for thinking that "because a man can make silly women cry, he can dictate the principles of law and government to grown men" (quoted in Bevington , 1941, p. 161).[5] Merle Bevington, the journal's historian, summarizes its position on women's status: "The *Saturday Review* assumed as a fact that women were inferior to men. It found the best evidence for this assumption in the history of literature and the arts, where the first rank has 'never, or next to never' been attained by a woman, though many have done excellent work of the second rank" (1941, p. 116). Many women writers deliberately eschewed serious literary stature, claiming for themselves a place in the "second-rank" where the *Saturday Review* said they belonged. Thus, Mrs Oliphant is proud to claim for women writers a high position in the class of second-rank novelists: "This . . . is the age of female novelists, and women, who rarely or never find their way to the loftiest class, have a natural right and claim to rank foremost in the second" (Nadel, *Victorian Fiction*, 1980, p. 555).

In 1865, the *Saturday Review* came up with another popular stereotype to explain why women were not (and should not try to be) first-rate novelists: "Female nature, mental as well as physical, is essentially receptive and not creative" (quoted in Helsinger, et al., 1983, vol. 3, p. 16). This attitude about appropriate female nature may explain the often gallant critical reception (remember Chorley's fondness for undistinguished literary women) that mediocre works by women received, compared with the sterner reception of striking female talent. George Eliot complains bitterly about this journalistic tendency in her essay "Silly Novels":

> We are aware that the ladies at whom our criticism is pointed are accustomed to be told, in the choicest phraseology of puffery, that their pictures of life are brilliant . . . No sooner does a woman show that she has genius or effective talent, than she receives the tribute of being moderately praised and severely criticized. By a peculiar thermometric adjustment, when a woman's talent is at zero, journalistic approbation is at the boiling pitch; . . . if ever she reaches excellence, critical enthusiasm drops to the freezing point. (Nadel, *Victorian Fiction*, 1980, p. 400)

If women writers kept to their "proper sphere" in conforming to stereotypes about femininity, much like middle-class people not copying their "betters", critics could thus be pleasantly condescending, rather than feel threatened.

If "feminine" was often a condescending or insulting adjective when used to describe writing, implying domestic, didactic, limited, silly, superficial and second-class, "masculine" was usually a complimentary adjective, except, of course, when used in reference to women's writing. Masculinity was identified with high culture (and male readers), rather than with popular culture (and female readers); masculinity was also associated with intellectual qualities, with originality, with power, and with truth; whereas, as we have seen, femininity was associated with stereotypically female qualities such as weakness or feebleness, and lack of significant power, intellect or ideas. These binary associations according to gender are evident throughout Victorian literary criticism, whether explicit or implicit, and are applied both to writers and to readers. Charles Reade, for example, claimed that his "true" novels were excluded from the small circulating libraries, which "will only take in ladies' novels" (quoted in Gettmann, 1965, p. 248); here "true" is identified with male, and "false" with female. The qualities valued by the *Saturday Review* invariably reflected gender hierarchies. Ellen Casey states that *Saturday* critics "valued strength, originality, cleverness, and power" in novels ("Weekly Reviews",p. 10); in 1857, the *Saturday Review* lamented the tendency of novels to confine themselves to domestic scenes, "a low range of thought", and their failure "to investigate the great problems of life" (quoted in Bevington, 1941, p. 155).

Even critics unusually sympathetic to women's writing, such as Lewes, divided literary qualities rigidly down gender lines, as in the 1852 essay "The Lady Novelists", for the *Westminster Review*[6]: "To write as men write, is the aim and besetting sin of women; to write as women is the real office they have to perform . . . women [succeed] better in finesse of detail, in pathos and sentiment, while men generally succeed better in the construction of plots and the delineation of character" (pp. 133–4).

The term "masculine" was short-hand for a thumbs-up sign of critical approval. George Meredith's The *Ordeal of Richard Feverel* was praised by the *Saturday Review* in 1865 for its "admirable manliness". Thomas Hughes's story of life at a boys' school, *Tom Brown's Schooldays*, was praised by the same periodical for its noble masculinity. Oliphant describes the style of Thackeray's *Vanity Fair* as "winning, easy, masculine, felicitous and humorous . . . The author indulges in no sentimentalities" (Nadel, *Victorian Fiction*, 1980, p. 315). A man was morally obliged to be "manly" in his writing, as is evident in the *Spectator*'s attack of Swinburne's work: "it is precisely the unmanliness of the book . . . that is so suffocating . . . We hold that, in this volume at least, Mr Swinburne is both unmasculine and unfeminine. He is unmanly, or effeminate, which you please, and they mean morally the same thing" (quoted in Helsinger et al., 1983, vol. 3, p. 156). This reaction to Swinburne is an interesting illustration of the gender-based constraints that men suffered in Victorian literary criticism.

Men also had gender-derived limitations on their work. They were expected to excel in their depiction of male characters, although they were also thought capable of creating believable heroines. Men were expected to centre their books upon male characters, and were accused of effeminacy if a woman was the focus of their work.[7] Some male writers, as we have seen above, were attacked for being insufficiently masculine in their subject-matter, in their treatment of emotion, or in their tone.

When a critic was uncertain about the sex of a particular writer, sometimes because of an apparent discrepancy between the style or content and the sex of the name or pseudonym of the author, or sometimes because it was an unknown author's first book and the critic wondered whether a pseudonym was being used, he or she would construct a picture of the author in question, based on his or her interpretation of the novel. Eliot was generally felt to possess a masculine style, perhaps more so than any other female Victorian novelist, as Mrs. Oliphant argues in an *Edinburgh Review* article: "George Eliot's books remain (with the exception of *The Mill on the Floss*), less definable in point of sex than the books of any other woman who has ever written. A certain size . . . and freedom in the style, an absence of that timidity, often varied by temerity, which, however disguised, is rarely absent from the style of women, seems to us to obliterate the distinctions of sex; and her scientific illustrations and indications of scholarship, more easy and assured than a woman's ordinary furtive classical allusions no doubt added greatly to this effect" (quoted in Tuchman, *Edging*, 1989, p. 186).

Eliot herself, however, in an 1854 *Westminster* article, finds fault with women writers for what amounts to dressing in drag: "With a few remarkable exceptions, our own feminine literature is made up of books which could have been better written by men . . . when not a feeble imitation, they are usually an absurd exaggeration of the masculine style, like the swaggering gait of a bad actress in male attire" (quoted in Helsinger et al., 1983, vol. 3, p. 59). An 1861 *Dublin*

University Magazine article makes an unusually revealing attack on women writers acting like transvestites; the frequency of this strange image indicates the remarkable extent to which literary qualities and characteristics were gendered, and has important implications for the study of literary reception at this time:

> Why are female novelists so prone to masquerade in garments borrowed from the sterner sex . . .? It is a poor compliment to male critics to suppose that the putting of a man's name in the first page of a new novel will therefore blind them to the real authorship of that novel . . . None but shallow or one-sided dogmatists would speak of women's books with an air of conscious patronage or affected reserve . . . A true woman's book will reveal its own special charm . . . Like woman herself, it be nothing unless it be "pure womanly,' . . . striving to copy the man's free carriage, deep tones, and hard reasonings, she can only succeed in behaving like a better sort of monkey.   (Quoted in Helsinger et al., 1983, vol. 3, p. 65)

It is of course well known that the Brontë sisters were among many female novelists who adopted male or androgynous pen-names in an effort to escape negative judgement. It is less well known that some male novelists adopted female pen-names in mid-nineteenth-century England in an attempt to capitalize on the commercial popularity of books by women in this period. Q. D. Leavis argues that the Victorian male novelist "must adopt a false personality and the falsetto voice that goes with it" (1965, p.253). Tuchman believes that "solid data seem to support the assumption that many male writers masqueraded as women in the novel's heyday" (*Edging*, 1989, p. 53). While it would help to see this data, it does seem possible that the proportion of women readers and the commercial imperative of being accepted by the circulating libraries might have led some male novelists to attempt the best-selling domestic genre, disguised with a "female" voice to enhance their credibility.

As Oliphant and so many modern critics note, female novelists were extremely popular in Victorian England, despite the limiting implications of feminine stereotypes for feminine authors. Tuchman points out that, in the *Dictionary of National Biography*, 88 per cent of all listed novelists born between 1750 and 1814 were women ("When the Prevalent", p. 148). Indeed, by the mid-nineteenth century, novel-writing was associated with women, with women readers as well as with women writers.

George Eliot, objecting strongly to being written about in the context of other women writers such as Mrs Mulock, sought to differentiate herself from their ilk by complaining that Mrs Mulock was "a writer who is read only by novel-readers, pure and simple, never by people of high culture" (quoted in Tuchman, "When the Prevalent", p. 155). Novel-readers are obviously identified with women, while "people of high culture" are identified with men. Publishers' reports reveal the same dichotomies along gender lines as are found in literary criticism: Morley's reaction to Mrs Molesworth's *Heathercourt Rectory* is that "few men would get through it, and the ladies who read it would hardly think the better of their own minds if they liked it strongly" (quoted in Tuchman, *Edging*, 1989, p. 83). Part of what critics wrote and thought about the novel was predicated on gender associations with its readers. Some critics felt that the subject-matter and style of novels was too closely directed towards the women readers who formed the majority of Mudie's subscribers.

Gaining Mudie's approval was a vital factor in the success of a novel, and Mudie was acutely anxious not to offend or corrupt his middle- and upper-middle-class readers. His advertisements proclaimed that "[n]ovels of objectionable character or inferior ability are almost invariably excluded" (quoted in Sutherland, *Victorian Novelists*, 1976, p. 26). Because of Mudie's role in the literary success of a work, publishers and novelists tried desperately to please him, and this involved careful screening for "objectionable" material. In 1859 *The Bookseller* reported a rumour that publishers sent novel proof sheets to Mudie for approval. It was important not only that Mudie accept a novel, but that he order large numbers of copies.[8]

Many Victorian novelists complained about Mudie's censorship and its effect on novel-writing. Because of the "young girl standard", men were expected to write morally pure books, books which would not bring a blush to the cheek of the parson's daughter, and many felt that this was an emasculating limitation.[9] George Moore, for example, complained that "[l]iterature and young girls are irreconcilable elements, and the sooner we leave off trying to reconcile them the better. At this vain endeavor the circulating library has been at work for the last twenty years . . . [The criterion is] 'would you or would you not give that book to your sister of sixteen to read'" (quoted in Griest, 1970, p. 138). Fitzjames Stephen's article in the *Saturday Review* of 11 July 1857 is representative in its disapproval of the young girl standard:

Surely it is very questionable whether it be desirable that no novels be written except those fit for young ladies to read . . . why should
works of imagination [be considered] such mere toys that they ought
always to be calculated for girlish ignorance? Novelists, in acqui-
escing in the crippling restrictions placed upon them, seem to think
that . . . [their] highest function . . . is the amusement of children;
but we are by no means prepared to say that in literature,
emasculation produces purity.   (IV, pp. 40–1)

The following chapters analyze critics' gender "processing" in contemporary critiques of Reade, Emily Brontë, Trollope, and Yonge,
exploring what, for example, constitutes literary "emasculation",
assessing what qualities in a book's content and style are perceived
as inscribed masculinity or femininity, how the reviewers conceptualize the gender of the actual reader, and how these gendered con-
cepts figure in the Victorian horizon of expectations.

2

The "Virile Creator" versus the "Twaddlers Tame and Soft": Charles Reade's *It Is Never Too Late To Mend*

CHARLES READE
Rupert of Letters! Stilled that fiery tongue
As trenchant as the trooper's steel! And yet
No passion-dainty Poet ever sung
  Whose heart was tenderer. Round the world regret
Will rise on hearing that distinctive voice
  Is mute which gave to Fiction and the stage
Virile creations, made the oppressed rejoice,
  And vindicated with a noble rage
The master-virtue, Justice, stabbed too oft,
  Like Caesar, by its trusted seeming friends.
The world, o'er full of twaddlers tame and soft,
  Will miss his leonine style, who roars and rends
With Samson zest, yet yields from strenuous might
"Sweetness" of Pity and victorious Right.

"Charles Reade", Punch, 19 April 1884, p. 181

January 12, 1857 – Reading Never Too Late To Mend, *one of the weightiest events of late. Oh those prison scenes! how they haunt one!*

The Journals of Caroline Fox, 1835–71,
ed. Wendy Monk, p. 224

Charles Reade's *It Is Never Too Late To Mend* was one of the nineteenth century's best-selling and critically esteemed novels. It caused a sensation when it first appeared in August 1856; it was "praised and purchased by everyone from shopkeepers . . . to writers and philanthropists" (Burns, 1966, p. 174). In *My Literary Passions*, W. D. Howells's chapter on Reade is sandwiched between chapters on Goethe and Dante: "We were all reading his jaunty, nervy, knowing books," he writes, "and some of us were questioning whether we ought not to set him above Thackeray and Dickens and George Eliot . . . so great was the effect that Charles Reade had with our generation" (Howells, 1895, p. 144). Many contemporary critics felt, like Walter Besant, that "Reade [took] rank with Fielding, Smollett, Scott, Dickens, and Thackeray" (Besant, "Charles Reade", p. 200). As recently as 1940, George Orwell declared that *It Is Never Too Late To Mend* was one of three novels by Reade "which I personally would back to outlive the entire works of Meredith and George Eliot" (1968, p. 37).

In recent years, however, Reade has become an increasingly shadowy figure whose main claim to fame is the bibliographic entry in *Victorian Fiction* that laments the continued absence of critical studies or attention dedicated to him. Reconstructing the critical context of the original reception of Reade reveals a great deal about Victorian criteria for literary value, and it especially exposes the role of gender associations within those criteria.

It Is Never Too Late To Mend was Reade's first full-length novel after two shorter works that had received only limited notice, and Reade was determined to make it establish his reputation. He spent two years writing it, and constructed a "great system" in which he placed enormous faith; the "system" involved basing the novel on historical facts as much as possible, whether these came from the "blue books" on prison reform, newspaper articles, books on Australia, or interviews with former Australian gold-miners. Reade intended *It Is Never Too Late To Mend* to follow in the epic tradition, with focus on theme and action rather than on character analysis. Burns describes him as "consciously abjuring the techniques of Trollope and the domestic novelists (whose works he dismissed as 'chronicles of small beer') in an effort to create epic characters equal to what he conceived to be his epic theme" (1961, p. 159).

There are three plots in *It Is Never Too Late To Mend*: one of which deals with prison reform, one with gold digging in Australia, and one with love. The novel opens with the romantic plot: George Fielding is an honest but poor farmer who decides to seek his fortune in Australia so that he will be an acceptable suitor for Susan Merton, his beloved. The central and main plot is devoted to prison reform, and takes us with Fielding's lodger, Robinson, to a corrupt prison modelled on the contemporary scandal of Birmingham gaol.[1] Prison atrocities are painted in excruciating detail, as is the heroic and eventually successful endeavour of the prison chaplain to expose and rectify the situation, bringing the sadistic governor, Hawes, to justice. Robinson (now reformed) and Fielding end up together in Australia, where, after many adventures, they make their fortunes, and return to England just in time for Fielding to save Susan Merton from being tricked into marriage with his unprincipled rival.

The success of Reade's epic action novel established his reputation. It went through five editions in England from 1856 to 1857, sold 2,700 copies of Bentley's cheap edition in just two days, and 25,000 copies of Bentley's original edition in a few months. The reviews were mostly flattering, but Reade fired off outraged letters to the press at any hint of criticism, thus contributing to the novel's publicity as well as to his own growing reputation for being irascible and belligerent. (One letter, to the *Saturday Review*, for example, began thus: "You have brains of your own and good ones. Do not you echo the bray of such a very small ass as the *Edinburgh Review*. . . . Reflect!" [*Readiana*, 313].)[2] Evaluations of *It Is Never Too Late To Mend*, whether formed by reviewers or written by Reade in response to these reviews, are overtly or implicitly framed and structured by a highly gendered aesthetics. Critics saw *It Is Never Too Late To Mend* as a quintessentially "masculine" novel and evaluated it accordingly.[3]

Victorian reviewers asserted, for example, that the primary audience for this book would necessarily be men. They compared the novel with other "masculine" novels and contrasted it to "feminine" works. They commented on the relative merits of character depiction versus plot, and evaluated the portrayal of male versus female characters. Each of these "framings", to a varying extent, reveals the gender schema the reviewer deploys. It was an especially popular Victorian practice to compare and contrast Reade with George Eliot, a type of framing that accentuated gender associations.

The adjectives used to praise Reade are more obviously patterned along gender lines than the implicit gender framing brought to critical discussions of Anthony Trollope, for example. Readers consistently associated Reade's style with traits that were considered quintessentially masculine in Victorian England. The following descriptions of his writing are typical: "rough", "powerful", "lusty", "forcible", "vigorous", "superb physical strength", "daring", "imperious", "vehement", "crude". Reade's *Punch* obituary contrasts his

"virile creations" and "strenuous might" with the effeminacy of "twaddlers tame and soft" (19 April 1884, p. 181). For contemporary Victorian
critics, Reade distinguished himself from female novelists through
his "intellectual power" and "originality". As the *Examiner* put it, he
was "no mere confectioner of novels"; instead he was "a man with
real originality of thought, shrewd in invention, powerful in expression" (23 August 1856, p. 534).

When reviewers sought to label *It Is Never Too Late To Mend*, they
turned first to its subject and plot. The subject matter of the novel,
prison reform, Australian gold digging, and, to a lesser extent, moral
transformation, is admired as profound and important, and is seen
as justification in and of itself for taking the novel seriously. Although
women were part of the reform movements, prison reform was a
weighty public issue that was certainly male territory in terms of leg-
islative responsibility. The gendered associations of the novel's subject give it a certain prestige and dignity for the reviewers. The *Spectator*,
for example, argues that Reade's work extends the clichéd limitations
of conventional novels in its depiction of the battle "between good
and evil":

> The minds of thoughtful Englishmen have been much turned of
> late to schemes for reforming the criminal classes of our popula-
> tion, to systems of prison discipline, and to institutions for com-
> bining the education of the criminal with the punishment of his
> crime. It might once have been a question whether a subject of such
> stern practical importance, involving so much that is saddening
> and even revolting to the heart and to the taste, and demanding for
> its treatment any qualities rather than one-sided sentimentality, is
> well adapted to give that pleasure which readers look for at the
> hands of the novelist. But . . . nothing but genius and true earnest-
> ness . . . are required to move the heart of mankind to fervid sym-
> pathy with the real, vulgar, everyday suffering of their brethren,
> far more strongly and truly than with the sentimental woes and
> drawingroom distresses which form the staple of so much of our
> circulating library fiction.   (16 August 1856, p. 877)

The gendered distinctions of this review emphasize that the phrase
"minds of thoughtful Englishmen" is indeed intended as male-
specific, and that "stern", "practical", "revolting to the heart and taste",
"strongly", and "truly" are contrasted to the feminine implications of
"sentimentality", "sentimental woes", "drawing room distresses",

and "circulating library fiction". The elevation of one set of terms against the others stresses the critical advantages Reade gains by distinguishing himself from women writers, and has interesting implications for the gendered associations and status of the novel as a genre. The reviewer implies that the days of the novel as a sentimental, domestic, and feminine genre are numbered, and that Reade may herald a new age of vigorous, masculine, important novel-writing which even women will come to emulate.[4]

Victorians strongly identified women with novel-reading in general and with circulating library membership in particular. As Guinevere Griest documents in *Mudie's Circulating Library*, Mudie's "years of eminence" in the mid- to late nineteenth century, coinciding with the "years of great development in the English novel", rendered Mudie "the single most important distributor of fiction . . . exert[ing] such a profound influence that its creator [was] a symbolic "Dictator of the London Literary World' " (1970, p. 27). Mudie's typical subscribers were identified with young women and the " 'British Matron' ", and the Library's standards were designed accordingly (pp. 137–40).

Consequently, when many contemporary reviewers suggested that Reade's novel was one that could be enjoyed by readers who were intelligent and informed and who did not normally read novels, they were, I believe, distinguishing between Mudie's female subscribers and male readers. George Eliot, writing for the *Westminster Review*, holds that it is "one of the exceptional novels to be read not merely by the idle and the half-educated, but by the busy and the thoroughly informed" (October, 1856, p. 315). (Again, Eliot is surely equating "idle" and "half-educated" with middle-class Victorian women of leisure, in contrast to University-educated and "industrious" Victorian middle-class men.) G. H. Lewes makes a surprisingly similar point in the *Leader*, raising questions about the mutual influence of Eliot and Lewes: "with these qualities we ought to see him produce a novel which would not simply amuse that unfastidious class of readers subscribing to circulating libraries, but also that other class, larger and more cultivated, which reads with gratitude a good novel, but seldom troubles the library. *It Is Never Too Late To Mend* is such a novel, though not ranking high in the class" (23 August 1856, p. 810).

Information about readership has often to be inferred, as we have no statistical data comparing gender patterns in readership, but reviews and critical commentaries dedicated to Reade do suggest that while *It Is Never Too Late To Mend* was read by both sexes, the proportion of male readers was very high. An 1857 *Edinburgh Review* article by Fitzjames Stephen takes issue with Reade for trespassing beyond the usually domestic, and by implication feminine boundaries of the novel. Reade's novel and Dickens's *Little Dorrit* "address themselves almost entirely to the imagination upon subjects which properly belong to the intellect . . . they caricature instead of representing the world. This applies even to those ordinary domestic relations which are the legitimate province of the novel. . . . The representations of novelists are not only false, but often in the highest degree mischievous when they apply, not to the feelings, but to the facts and business transactions of the world" (July 1857, p. 65). Stephens worries particularly about the effect on inexperienced young men attracted to the novel by its subject-matter: "men of the world may laugh at books which represent all who govern as fools, knaves . . . whilst the young and inexperienced are led to think far too meanly of the various careers which the organisations of society places before them" (p. 68). Mrs Oliphant defines the main readership of *It Is Never Too Late To Mend* as boys: "the chief scenes to all boys and wholesome minded persons who love a story can never lose their excitement" (*The Victorian Age*, 1892, p. 481).

The most explicit identification of Reade's readership as predominantly male comes from Walter Besant, in an 1882 *Blackwood's Edinburgh Magazine*.[5] Besant was a fervent admirer of Reade's, and felt that the author had been unjustly neglected by English critics in favour of women writers. He concludes that the reason for this neglect is that Reade is a novelist for men, and implies that such writing is currently out of vogue in England: "it is perfectly understood that of all living men who write novels, he is the most widely known, the most read, and the most admired. Remember that there are the people in America, in India, and in our colonies, to consider, besides the subscribers to our circulating libraries. In the quiet plantations, on the coffee, tea, sugar, and indigo estates, on the silent sheep runs, in faraway farm-houses, in the States and Canada and the colonies everywhere, the men read novels. Here, in this country, there are more women readers of novels than men" ("Charles Reade", p. 199). Gaye Tuchman argues in *Edging Women Out* that women novelists had such a wide commercial popularity in Victorian England that male novelists sometimes adopted female pen-names. The defensive tone of Besant's comments suggests such a situation.[6]

Most of the reviewers of *It Is Never Too Late To Mend* believed that the novel distinguished itself from other contemporary works. The

Critic called it "one of the very few first-rate works of fiction which we have met with in our life" (15 August 1856, p. 395). The *Athenaeum* termed it "the most vigorous and various novel which has till now appeared this year" (9 August 1856, p. 990), and the *Examiner* echoed these terms, finding it to be "a book of considerable mark, being a novel written with unusual vigour and intensity of feeling" (23 August 1856, p. 533). Reade's "vigour" is identified with both the book's content and style, neither of which are seen as typical of conventional novels, and both of which become contrasted to women's "drawing-room" fiction and the predominantly female readers of circulating libraries. Reade is not confined to conventional domestic scenes, as were so many women novelists; instead, as G. H. Lewes puts it in the *Leader*, "he has seen varieties of life, and has had his eyes open" (23 August 1856, p. 809).

The following review from the *Critic* is structured around gender division and hierarchy: Reade's work is compared with "boys' own" type adventure stories, and contrasted to fatuous and frivolous works by women writers. The *Critic* reviewed the following novels, in this order: *Horatio Howard Brenton: A Naval Novel*, by Captain Sir Edward Belcher; *The Quadroon; or A Lover's Adventures in Louisiana*, by Captain Mayne Reid; *Helen Lincoln*, by Carrie Capron; *It Is Never Too Late To Mend*, by Charles Reade; *Sunshine and Shadow*, by the Author of *Mabel* (15 August 1856, p. 394). The first novel "is intended to convey the opinions of its author upon manly matters pertaining to the 'service'" (p. 394); "always writing like a gentleman", Captain Reid tells the story of a man who is "blown up in a Mississippi steamer, stabbed with a bowie knife, stung by a rattle-snake, hunted by sleuth-hounds" (p. 394); Carrie Capron's novel, on the other hand, exhibits "no very remarkable power" (p. 394); Reade's novel is praised as "impossible to lay down until it is concluded", an important and powerfully distinguished work. "A perfect contrast to this admirable work," the reviewer writes scathingly, "is *Sunshine and Shadow*, by the anonymous author of *Mabel*. Anything more vapid, more pointless, and more unnatural than this composition it would be difficult to conceive. We suppose that it is intended to belong to that class of fictions which are termed fashionable novels, of which Carlyle has said that they, of all the other productions of literature, most nearly approach absolute fatuity" (p. 395). Clearly, Reade is seen as admirable for the ways in which his work resembles but transcends the male adventure stories. Like them, his plot is full of exciting adventure, but his power lies also in his novel's social significance. Regardless of the

vexed question of "true" literary merit, the *Critic*'s reviewer associates literary power and interest with Reade and Captain Mayne Reid,
and "vapidity", "fatuity", and lack of literary power with the "fashionable" world of women novelists.

The only woman novelist with whom Reade is compared is Harriet
Beecher Stowe, and that connection was made only because *Uncle
Tom's Cabin* had appeared recently, to great popular acclaim, and like
Reade's novel it was a "principle" novel aimed at exposing social
wrong. Reade was criticized for being more violent than Stowe, and
less sensitive to the imaginative subtleties of character development.
George Eliot felt that Reade lacked Stowe's imaginative sympathy
and ability to portray characters. Stowe, unlike Reade, "attains her
finest dramatic effects by means of her energetic sympathy, and not
by conscious artifice" ("Three Novels", p. 315). In this comment, as
in the ubiquitous later comparisons of Reade and Eliot, is the half-
hidden assumption that women writers can, through a natural extension of their innate nature and Victorian role, exercise a negative
capability – more easily forget themselves and their egos than male
writers – and enter sympathetically and selflessly into the hearts and
minds of their characters.[7]

Several other critics, however, including Besant, explicitly
contrast Reade with women novelists, usually to the detriment of the
latter, and usually to make some point about the unjust neglect of
Reade in favour of weak and inferior female novelists. Besant complains that publishers are biased towards female writers: "there are
a dozen women who read novels to one man; most women, like most
men, are lacking in imagination, and therefore like to have things
presented from their own, the feminine, point of view . . . one can very
well understand how those books which prophesy smooth things,
accept all the little social make-believes . . . may be more delightful to
many people than those which set forth the grave and terrible realities of the world" ("Charles Reade", p. 198). Besant's own language
reveals a distinct bias towards Reade's "serious" and important male
work, in comparison with what he sees as popular feminine frivoli-
ty. Critics, he believes, are sheep-like in their slavish pandering to
women writers: "while we have been inundated with essays on the
genius of George Eliot, Miss Thackeray, and others, I do not remember to have read one single serious effort to explain Charles Reade's
success"(p. 199). Besant goes on to rectify this omission by arguing
that Reade's success is due to his being a scholar, to knowing Latin
and Greek, to having a strong style, to preparing for authorship by

"life among men", by "cultivated talk in the Fellows' Common Room" (p. 204).

An 1869 *Blackwood's Edinburgh Magazine* article also complains that Reade has received less attention than that accorded female novelists, despite deserving more: "The works of the distinguished novelist . . . whom we are about to discuss, have, we believe, been less commented on by the critics of the day than those of . . . Miss Braddon or Ouida, or others of like calibre. And yet it would take half a hundred ordinary novelists to make up a shadow of the power . . . and splendid graphic force of the author of the "'Cloister and the Hearth'" (October 1869, p. 488).

In general, then, Reade is praised for the power, excitement, and rapidity of his plot, and likened in these respects to other male action and adventure novelists such as Dumas, Ainsworth, Fielding, and Walter Scott. As the *Spectator* puts it, "he has shown in the suspension of the denouement, and in the invention of the incidents that carry on this plot, the sort of talent that distinguishes Dumas the elder and our own Harrison Ainsworth" (16 August 1856, p. 77). Reade is faulted for his inability to reveal psychological depth and complexity, an ability that is frequently, though not exclusively, associated with women novelists, such as Harriet Beecher Stowe and George Eliot.

Reade was vehement that the importance of his novel lay in the plot, not in the characters, and particularly not in the female characters. One is reminded of his contemptuous disregard for the domestic novelists' "chronicles of small beer", and for Eliot's character analysis, which he felt "microscoped poodles into lions" (quoted in Burns, 1961, p. 161). He, on the other hand, was aiming determinedly at an epic roar, and was candid about his failure to make Susan three-dimensional. In his account of how he changed the initial title of his novel from *Susan Merton*, he states that *"Susan Merton* is a very bad title, because under that title, the book is a failure, Susan Merton being a third-rate character in point of invention and colour" (quoted in Elwin, 1931, p. 112).

When his characters were praised, they were admired for conforming to gender stereotypes, though contemporary critics did not, of course, use such terminology. The *Critic* likes the "charming contrast" between George Fielding and Susan Merton: "he a manly, real rustic; she a simple, loving maiden" (15 August 1856, p. 395). The male characters were generally acknowledged to be superior, though Besant claims, strangely, that Reade "invented the True Woman", and that his portrayals of women are far superior to those of women novelists: "there are plenty of sweet women in stories . . . the conventional girl of the better lady novelists, the detestable girl of the worser lady novelists; but Reade has found the real woman. She is always in the house . . . what he loves most is the true, genuine woman with her perfect abnegation of self" ("Charles Reade", p. 202). Reade, in other words, successfully replicates conventional middle-class notions of Victorian womanhood. Ouida, however, is equally convinced that Reade's female characters, while perhaps resembling female stereotypes, have little relation to actual upper-class women: "Of the woman who is essentially of our time, the woman of high culture, of artistic taste, of profound knowledge of men and manners . . . he has never had even the faintest imagination" ("Charles Reade", p. 495).

The most pointed and interesting gender-based comparison between Reade and women authors is the comparison and contrast with George Eliot. This comparison developed into an occasionally ugly Victorian controversy, into which Reade hurled himself whole-heartedly. Perhaps Eliot's fairly critical 1856 review of *It Is Never Too Late To Mend* was the start of Reade's animosity towards her; her opinion of him is transparent in a letter in 1858 to a friend: "How could you waste your pretty eyes in reading *White Lies*? Surely they are too precious to be spent on the inflated plagiarisms of a man gone mad with restless vanity and unveracity" (Haight, II, 1954, p. 422). Reade's rivalry towards Eliot is also revealed in the following anecdote from Justin McCarthy's *Reminiscences*: "To speak the truth frankly, Reade was an extremely self-conceited man . . . he once wrote indignantly to the editor of an American monthly magazine complaining of an article on English novelists which appeared in its pages because the writer of the article put Charles Reade on a level lower than that of George Eliot" (1900, p. 356).

By the 1860s and 1870s, comparisons of Reade and Eliot had become "fashionable", in Swinburne's words ("Charles Reade", p. 554). The controversy was fuelled by the proximity of their two historical novels, both of which had medieval/Renaissance Italian settings: Reade's *The Cloister and the Hearth* appeared in 1861, closely followed by Eliot's *Romola* in 1862. Swinburne's commentary in the *Nineteenth Century* is more restrained than most in this respect, but he does express preference for Reade's novel, and this preference is expressed in language with gender-laden implications: "when we come to collation of minor characters and groups the superiority of the male novelist is so obvious and so enormous that any comparison between the full robust proportions of his breathing figures and the stiff thin outlines of George Eliot's phantasmal puppets would be unfair if it were not unavoidable. The variety of life, the vigour of action, the straightforward and easy mastery displayed at every step in every stage of the fiction would of themselves be enough to place *The Cloister and the Hearth* among the very greatest masterpieces of narrative" (p. 556).[8]

Charles Reade's own assessment of the respective merits of *The Cloister and the Hearth* and *Romola* is painfully apparent in a letter he wrote to the *American Galaxy*, after it had printed an article comparing the two authors – the same letter referred to above by McCarthy. What is perhaps most striking about the letter, apart from its vitriolic fury, is the extent to which Reade's sense of his own superiority over Eliot is phrased according to gender hierarchies and distinctions; his own explicitly gendered self-assessment is exaggerated to the point of caricature. Eliot, he believes, has little or no power, and what power she does possess is "feeble": "She has no imagination of the higher kind, and no power of construction, nor dramatic power. She has a little humour, whereas most women have none" (*Bookman*, November 1903, p. 253). The implication is that men have a monopoly on the highest creative power, whereas women tend to demonstrate a secondary imitative kind of imagination. Also evident is the way in which Reade formulates his sense of irritated pride into a gender war; his own self-esteem as a writer seems to be inextricably caught up with his own male-gendered identity and the associations he has with masculinity. Thus Eliot's claim to fame is really due to another man: "her greatest quality of all is living with an anonymous writer [Lewes], who has bought the English press for a time and puffed her into a condition she cannot maintain and is gradually losing" (p. 253). He proceeds to contrast *Romola* with *The Cloister and the Hearth*, calling the "Middle Ages" "a gigantic theme" which the "unhappy scribbler" [Eliot] has "dwarfed . . . to her own size" (p. 253). Eliot, "his fair pupil", has, he writes condescendingly, copied all her best ideas from him. It is perhaps not surprising, considering Reade's personality, that he should have written about Eliot in such terms; what is more startling is the number of others who also accused Eliot of at most plagiarizing or at least being inspired by Reade.[9]

Once A Week devoted an 1872 article to arguing the superiority of Reade over Eliot, and to listing alleged plagiarisms. The *Once A Week* article actually juxtaposes scenes by Eliot and Reade in order to "prove" Eliot's plagiarism, but does not make a convincing case.[10] Like Reade in his letter, this article uses gendered adjectives to validate male qualities and male authors and denigrate female qualities and female authors. One alleged incident of plagiarism, the boat scene in *The Mill on the Floss*, is "petty and womanish by comparison with her [Eliot's] model" (20 January 1872, p. 83). *Romola*, unlike *The Cloister and the Hearth*, has no power, and presents an "emasculated" Savanarola: "One great historical figure, Savanarola, is taken, and turned into a woman by a female writer: sure sign imagination is wanting. There is a dearth of powerful incidents, though the time was full of them, as *The Cloister and the Hearth* is full of them" (p. 85). And the character portrayal is "delicate" (p. 85); needless to say, this adjective is not intended to be complimentary. Finally, the author refers to Reade's style as "masculine": "They [his books] are written in English as pure, as simple, and as truly Saxon as any this century has produced: in a literary style – nervous, vigorous, and masculine – with which the most captious and partizan critic cannot find any fault" (p. 87).[11]

What is it about Reade's style that is identified as masculine? Part of the answer involves readers' gender associations with Reade's dominating persona as narrator. His writing is often described in terms of physical strength; "forcible" is one of the most common adjectives used. Readers often expressed an ambivalent admiration for Reade's ability to hypnotize or cast a spell on them as readers. Some submitted happily to this spell, finding it exciting. The *Examiner* says that the book "commands the reader's unbroken attention from the first page to the last" (23 August 1856, p. 533). Other readers felt uneasy at this display of power. Lewes, for example, states that "the scenes of prison-life have strange fascination, and in many respects are painted with strange power" ("Charles Reade's New Novel", p. 809). Others feel that the spell is "harrowing", or "horrible", and readers who react this way feel puzzled or annoyed at being forced into a submissive role by Reade.[12] Both Lewes and Eliot objected to what they saw as Reade's inability to control his anger, to his semi-hysterical and "puerile" style. (In their use of "puerile" we see how masculinity can also have negative connotations.)[13]

An exploration of the following representative passage from *It Is Never Too Late To Mend* allows a more specific analysis of the gendered style of Reade's writing for Victorian readers:

God has been bountiful to the human race in this age . . . He has given us warlike heroes more than we can count . . . and valor as full of variety as courage in the Iliad is monotonous. . . .

He has given us to see Titans enslaved by man; steam harnessed to our carriages and ships . . . and now, gold revealed in the east and west at once, and so mankind now first in earnest peopling the enormous globe. Yet old women and children of the pen say this is a bad, a small, a lifeless, an unpoetic age: and they are not mistaken. For they lie.

As only tooth-stoppers, retailers of conventional phrases, links in the great cuckoo-chain, universal pill-venders, Satan, and ancient booksellers' ancient nameless hacks can lie, they lie.

It is they that are small-eyed. Now, as heretofore, weaklings cannot rise high enough to take a bird's-eye view of their own age, and calculate its dimensions.

The age, smaller than epochs to come, is a giant compared with the past, and full of mighty materials for any great pen in prose or verse.

My little friends aged nineteen and downwards – four-score and upwards – who have been lending your ears to the stale little cant of every age as chanted in this one by Buffo-Bombastes and other foaming-at-the-pen old women of both sexes – take, by way of antidote to all that poisonous soul-withering drivel, ten honest words.

I say before heaven and earth that the man who could grasp the facts of this day and do an immortal writer's duty by them . . . would be the greatest writer ever lived. . . . I say that he who has eyes to see may now see greater and far more poetic things than human eyes have seen since our Lord and His apostles and His miracles left the earth.

It is very hard to write a good book. . . . Bunglers will not mend matters by blackening the great canvases they can't paint on, nor the impotent become males by detraction . . . . the Titan events that stride so swiftly past IN THIS GIGANTIC AGE.   (pp. 76–8)

Through allusions to the epic tradition, as well as through reference to momentous historical developments, particularly those concerning the industrial revolution and the Empire, Reade clearly aligns himself with the masculine world. As the *Saturday Review* pointed out in 1857, many critics felt that the subject-matter and style of novels were too much directed towards women readers, and complained about the tendency of novels to concentrate on domestic issues, show-ing "a low range of thought", and failing to "investigate the great problems of life" (quoted in Bevington, 1941, p. 155). In contrast to domestic novels, Reade strikes a pose as a "man who could grasp the facts of the day" (p. 77), a "warlike hero" who might rival those of the *Iliad*. It is not surprising that this kind of declaration about the con-tent of his novel could lead his work to be perceived, as E. W. Hornung put it in 1921, as "the writing of a gentleman in his shirt-sleeves" ("Charles Reade", p. 162).

The gendered implications of the content and the references to epic are only intensified by the explicit references to gender in this pas-sage; these allusions play a helpful role in clarifying the importance of male-gendered connotations to Reade's own sense of identity as a writer. Reade juxtaposes his own epic vision of the Victorian age with the limited and lying vision of "old women and children of the pen". Apart from the obvious self-declaration as a "man" of the pen, and the clearly derogatory association of women with children and with the "old", women writers, as well as those male writers unfortunate enough to resemble women in this respect, are depicted as powerless and lacking in insight and vision. They are "retailers of convention-al phrases" – conventional probably being short-hand for popular domestic fiction by women, as it was in so many Victorian reviews – "weaklings", and "foaming-at-the-pen old women". In the final para-graph, Reade refers furiously to critics of writers such as himself, who are trying to "write a good book", as the "impotent" trying to "become males by detraction". Once again, masculinity and sexual vigour or power recur as self-defining characteristics of the author, and femi-ninity, effeminacy, and impotence become the associations in oppo-sition to which he defines himself.

Also notable in this passage, as in so much of *It Is Never Too Late To Mend*, is the constant use of images of size as a mark of evaluation; these images are clearly related to the masculine/feminine dichoto-my identified above. Thus the globe is "enormous", and the age is "gigantic" rather than "small". Not only is the age "a giant compared with the past", but it is also "full of mighty materials for any great pen in prose or verse". Predictably, size is again equated with power, and "mighty" is contrasted to his "little" friends who listen to the "little" cant produced by "old women of both sexes". The man who can see may now see "greater" things than have existed since Biblical days, and is in a position to be "the greatest writer ever lived". The canvas of such a book is also "great", as are "the Titan events" of what, not surprisingly printed in capital letters, is "THIS GIGANTIC AGE". Contemporary critics expressed amazement at such use of typography, but it seems a natural extension of Reade's overwhelming desire to be perceived as "great", and to be taken seriously as a contemporary chronicler of epics. Given Reade's conscious and strident assumption and equation of masculinity and greatness, it is perhaps not surprising that critics followed suit in the gendered adjectives they used to describe *It Is Never Too Late To Mend*.[14]

Despite their frequent irritation, the reviewers basically accepted Reade's domineering style because it conformed to their gender associations with his subject-matter and with him as a "masculine" writer.[15]

Analysis of Victorian critical commentary on Reade reveals a striking correlation between the content and style of *It Is Never Too Late To Mend* and contemporary perceptions about gender-appropriate writing. Indeed, as the above excerpts from reviews show, the degree to which gender associations and perceptions structure, frame, and dominate discussions of Reade is remarkable – it is no exaggeration to say that gender played a primary role in Reade's contemporary reception, and that the qualities critics valued in Reade are ordered by a gender-stratified way of approaching and evaluating literature.

What is also remarkable is the degree to which *It Is Never Too Late To Mend* is itself saturated with gender stereotypes; it depicts conventional Victorian gender associations, confirming the gender framework of the contemporary reader. One could perhaps conclude that reactions to Reade's novel were provoked and influenced by the style of writing to which they were responding. Norman Holland believes that, "all of us, as we read, use the literary work to symbolize and finally to replicate ourselves" ("Unity", p. 124). In the way in which the novel confirms the gender framework of the contemporary reader, it allows the reader to replicate himself and project a mirrored identity theme. My use of the generic male pronoun is not incidental – it would seem easier for male readers to have this psychological reaction to the text, which might account in part for Reade's popularity among male readers.

The extent to which Reade's novel echoed and exaggerated conventional Victorian gender stereotypes is, I believe, partly responsible for both its popularity and its subsequent critical demise. Jauss argues that the artistic value of a work is directly correlated to its distance from the expectations of its first readers, and that literary success, as opposed to artistic value, occurs when a book presents readers with their own images: "literary success presupposes a book which expresses what the group expects, a book which presents the group with its own image" (*Toward*, 1982, p. 26). *It Is Never Too Late To Mend* was extremely close to reader expectations, both in its topical content and in its gender constructions, and in this sense it did present readers with their own images. Jacques Leenhardt's research is consistent with that of Jauss. His investigation of the "unifying cultural schema" that help readers form patterns to understand a text, cites a survey in which French respondents expressed a preference for novels that contained material stereotypically close to their own preconceived ideas (*"Toward"*, pp. 205–23). Both Jauss's and Leenhardt's theories suggest that Victorian recognition of popular gender stereotypes in Reade's work was, at least in part, responsible for his success.

The gendered extremes of Reade's technique and content express a fervency that betrays a moral or religious urgency. This would suggest that Reade's work possessed an overtly ideological "function". Louis Althusser defines ideology as a system of representations in which the individual comes to recognize his or her position in the social formation, not as historically specific and socially constructed, but as "natural" and universally "true" ("Ideology", in 1971, pp. 162–83). Without broaching the problems of Althusser's aesthetics (see Bennett, 1979, pp. 118–31), it is clear that the difference between the gendered world of *It Is Never Too Late To Mend* and that of, say, *Barchester Towers* is that while the latter naturalizes gender roles, the former renders them visible – not to problematize Victorian constructions of gender, but to idealize them. In other words, as the blatantly gendered terms critics used to "evaluate" Reade would indicate, Victorian readers were well aware that Reade's "masculine" themes and qualities were foregrounded – that is, the ideology was easily "perceptible". However, this visibility did not function to distance the ideological from the "real", to make the representations "strange" and questionable, but rather it worked to valorize the gender constructions represented, re-infusing them with cultural value, rendering them not only natural, but heroic.

My examination of the gender constructions in Reade's novel, along with investigations of reviewers' use of the fundamental framework of gender assumptions, opens a window on the somewhat murky and often generalized realm of the influence of gender on reception, and proves that, in the case of *It Is Never Too Late To Mend*, reviewers were certainly not analyzing and evaluating from ideologically neutral positions, but in a historical context that evaluated literary works according to gender hierarchies.

In her discussion of the process of canonization, Herrnstein Smith suggests that "we make texts timeless by suppressing their temporality" ("Contingencies", p. 32), that we make "potentially alienating ideology" tolerable by interpreting it and allegorizing it "in terms of current ideologies" (p. 32). Reade foregrounds his "alienating" ideology so prominently that the text becomes resistant to such suppression or allegorization; ultimately we cannot repress our repulsion for Reade's designation of "old women and children of the pen" as a contemptible literary under-class.

3

The Unveiling of Ellis Bell: Emily Brontë's *Wuthering Heights*

And as a rule, the mass of women writers do write badly. . . . At the first blush, they seem to have many things in their favour. In the first place, they are refined and tender-hearted. . . . No woman would think of letting a character in her novel be a genuine hero who was cruel to flies, or who did not like babies, or who did not hate treading on a snail. Their books have generally a moral purpose . . .

> ("Authoresses", *The Saturday Review*,
> 11 November, 1865, p. 602)

In the midst of the reader's perplexity, the ideas predominant in his mind concerning this book are likely to be brutal cruelty and semi-savage love. What may be the moral which the author wishes the reader to deduce from his work, it is difficult to say

> ("Review of *Wuthering Heights*", *Douglas Jerrold's Weekly Newspaper*, 15 January, 1848, p. 77)

If we read it [Wuthering Heights] at all, we read in haste, and with a prior sense of repulsion, which dropped a veil between book and reader and was in truth only the result of an all but universal tenor of opinion amongst our elders

> (Mrs Humphrey Ward, quoted in Collister,
> "After 'Half a Century' ", p. 416)

Elaine Showalter's 1977 work *A Literature of Their Own* explored, among other things, the Victorian double standard in periodical reviewing, which was particularly strong, she argued, from the 1840s to the 1860s. Women, she wrote, were thought "to possess sentiment, refinement, tact, observation, domestic expertise, high moral tone, and knowledge of female character; and thought to lack originality, intellectual training, abstract intelligence, humor, self-control, and knowledge of male character" (1977, p. 90).[1] Carol Ohmann's 1971 article "Emily Brontë in the Hands of Male Critics" argued that the reception of *Wuthering Heights* was dominated by sexual prejudice. One of the most recent biographies of Emily Brontë, a 1990 work by Katherine Frank, reiterates Ohmann's emphasis on a sexual double standard in the reception of *Wuthering Heights*: "The sex of both Ellis and Currer Bell was almost as important to their early reviewers as the power of their stories. Indeed, a double standard clearly operated in the reactions to the novels" (1990, p. 237).

Neither Ohmann, nor Showalter, nor Frank offers an adequate account of the role of gender in the reception of *Wuthering Heights*. The straightforward and somewhat essentialist nature of Ohmann's thesis, combined with space constraints (in seven pages she accounts for the sexual double standard in both the nineteenth and twentieth centuries) limits complexity of analysis. Showalter addresses the Victorian sexual double standard in general, and does not focus on the specific case of *Wuthering Heights*. Frank fails to differentiate between the 1847/8 reviews of *Wuthering Heights*, written under the assumption that Ellis Bell was male, and the 1850 reviews of the second edition, written once Charlotte Brontë's "Biographical Notice" had unveiled Ellis Bell as Emily Brontë. Gender was indeed central to *Wuthering Heights*'s reception, and the implications of its role merits a more developed exploration. Recent approaches to *Wuthering Heights*, whether feminist, biographical, or Marxist, do not devote any sustained attention to the issue of gender and reception.[2]

A close examination of Charlotte Brontë's 1850 "Biographical Notice" and "Preface", probably the most influential "review" of all, is essential to a comprehensive study of the role of gender in the reception of *Wuthering Heights*. By now an intrinsic part of the Brontë myth, these two prefatory essays unveil the identity of Ellis Bell, give the circumstances of Emily Brontë's authorship and subsequent death, and make it clear that, despite rumours of Ellis and Currer Bell being pseudonyms for the same author, Emily Brontë alone was responsible for *Wuthering Heights*. Charlotte Brontë emphasizes not only that she had no part in her sister's novel, but that she is herself ambivalent about both its literary merit and its morality. In my judgement, both the "Biographical Notice" and the "Preface" were prompted by

a conscious or unconscious desire on Charlotte Brontë's part to distance and dissociate herself from the unfeminine "coarseness" of her
sister's novel, and to prevent critical attacks on *Wuthering Heights* from
spreading contagiously to *Jane Eyre*, already vulnerable to such accusations.[3] Charlotte Brontë's own gender preconceptions and anxiety
about her own reputation as a woman novelist influenced her public
assessment of *Wuthering Heights*. As I will argue below, Charlotte's
depiction of both Emily and herself exploit what, in reference to the
tone of eighteenth-century women novelists, Showalter terms "a
stereotype of helpless femininity to win chivalrous protection from
male reviewers and to minimize . . . unwomanly self-assertion" (1977,
p. 17).

The "Biographical Notice" and "Preface" provided a critical context for what was perceived as a tantalizingly unplaceable work in
1847, but the gender messages of this new context affected the tenor
and content of subsequent critical assessment. The 1850 reviews
focused primarily on the biographical information in Charlotte
Brontë's prefatory essays. After critics had recovered from the shock
of discovering Ellis Bell's identity, and after they had speculated chivalrously on the biographical material, they turned their attention to the
eccentricity, for some the impossibility, of *Wuthering Heights* as a
woman's novel; this led, at its most extreme manifestation, to rumours
that the novel had really been written by Patrick Branwell Brontë,
Emily Brontë's brother, who had then dictated the novel to Emily.

Jonathan Culler argues that readers' interpretations of a text depend
not on the text itself, but on the reading conventions and sign systems
they apply to literature; literary competence involves focusing on
publicly held definitions of appropriate interpretations.[4] Gender
schema, as Mary Crawford and Roger Chaffin demonstrate, provide
one framework for the construction of meaning. In Victorian culture,
with its rigidly demarcated gender roles, readers had different expectations of writing by men and by women.[5]

Women's writing was expected to form a natural extension of female
domestic roles; in the 1840s "domestic realism" formed the most prevalent female genre.[6] In such a context, it is not surprising that, on
its first appearance, *Wuthering Heights* was thought of as over-
whelmingly masculine; there was little question in the minds of the
reviewers that Ellis Bell was male. *Wuthering Heights* explodes the safe
and idealized domestic world represented by Victorian women and
portrayed in conventional domestic novels, with its story of frustrated
love, violence, and death; its strength of language (its intensity and

its profanity) reflects the unconventionality of the plot. *Wuthering Heights* is, in fact, a radical transformation of the genre. Even as the work of a man, *Wuthering Heights* was shockingly unusual. David Cecil goes so far as to argue that, if measured against Dickens, Thackeray, Trollope, and Gaskell, *Wuthering Heights* makes no sense as a Victorian novel: "she [Emily Brontë] stands outside the main current of nineteenth-century fiction as markedly as Blake stands outside the main current of eighteenth-century poetry" (1934, p. 138).[7]

Critical reaction to the 1847/8 edition of *Wuthering Heights* under the gender-neutral pseudonym of Ellis Bell was one of irritated, frustrated bafflement. Critics tried desperately to label and define the novel, but the extent to which it defeated them is evident in the fact that it was invariably reviewed on its own (or with *Agnes Grey*, included in the three volume "set"), unlike Charles Reade's *It Is Never Too Late To Mend*, for example. (A reviewer from the *Examiner* compared Ellis Bell to an obscure male novelist by the name of Hooton who wrote a novel about a wandering tramp, and was, supposedly, in the tradition of Fielding.)[8] The sense of "mastery" that Culler identifies as part of finishing reading a book, when experience turns to knowledge and takes the reader outside the experience of reading, eluded the reviewers until 1850. With the "Biographical Notice" and "Preface" provided by Charlotte Brontë as introduction to the 1850 edition of *Wuthering Heights*, the tone of the reviewers changes from one of bewilderment to confidence, even to condescension. At this point gender frameworks and preconceptions take charge, and the tone of the reviewers often becomes protective and patronizing.

Elizabeth Flynn classifies readers into three groups: "submissive", "interactive", and "dominant". She argues that male readers tend to be more dominant than female readers, who are more likely to be interactive. Although her argument seems vulnerable to charges of being reductively schematic, her definition of dominant readers is helpful when discussing how reviewers related Brontë's prefatory essays to *Wuthering Heights*: dominant readers apply an externally derived framework to the text they are reading, and this framework allows them to remain emotionally and intellectually distant from the text, to the point of "silencing" it. As we shall see below, the 1850 reviewers of *Wuthering Heights* are "dominant" readers, readers whose ideas about gender create a barrier between themselves and the text, a barrier which is reflected in their focus on the biographical information rather than on the novel.

The sense of relief felt by critics as they are finally provided with a context for *Wuthering Heights* is tangible in the reviews: this new context forms part of a pre-existing and elaborately structured hierarchy and pattern of gender roles and rules, and allows the reviewers a means of controlling and containing the otherwise troubling and elusive *Wuthering Heights*. Norman Holland's psychoanalytical literary approach suggests that "we match inner defenses and expectations to outer realities [the text] in order to project fantasies into . . . significance" (Flynn and Schweickart, 1986, p. xxiii). In 1847, readers' defence mechanisms and frustrated expectations led to an ambivalent mix of confusion, shock, and admiration; the 1850 "Preface" functions as a strategy for "each individual reader . . . to [achieve] pleasure and [avoid] distress"(p. xxiii).[9]

According to some historical accounts, in 1847 *Wuthering Heights* was "passed over, disregarded", as A. Mary F. Robinson, one of Emily Brontë's first biographers, puts it (1883, p. 278), and was rejected unequivocally. In fact, Brontë's novel received a significant amount of critical attention, sold out of the first edition, and was not condemned totally or unanimously.[10] In fact, what is perhaps most striking in the early reviews is the reviewers' ambivalence about the quality and effect of *Wuthering Heights*. This ambivalence surfaces in the syntactic arrangement of individual critical assessments; the sentences are often composed with a "yes . . . but" structure, where an independent clause begins by admiring the "power" of the novel, but is quickly followed by a qualifying assessment. A representative example is the review from *Douglas Jerrold's Weekly Newspaper*, which states that "there seems to us great power in this book, but a purposeless power, which we feel a great desire to see turned to better account" (15 January 1848, p. 77). The *Literary Register* echoes this sentiment, praising the novel's "undoubtedly powerful writing," but lamenting that "it seems to be thrown away" (February 1848, p. 139). This sense of conflicting response is reflected in the *Examiner's* use of double negatives: "This is a strange book. It is not without evidence of considerable power, but, as a whole, it is wild, confused, disjointed, and improbable" (8 January 1848, p. 21).

The "literary competence" of the reviewers is challenged as they struggle in vain to judge the work by relating it to Victorian literary conventions. Such conventions include beliefs about the aim of art, the need for a moral, and the "proper" behaviour of characters in general, heroes and female characters in particular. Many reviews expressed the sense that novels should "modify and in some cases refine" the ordinary world, as the *Examiner* put it, and that, as *The Economist* stated, art should provide a "pleasing interest" (29 January 1848, p. 126). *Wuthering Heights* clearly deviated from such ideals. The *Athenaeum*, for example, found the novel "eccentric" and "unpleasant" in this respect, and other reviewers felt even more outraged at the "cruelty" and "inhumanity" of the work. Reviewers were frustrated by the novel's failure to replicate middle-class social ideals. Characters should be "civilized", should not be taken from "low-class" walks of life, and if intended to be the hero, should be suitably "moral" and well-behaved – *Peterson's Magazine* exclaims in confusion over Heathcliff, that the "hero is a villain" (June 1848, p. 229). The *Brittania*'s reviewer is alarmed to note that the female characters in the novel actually engage in physical fights.

Almost all reviewers diligently search for a moral, are troubled at their inability to find one, and sometimes invent their own in compensation. "What may be the moral which the author wishes the reader to deduce from his work, it is difficult to say," writes the critic from *Douglas Jerrold's Weekly Newspaper* (January 1848, p. 77). *The Literary Register* poses a series of questions to the novel which the novel stubbornly resists: "We want to know the object of fiction. . . . Do they [novels] teach mankind to avoid one course and take another? Do they dissect any portion of existing society? . . . If these questions were asked regarding *Wuthering Heights*, there could not be an affirmative answer given" (February 1848, p. 139). The *Union Magazine* is annoyed that there is "no attempt at placing the evil in its true deformity", and *Britannia* is one of several periodicals that goes so far as to invent a moral: "We do not know whether the author writes with any purpose; but we can speak of one effect of his production. It strongly shows the brutalizing influence of unchecked passion" (15 January 1848, p. 43).

Reviewers, then, felt that the absence of a moral, the subject-matter of the book, and the character portrayal broke the unwritten authorial contract with the reader, leaving the reader with only a partial map to a foreign country; the novel was not didactic, did not reflect Victorian middle-class society, and showed no sign of following in any literary tradition they could identify.

When *Wuthering Heights* first appeared, critics unanimously assumed the author was male. They admired *Wuthering Heights* for

its so-called masculinity, for the ways in which it diverged from conventional popular (and, by implication, feminine) novels, but they
also felt that the novel went too far in this direction, to the point of
being offensively unfit for social consumption.

The plot, characterization, and language did not correspond with
what G. H. Lewes termed typical productions of "The Lady Novelists",
novels formulated around "domestic experience", "Sentiment",
and "the joys and sorrows of affection" ("The Lady Novelists",
p. 133). Instead, the aspect of *Wuthering Heights* most frequently identified was its "power", a characteristic invariably associated in
Victorian literary criticism with male authors. Reviewers admired
the book's rejection of "effeminate frippery", as one critic called
it. The gender overtones of the praise given to *Wuthering Heights*
are explicit, keeping in mind Victorian associations with women's
writing. The "rough, shaggy, uncouth power" that the *Literary
World* found in *Wuthering Heights* makes another reviewer imagine
the author as "a rough sailor . . . not a gentleman", who mistakenly
believes he can understand women (quoted in Ohmann, "Emily
Brontë", p. 908). Certainly, "rough", "shaggy", and "uncouth" are
not qualities we would associate with decorous middle-class
Victorian womanhood. Similarly the "original energy" found by
the *Britannia*'s reviewer in this novel obviously coincides more
closely with Victorian ideas about male intellectual production
than with their ideas about female creativity.[11] An 1850 *Examiner*
review of *The Tenant of Wildfell Hall* assesses Ellis and Acton Bell
thus: "The Bells are of a hardy race. They do not lounge in drawing-
rooms or boudoirs. The air they breathe is not that of the hothouse or
of perfumed apartments . . . whatever may be their defects . . . they
are not common-place writers" (21 December 1850, p. 815). "Common-
place" is clearly identified with women writers, whereas, despite their
shocking qualities, the Bells are pleasingly and originally masculine.
The *Examiner* is beguiled by what it perceives as the masculine qualities of *Wuthering Heights*, though it warns the author against carrying this to an extreme: "We detest the affectation and effeminate
frippery which is but too frequent in the modern novel, and willing-
ly trust ourselves to an author who goes at once fearlessly into the
moors and desolate places for his heroes" (8 January 1848, p. 22).
Douglas Jerrold's reviewer grudgingly admires a style that is "apparently disdainful of prettiness" (15 January 1848, p. 77). (Region and
gender connect interestingly here: the North of England is commonly seen as intrinsically more rough, wild, and uncivilized than the

more domesticated and urban south, and these connotations have clear gender and class associations.)

Despite their admiration for the power of *Wuthering Heights*, reviewers abhorred its "coarseness" of plot, character, and language – Ellis Bell had gone so far in an otherwise admirable direction that he had over-stepped acceptable boundaries of taste. Nevertheless, many felt fascinated by *Wuthering Heights*, despite its "strange" and "dark" qualities, and more than one review expressed the sentiment that the reader was somehow compelled to read, despite being repelled – that the novel exerted a forceful and dominating effect on the reader, in the manner of Charles Reade. The *Literary World* refers to the book's power as a "strange magic": forcing the reader to "read what we dislike . . . . we are made subject to the immense power of the book" (29 April 1848, p. 243).

Most 1847 and 1848 reviews of *Wuthering Heights* were intrigued by the similarities they found between the novels by Currer and Ellis Bell. Usually, this worked to the advantage of *Wuthering Heights*, giving it a ready-made readership predisposed to find it interesting. As Elizabeth Gaskell states in her biography, "many critics insisted on believing that all the fictions published by the Bells were the works of one author, but written at different periods of his development and maturity. No doubt this suspicion affected the reception of the books" (1892, p. 277). T. Newby, Emily's publisher, and, by all accounts an unscrupulous businessman, exploited this confusion of authorship, realizing that it was bound to increase sales of *Wuthering Heights*, and apart from doing his best to spread the rumour in England, went so far as to claim, in the American edition, that *Jane Eyre* and *Wuthering Heights* were both products of Currer Bell.

The *Literary World* is typical of other periodicals in the way it links Ellis and Currer Bell: "The book throughout is characterized by the same mind whose peculiarities of thought and expression are stamped upon the work of Currer Bell" (29 April 1848, p. 243). The *Athenaeum* finds the "cast of thought, incident, and language" so similar to *Jane Eyre* that its "curiosity" is excited (25 December 1847, p. 1324). *Britannia* states that in "many respects they [*Wuthering Heights* and *Agnes Grey*] remind us of the recent novel of *Jane Eyre*. We presume they proceed from one family, if not from one pen" (43). However, even though its connections with *Jane Eyre* increased the readership of *Wuthering Heights*, the initial expectations of the reviewers of the latter, conditioned by their admiration for the former, caused them to be intensely disappointed by the shocking departure from convention in Emily's novel.

Wuthering Heights, then, reaped some advantages from the confusion of authorship; this was not the case for *Jane Eyre*, and Charlotte Brontë suffered bitterly from the associations drawn between her work and that of her sister. Although *Jane Eyre* had been extremely popular with the reading public and had received mostly positive reviews, some reviewers had found the work shocking and unfeminine – hence the controversy over the sex of the author. In December 1848, almost exactly a year after *Wuthering Heights* was first published, Elizabeth Rigby voiced the most outspoken protest against what she perceived as the revolutionary and unfeminine qualities of Currer Bell's work. Other critics and readers had expressed similar protests on *Jane Eyre*'s first appearance, albeit in more subdued terminology.[12] When reviewers read *Wuthering Heights*, they found it to be an exaggeration or caricature of the qualities they had been somewhat disturbed by in *Jane Eyre*, and this in turn made them think of *Jane Eyre* as more controversial, particularly when they thought of it as another work by the same author. *Peterson's Magazine* assesses the two novels in fairly typical terms:

> The novel reading world were taken by storm when *Jane Eyre* appeared . . . and the inquiry instantly arose as to who the anonymous author could be. The general opinion finally decided that Harriet Martineau was the writer. But the appearance of *Wuthering Heights* about a month after the issue of *Jane Eyre* changed this belief; for Miss Martineau, it was confessed, could never have written anything so coarse as *Wuthering Heights*. The hero is a villain . . . and the best characters are as bad as the worst in other books. We rise from the perusal of *Wuthering Heights* as if we had come fresh from a peat-house. Read *Jane Eyre*, is our advice, but burn *Wuthering Heights*. (June 1848, p. 229)

For reviewers convinced that Ellis and Currer Bell were one person, the appearance of Emily's novel ended the controversy over the sex of the author of *Jane Eyre*, since, if Currer Bell was the author of *Wuthering Heights*, he had to be male. As one reviewer put it, "we hope it will be proven to have been written by another hand than that which wrote *Jane Eyre*, but if the authorship should be identical, it will at least settle the much-discussed question of sex. No woman could write *Wuthering Heights*" (*The Union Magazine*, June 1848, p. 287).

The *Quarterly Review* and the *North British Review* both convey a clear sense of how much Charlotte Brontë stood to lose from the association of *Jane Eyre* with *Wuthering Heights*. One of the recurrent themes in this discussion is the supposed similarity between the characters of Rochester and Heathcliff. The *Quarterly Review* becomes almost speechless in its disgust at the way in which the characters in *Wuthering Heights* are, in its eyes, even more uncivilized and immoral than their so-called counterparts in *Jane Eyre*: "For though there is a decided family likeness between the two, yet the aspect of the Jane and Rochester animals in their native state, as Cathy and Heathcliff, is too odiously and abominably pagan to be palatable even to the most vitiated class of English readers" (Rigby, "A Review of *Jane Eyre*", p. 175). The *North British Review* states explicitly that its opinion of *Wuthering Heights* leads it to re-evaluate *Jane Eyre*: "But there are more latent objections to the tendency of this powerful book [*Jane Eyre*], which we are apt to overlook on a first perusal, and of the perniciousness of which we can only judge when we have seen them developed in other works professedly proceeding from the same source" (August 1849, p. 480).

Given the tone of the above reviews, and considering Charlotte Brontë's desire for her novel to be critically and socially acceptable, it is not surprising that she desired to distance herself from *Wuthering Heights* and Ellis Bell. Charlotte Brontë, already sensitive to the precarious status of *Jane Eyre*'s reputation, was far from delighted at being associated with such unfeminine coarseness. Romer Wilson describes Charlotte's initial response to the authorship confusion thus:

> Soon after these publications [*Wuthering Heights* and *Agnes Grey*] began that misattribution of authorship in the press that caused Charlotte so much agitation. The *Athenaeum* and other papers attributed *Jane Eyre* to Ellis Bell. 'Ellis Bell is strong enough to stand without being propped by Currer Bell,' said Charlotte, obviously nervous of appearing under that dark name. (1982, p. 277)

Charlotte Brontë's "Biographical Notice" and "Preface" should be read in the context of the author's anxiety about being associated with Emily. Read in this manner, they assume an altogether different tone and meaning, one strongly influenced by Charlotte's own ambivalence towards Victorian gender ideals and her sense of identity as a Victorian woman writer.[13] In turn, these 1850 prefatory comments were the most influential "review" of *Wuthering Heights* to date, and shaped subsequent reviews of, and reactions to, Emily Brontë's novel.

The ostensible purpose behind Charlotte's "Biographical Notice of Ellis and Acton Bell" was two-fold: to prove the actual authorship of the Bell novels, and "to wipe the dust off their [Emily's and Anne's] gravestones, and leave their dear names free from soil" (1850, p. 8). These two purposes were contradictory, forcing Brontë to adopt some rather strained arguments. The only person whose reputation would be "unsoiled" by a clarification of the real authorship was Currer Bell or Charlotte Brontë herself; this, in my judgement, is the main purpose of the "Biographical Notice", a purpose clearly at odds with its second declared intention. If we keep in mind the 1847/8 reviews, it becomes clear that Ellis Bell was redeemed somewhat by her association with Currer Bell, since critics who thought they were the same person usually imagined that *Wuthering Heights* was an earlier and "ruder" production than *Jane Eyre*, with the implication that its author was now more mature, civilized, and polite. Emily/Ellis benefited from the assumption that her earlier tendencies had become smoothed and refined. Most critics, however, have taken the "Biographical Notice" at face value, as in the following example from Winifred Gérin: "in nineteenth-century England Currer Bell felt obliged to make concessions to the Establishment to protect her sister's good name against possible charges of paganism" (1971, p. 263).

Once she distances herself from *Wuthering Heights* by explaining its real authorship, Charlotte Brontë attempts to act as "the interpreter" who "ought always to have stood between her [Emily] and the world" (1850, p. 8). Brontë's "interpretation" of Emily is filtered through her own self-image as a woman writer, and her own anxiety about the similarities between their books. She exaggerates the critical attacks on *Wuthering Heights*, and when she singles out a review for praise it is not one that is essentially complimentary to *Wuthering Heights*, even though we know from Charles Simpson's biography of Emily Brontë that one of the five reviews Emily kept in her desk was unequivocally flattering.[14]

Charlotte Brontë situates her defence of Emily within the context of Victorian ideas about women and women writers. If *Wuthering Heights* by Ellis Bell was too coarse, too suggestive, and too pagan, *Wuthering Heights* by Emily Brontë would clearly be open to charges of monstrous sex-role transgressions. What Charlotte does, then, is to recreate an image of Emily as, in some ways, a stereotype of the ideal Victorian woman: passive, nun-like, innocent, domestic, and ignorant of the outside world. In other ways, she depicts her as so strange that she cannot be held subject to Victorian ideas about social conventions: she is a child-like mystic, with a passionate attachment to the natural world.

The "Biographical Notice" explicitly foregrounds the Brontë sisters' perception of a Victorian double standard in literary criticism: "without at that time suspecting that our mode of writing and thinking was not what is called 'feminine' – we had a vague impression that authoresses are liable to be looked on with prejudice" (1850, p. 4). This extract is well known. What, however, is seldom if ever discussed is the way in which Charlotte Brontë's defence is itself informed by Victorian gender stereotypes. Nancy Armstrong probably comes closest in her remarks on Brontë's depoliticization of her sister: "Encouraging readers to locate the meaning of Emily's fiction in the secret recesses of her emotional life, the Preface dismisses such violations of the sexual contract as mere symptoms of imperfect gender definition. But in doing so . . . [it] brings the norms of gender to bear on the fiction in question and effectively feminizes, or removes that fiction from political controversy" (*Desire*, 1987, p. 46).[15]

If we take Armstrong's point further and examine the ways in which Brontë contradicts herself about gender roles, at once protesting against and endorsing Victorian social constructions of gender, Charlotte's public ambivalence towards Emily's work becomes increasingly apparent. The tensions in the argument only emphasize the problematic position of the Victorian woman writer. Two paragraphs before Charlotte delivers her famous comment on the Victorian literary double standard, she praises Emily's poetry for being "not common effusions, nor at all like the poetry women generally write" (1850, p. 4). Implied in this comment is a rigid gender-defined set of artistic criteria that coincide with what she subsequently complains about.[16]

Later in the "Biographical Notice" and "Preface", Charlotte draws a picture of Emily as conventionally feminine in her artistic passivity and innocence. In an attempt to exculpate Emily from any accusations of coarseness and immoral lack of femininity, she depicts her sister as the helpless victim of artistic inspiration: "the writer who possesses the creative gift owns something of which he is not always master – something that at times strangely wills and works for itself. . . . Be the work grim or glorious, dread or divine, you have little choice left but quiescent adoption. As for you – the nominal artist – your share of it has been to work passively under dictates you neither delivered nor could question – that would not be uttered at your prayer, nor suppressed or changed at your caprice" (1850, p. 12). This description of the "nominal artist" coincides with the common practice in Victorian literary criticism of granting men primary or creative imagination, and seeing in women's artistic works a lesser imagination, one characterized by a more passive, even imitative, inspiration.[17] Brontë creates an image of Emily as the victim of an aggressive visitation from the gods of inspiration.

One of Charlotte's other main concerns in these two prefatory essays was to deal with the suspicion that the "immorality" of *Wuthering Heights* stemmed from real-life experience and observation on the part of the author. Such a suspicion would have caused reviewers to reflect on the moral integrity of any writer, but with particularly problematic results for women, since female writers, it was thought, having less access to active intellectual talent, relied more on passive observation for the creation of their literary works.[18] Charlotte thus takes pains to emphasize her sister's total ignorance of the "world", overlooking Emily's stay in Belgium as teacher and pupil and perhaps trying to hide Branwell's drug and alcohol addiction as a possible artistic source: "I am bound to avow that she had scarcely more practical knowledge of the peasantry amongst whom she lived, than a nun has of the country people who sometimes pass her convent gates. . . . Having formed these beings [Heathcliff and Cathy] she did not know what she had done" (1850, p. 10).

An aura of sexual innocence is created by the "veil" image in these two essays. Their pseudonyms "veiled" (p. 4) their identities, and Anne's feelings were masked by a "nun-like veil which was rarely lifted" (p. 8). The nun and veil images emphasize that the unconventional attributes of the works of Emily and Anne should be exempt from usual Victorian associations. Any eccentricities critics might find in *Wuthering Heights* as a woman's novel must, Brontë implies, be attributed to innocence and lack of worldly and social experience. She also emphasizes the importance of region to an understanding of *Wuthering Heights*, claiming that the moors were a "wild workshop", partly responsible for any impression of strangeness and lack of femininity reviewers might derive from *Wuthering Heights*.

Apart from attempting to exonerate Emily from possible charges of immorality and coarseness, Brontë also uses the "Biographical Notice" and "Preface" to distance herself from Emily's work by making clear her own misgivings about *Wuthering Heights*. Her own doubts as a "reviewer" are evident in her selection of Sydney Dobell's *Palladium* article as the exception that recognized Emily's talent, in her strong qualifications of any praise granted to Emily, and in her exaggeration of the negativity of the reviews.

Dobell's essay on "Currer Bell" was written under the impression that *Wuthering Heights* was an inferior early effort of Currer Bell.

Apart from establishing the "absolute superiority" of *Jane Eyre*, Dobell also mixes his praise of *Wuthering Heights* with criticism. "The authoress [Dobell writes] has too often disgusted, where she should have terrified, and has allowed us a familiarity with her fiend which has ended in unequivocal contempt" ("A Review", p. 218). Considering Dobell's attitude towards *Wuthering Heights*, and bearing in mind that there were more flattering reviews of Emily's work, Charlotte's decision to single out Dobell as the only "seer" demonstrates at best an ambivalence towards *Wuthering Heights* and towards her sister's reputation as a writer, and, at worst, a desire to differentiate her own work from that of her sister, establishing her superiority over Emily.

Shortly after she praises Dobell's "fine sympathies of genius" (1850, p. 6), Charlotte proceeds to call Emily's mind "original", only to qualify this with the following comment in parentheses: "however unripe, however inefficiently cultured and partially expanded that mind may be" (p. 6). Despite the ostensible effort to praise her sister, the instinct to qualify this praise seems to assume a more prominent place, and consume a greater amount of energy.

Finally, Charlotte exaggerates the negativity of the 1847 and 1848 reviews, as both the *Leader* and the *Examiner* point out in their reviews of the 1850 edition of *Wuthering Heights*. She argues that "critics failed to do [*Wuthering Heights* and *Agnes Grey*] justice. The immature but very real powers revealed in *Wuthering Heights* were scarcely recognized; its import and nature were misunderstood; the identity of its author was misrepresented" (p. 5). My excerpts from the early reviews above indicate that while reviewers were shocked and confused by Emily's novel, they did, in many cases, explicitly recognize its "real powers" – more so in fact than Charlotte Brontë does in the prefatory essays. Charlotte Brontë claims that *Wuthering Heights*'s reputation suffered by its being thought of as an author's attempt to "palm off an inferior and immature production under cover of one successful effort" (p. 5). In fact, as I argued above, and as the following excerpt from a *North British Review* essay confirms, *Jane Eyre* was the work that suffered from the juxtaposition: "Of the many among whom *Jane Eyre* made a sensation, not a few professed themselves a little shocked. . . . Especially was this antipathy a force at a time when she [Currer Bell] was the accredited author of that wild wicked wilful tale, *Wuthering Heights*" (quoted in Winnifrith, 1973, p. 128). When critics compared the two works, they sometimes commented disapprovingly on the similarity they found between Rochester and Heathcliff.[19] With this in mind, Charlotte's explicit criticism of the creation of

Heathcliff in the "Preface" can also be read as a defensive move: "Whether it is right or advisable to create beings like Heathcliff I do not know: I scarcely think it is" (1850, p. 12).

A. R. Brick argues that Charlotte saw herself as guardian of her sisters' reputations, and was just as concerned that their reputations should not be over-valued as under-valued ("Lewes's Review", p. 356). Charlotte was, of course, the oldest sister, and as such played a maternal role to her younger siblings; at the same time, however, she must have felt somewhat ambivalent towards the literary success of her sisters given that her *The Professor* was rejected in favour of *Wuthering Heights* and *Agnes Grey*, which were accepted before *Jane Eyre* was even published. Charlotte was concerned, then, that her sisters' literary reputation should not be over-valued, and with establishing her own reputation as a moral and respectable Victorian woman writer, while at the same time assuming an acceptably conventional public role as interpreter, guardian, and protector. Part of this motivation may well have been unconscious, however, and Charlotte's "unveiling" of Emily does attempt to salvage Emily's moral reputation as much as possible while simultaneously, and, as I suggested above, somewhat contradictorily, salvaging her own.

The 1850 reviews of the second edition of *Wuthering Heights* are dominated by Charlotte Brontë's two prefatory essays. What is perhaps most obvious in their tone is an overwhelming sense of relief that finally a context has been provided in which to place *Wuthering Heights*. The reviews focus far more on the "Biographical Notice" than on *Wuthering Heights* itself, and when they do re-examine the novel, it is through the focus of Charlotte's perspective, a biographical focus that has characterized writing about Emily Brontë's novel to the present day. Reviewers follow Charlotte Brontë's lead in responding to and echoing Charlotte's comments about Emily's innocence, the isolation and eccentricity of her lifestyle, and the effects of the region on her work.

The *Leader*, the *Examiner*, the *Eclectic Review*, and *The Economist* all express gratitude for the provision of a context for *Wuthering Heights*. The *Examiner* refers to "the author of *Jane Eyre* partially [lifting] the veil from a history and mystery of authorship which has occupied the Quidnuncs of literature for the last two years" (21 December 1850, p. 815). *The Economist* is "glad to see the mystery that hung over the authorship of these works and of *Jane Eyre* cleared up" (no. 9, 1851, p. 15). The *Eclectic Review* expresses, though in a more unabashed way, the sentiments of all the critics when it finds the "Biographical Notice" more interesting than *Wuthering Heights* itself: "We purpose dealing rather with the Biographical Notice prefixed to this volume, than with the two works which it contains. . . . It is sufficient to say that the former interests us deeply, which the latter do not" (February 1851, p. 222).

Both the *Leader* and the *Examiner* find fault with just one aspect of the "Biographical Notice", Charlotte's description of the critical reception of *Wuthering Heights*. The *Leader* argues that "to judge from the extracts given of articles in the *Britannia* and *Atlas*, the critics were excessively indulgent" (Lewes, "Review", p. 953). The *Examiner* reprints an excerpt from its previous review in order to demonstrate Charlotte's exaggeration, and makes the telling point that Charlotte's comments in her prefatory essays are themselves similar in tone to that of the reviews: "Did it [the *Examiner*'s original review of *Wuthering Heights*] 'misunderstand' or 'misrepresent' them? If so, Currer Bell must herself share the reproach, for the language in which she speaks of her sister Emily's early habits and associations, as explaining what was faulty as well as what was excellent in her writings, does not materially differ from this which has just been quoted" (21 December 1850, p. 815). I would agree with the *Examiner* in this, and think that Charlotte aligns herself clearly with the reviewers in terms of outlook, tone, and language, part of her attempt to establish herself as a legitimate and respectable Victorian author.

After critics were told that Ellis was a woman, their attitudes towards *Wuthering Heights* shifted accordingly. *Wuthering Heights* by Emily Brontë was somehow different from *Wuthering Heights* by Ellis Bell. Reviewers began discussing Brontë as a female novelist, a sub-group regulated by other rules than those for male novelists. The 1851 *Athenaeum* review refers disparagingly to "isolated women writers"; *The Economist* remarks that "without a knowledge of their [the Brontës'] lives English literary history would have been deficient of a remarkable chapter concerning female authorship" (no. 9, 1851, p. 15). Even though critics previously had no doubt that the author was male, they now see internal evidence of female authorship, as in the following excerpt from the *Eclectic Review*: "It appears to us impossible to read them without feeling that their excellences and faults, their instinctive attachments and occasional exaggerations, the depths of their tenderness and their want of practical judgment all betoken the authorship of a lady" (February 1851, p. 223). Similarly, the *Leader* now reads *Wuthering Heights* as a love story, and with its choice of adjectives could be describing a conventional feminine romance: "we feel the truth of his [Heathcliff's] burning and impassioned love for Catherine, and of her inextinguishable love for him . . . although she is ashamed of her early playmate she loves him with a passionate abandonment which sets culture, education, the world, at defiance. It is in the treatment of this subject that Ellis Bell shows mastery" (Lewes, "Review", p. 953).

Critics approached both Emily Brontë's life and her book with a mixture of fascination and chivalric condescension. The 1850 reviews often constructed their own elaborate fantasy upon the biographical context, a fantasy clearly shaped by their preconceptions about gender roles. *The Economist*, for example, feels that the biographical drama increases the interest of Wuthering Heights since

> it explains to us also some of the peculiarities of *Jane Eyre*, and gives us a beautiful picture of three young women, living in a remote place, animated by a heroic desire for distinction by useful and honourable labours. . . . In them it must have been the offspring of knowledge and reflection – an intellectual desire, which of itself designates strong, if not peculiar minds.   (vol. 9, 1851, p. 15)

Similarly, the *Eclectic Review* waxes lyrical when it contemplates the biographical background of the Brontë sisters, and converts this picture into a conventionally sentimental Victorian scene of "domestic harmony and love":

> It [the Biographical Notice] has much literary interest, but to us it is yet far more interesting in the picture it exhibits of domestic harmony and love, broken in upon and shaded by the presence of "the king of terrors". . . . May the survivor combine, with her intellectual occupations, the faith and devotion which stand in intimate connexion with joys unspeakable and divine! (February 1851, p. 227)

The new awareness of Ellis Bell's way of life, innocence, and regional isolation led to an increased sympathy with her novel, a tendency to excuse the author from normal standards of literary and female propriety. Emily Brontë's death, described so poignantly in Charlotte's 1850 "Biographical Notice", may also have led critics to be more lenient in their treatment of her. Consequently, *Wuthering Heights* was not judged as severely in 1850 as it had been in 1847 and 1848.[20]

Once the initial amazement with the biographical circumstances of

Emily's composition had been somewhat dispelled, critics returned to the problems raised by the new context, focusing their confusion on the matter of sex and asking how a woman could have written such an unfeminine work. The *Eclectic Review* imagines that the female minds behind *Wuthering Heights*, *Jane Eyre* and *Agnes Grey* are atypical of the Victorian feminine ideal:

> In their perusal, we are in the company of an intelligent, free-spoken, and hearty woman, who feels deeply, can describe with power, has seen some of the rougher sides of life, and, though capable of strong affection, is probably wanting in the 'sweet attractive grace' which Milton so beautifully ascribes to Eve.   (February 1851, p. 223)

The *Leader* also struggles to imagine Ellis Bell as a woman:

> Curious enough it is to read *Wuthering Heights* and *The Tenant of Wildfell Hall* and remember that the writers were two retiring, solitary, consumptive girls! Books, coarse even for men, coarse in language and coarse in conception, the coarseness apparently of violent and uncultivated men – turn out to be the production of two girls living almost alone, filling their loneliness with quiet studies, and writing these books from a sense of duty, hating the pictures they drew, yet drawing them with austere conscientiousness! There is matter here for the moralist or critic to speculate on (Lewes, "Review", p. 953).[21]

This "curious" contradiction that a woman, an innocent and inexperienced woman, could be responsible for the extremely "masculine" "language" and "conception" of *Wuthering Heights* was a fundamental challenge to Victorian gender stereotypes, and set the tone of writing on *Wuthering Heights* for the rest of the century, as well as for much of the twentieth-century.[22] As Alice Law states, Victorians struggled with varying degrees of bafflement to see *Wuthering Heights* as the production of a woman: "Charlotte, in her preface to the 1850 edition, had given the stamp of her authority to Emily Brontë's authorship, which was henceforth accepted, though rather grudgingly, by many of the critics who still averred it could never have been written by a woman, and indeed only by a very exceptional man" (1974, p. 150).

One of the ways in which critics attempted to reconcile the "unfeminine" qualities of *Wuthering Heights* with the sex of its author was by attributing androgynous or male qualities to Emily Brontë; this practice also continued well into the twentieth century. Perhaps Charlotte Brontë started the trend by implying in her "Biographical Notice" that it was impossible to classify Emily Brontë according to conventional gender (or other) schema: "Stronger than a man, simpler than a child, her nature stood alone" (1850, p. 7). Probably the most frequently repeated observation about Emily Brontë was made by Monsieur Héger, the Brontës' teacher in Brussels: "He considered that had she been a man, she would have been a great explorer or navigator; as a writer, he thought she might have been a great historian" (Simpson, 1929, p. 164). The most bizarre example of the "Emily as man" school of criticism is found in Herbert Read's 1903 essay on the Brontës:

> In the case of Emily, the same causes [as Charlotte] produced a 'masculine protest' of a more complex kind, showing, indeed, the typical features of what I think we must, with the psycho-analyst, call psychical hermaphroditism. The outward expression of this state was evident enough. In her childhood the villagers thought her more like a boy than a girl. 'She should have been a man: a great navigator!' cried M. Héger. . . . Charlotte refers to 'a certain harshness in her powerful and peculiar character. . . . Yet Emily . . . was . . . of a shy, introspective cast, from which clue the psychologist will realize how much deeper and more powerful must have been the masculine assumptions of her mind. These found their fit expression. . . in *Wuthering Heights*. ("Charlotte and Emily Brontë", p. 163)

Muriel Spark adheres to essentialist Victorian gender-stratified definitions, feeling the need to state that "Emily was definitely of the female sex. . . . A few people remembered, after her death, that she had masculine qualities, but this seems to be pure myth, built up from an overlying impression of *Wuthering Heights*. Her latter day 'stoicism' possibly contributed to this idea, although in fact, her final gestures were more feminine than masculine" (1953, p. 93). A 1990 book by Irene Tayler entitled *Holy Ghosts: The Male Muses of Emily and Charlotte Brontë* perpetuates these gender-typed ideas of authorship, although from a different perspective:

> Perhaps, in the story of Heathcliff's survival after Catherine's death we may hear Emily saying that her own essence had

departed the world already, and that only her 'disbranched' masculine energy remained to write this novel for publication – a hurt and angry muse indeed. 'He' wrote this book with a furious intensity, as we know from the speed with which the book was finished but also from the harshness of its style and story, which critics have complained of from Charlotte on down. (1990, p. 93)

Everything about *Wuthering Heights* – subject-matter, characterization, and language – was perceived as masculine, although, as noted above, critics did discover some so-called "feminine" traits after they learned the author was female. Tayler refers to the "harshness of its style and story", and certainly these terms, though vague, recur frequently in this debate. For the 1851 critic in the *North British Review*, it is specifically the "coarseness of diction and even of sentiment" that is objected to as unfeminine, along with a "gratuitous use of blackguardism in phraseology" (quoted in Winnifrith , 1973, p. 128). An 1867 *Halifax Guardian* article quotes an earlier article that asked who could imagine that " 'Heathcliff, a man who never swerved from his arrow-straight course to perdition . . . had been conceived by a timid and retiring female?' " (15 June 187, p. 98). Here we see the character depiction being objected to, under the assumption that lived experience dictates the creation of character, and that such a character should be therefore beyond both the experience and the imagination of a woman. The author of the *Halifax Guardian* article reiterates this sentiment: "There is besides, I think, internal evidence, notwithstanding Charlotte's positive assertion to the contrary, that the novel in question never could have emanated from the pen of a young female. A character so revolting as the principal personage in that strange work, it is beyond the imagination of an inexperienced girl to conceive" (p. 99).[23]

In comments like these, we see how Charlotte's assertion of Emily's innocence and lack of worldly experience, designed to make her work more acceptable as the production of a woman, in fact makes it sometimes implausible to the point of impossibility for some critics. Here again, the *Saturday Review*'s discussion of women's literary disadvantage due to lack of worldly experience becomes relevant:

Those exceptional geniuses among them who have qualified themselves for authorship by tasting of the tree of knowledge, have sacrificed on one side what on another they have gained . . . nothing except genius can make up to the world what the world would

lose if women were less virginal and primitive.   (11 November
1865, p. 602)[24]

The first four chapters tend to be the ones discussed as most unfeminine, when critics are specific. For Alice Law, it is the "masculine
expressions" which make it almost impossible to see the work as the
production of a woman: "Some other masculine expressions occur in
the first chapters which no gentlewoman of the prim and prudish for-
ties would have dreamed of using: the reference to the figures of Loves
and Cupids over the doorway as 'shameless little boys' . . . the curs-
es, the brutal language . . . all these could never have been introduced
into the first novel by a quiet, reserved young woman like Emily
Brontë" (159). Mr Justice Vaisey, as late as 1946, believes that the tone
of "chapters 1, 2, and 3, and the early part of chapter 4, is not the same
as the rest of the book" (*"Wuthering Heights"*, p. 14), and he finds it
hard to believe that a woman could have been responsible for the
description of Mr Lockwood's "ridiculous love affair", and for
Lockwood's statements such as "I knew through experience that I
was tolerably attractive" (p. 14).[25] The Latin references ("previous to
inspecting the penetralium", for example) were also seen as strangely learned for a woman writer.

In a letter in 1856 to George Smith, Charlotte Brontë's publisher,
Mrs Gaskell attributes the coarseness of *Wuthering Heights* to Branwell's
influence: "it is a horrid story [Branwell's notorious affair with Lady
Trevelyan], and I should not have told it but to show the life of pro-
longed suffering those Brontë girls had to endure, and what doubt-
less familiarized them to a certain degree with coarse expressions,
such as have been complained of in *Wuthering Heights*" (*The Letters*,
1966, p. 432).[26]

The difficulties, and frequently the impossibility, of reconciling
Emily Brontë's work with popular notions of what a woman writer
could and should produce led to a rumour, often taken seriously, that
Emily's brother, Patrick Branwell Brontë, was the real author of
Wuthering Heights. The 1867 *Halifax Guardian* article alluded to earli-
er was entitled "Who Wrote *Wuthering Heights*?" and alleged that
Branwell read to his friends a story that sounded remarkably like
Wuthering Heights a few years before its publication. This rumour,
combined with the "internal evidence" of masculinity, leads the author
of the *Halifax Guardian* article to assume that Patrick Branwell Brontë
was the true author of *Wuthering Heights*. The argument that Branwell
Brontë was really responsible for *Wuthering Heights* surfaced in

several forms throughout the second half of the nineteenth century, inspired by the conviction that, as Alice Law, who subsequently wrote a book on the subject, put it, "its [*Wuthering Heights's*] appearance as coming from Emily Brontë is only less marvellous than Jove's reputed production of Minerva from his brain: on the other hand, if Branwell wrote it, there is no marvel" (1923, p. 131).

A. Mary F. Robinson, Emily's first biographer, is one of the critics who speculate on Branwell's possible involvement in part or all of Emily's book. She quotes T. Wemyss Reid on "some striking verbal coincidence between Branwell's own language and passages in *Wuthering Heights*" (1883, p. 217). Ultimately, Robinson dismisses the rumour as caused by those

> lovers of sensation who prefer any startling lie to an old truth. Their ranks have been increased by the number of those who, ignorant of the true circumstances of Emily's life, found it impossible that an inexperienced girl could portray so much violence and such morbid passion. On the contrary, given these circumstances, none but a personally inexperienced girl could have treated the subject with the absolute and sexless purity which we find in *Wuthering Heights*. (p. 219)

Alice Law collects the various rumours about Branwell's involvement in Emily's work and argues that he was the real author. Ironically, she idealizes Emily Brontë as a domestic Victorian angel, and argues that exonerating her from authorship of *Wuthering Heights* constitutes a defense of her character:

> We see in her one of the helpers of the world, a lifter of other people's burdens. . . . And yet it is this bright and brave creature, hating every species of depression, who is to be credited with the creation of the dark, hopeless, tragic story unfolded in . . . *Wuthering Heights*. (1923, p. 121)

Emily, she argues, was too pure and too retiring and private to write such a work; her heroine is instead a passively self-sacrificing scribe for her brother: "it is not very far-fetched to suppose that this generous sister undertook to help him, both by making a fresh copy of what he had done and by copying out the remainder until he had finished it: she may have written some connecting portions of the work" (p. 136). Apart from anecdotal evidence about Branwell's involvement in *Wuthering Heights*, Law bases her argument on an assumption of the inherent masculinity of *Wuthering Heights*, seen in plot, character, and style, and on the impossibility of a woman – especially Emily – writing such a book.

Although Law's argument, and others like it, seem ludicrous now, and although they were a distinct minority throughout the second half of the nineteenth century and the first half of the twentieth century, they were taken seriously enough at the time to be kept alive. Law's work even inspired a rejoinder by Irene Willis in 1936. It is also important to remember that, as bizarre as this rumour may sound today, it was in fact, though taken to extreme, a logical extension of the assumptions and preconceptions that governed the nineteenth-century critical response to the unveiling of Emily as a woman writer.

Wuthering Heights is an interesting test case for feminist criticism. Since it was thought, at different times, to be by a male author and by a female author, an analysis of its reception gives a particularly clear idea about how the sexual double standard operated in Victorian literary criticism. When *Wuthering Heights* was thought to be by a man, it was praised for its "masculine" power and originality. The problem was that it went too far in this direction – it was too "masculine", and perhaps therefore not suited for a "feminized" reading public. With the provision of the new biographical context, ideas and preconceptions about women writers formed the lens through which *Wuthering Heights* was subsequently viewed. As a glance at the *Saturday Review* article on "Authoresses", or at Mrs Humphrey Ward's account of reading *Wuthering Heights* as a girl, demonstrate, the book was shocking to the point of being sensational.[27] Whether critics thought the author male or female, Victorian gender schema functioned as a primary structuring framework for literary criticism on *Wuthering Heights* throughout the nineteenth century.

The *Saturday Review* article on "Authoresses" argues that only in the case of genius can a woman author be excused from the unwomanly transgressions involved in constructing an excellent work of art. Until the early twentieth century, most critics could not transcend the issues surrounding the "prescriptive barriers of sex" sufficiently to consider Emily Brontë a genius – instead, as I have demonstrated, critics focused on her as a woman.[28] In 1926, C. P. Sanger's groundbreaking article on *Wuthering Heights*, "The Structure of *Wuthering Heights*", actually argued that the novel was a meticulously crafted work of art. Although Sanger's treatment of *Wuthering Heights* as an aesthetic object was still accompanied by other discussions, such as

Alice Law's, of Emily Brontë as a woman writer, Sanger's article marked perhaps the main turning point from which critics began to consider the work as one of genius, one that therefore permitted them, according to the argument of the *Saturday Review*, to overlook questions of sex.[29] Inga-Stina Ewbank's 1966 work, *Their Proper Sphere*, argues that "whether she was a perfect woman or not, the art of Emily Brontë makes us see that there is an order of creative genius where the sex of its possessor ceases to matter" (1966, p. 155). As *Wuthering Heights* attained canonical status, then, it transcended gender biases.

4

"Something both More and Less than Manliness": Anthony Trollope's Reception

We state our opinion of it [Barchester Towers] as decidedly the clever-est novel of the season, and one of the most masculine delineations of modern life . . . that we have seen for many a day.

(*Westminster Review*, 1857)

My husband, who can seldom get a novel to hold him, has been held by all three [The Warden, Barchester Towers, and The Three Clerks], and by this [The Three Clerks] the strongest. . . . What a thorough-ly man's book it is! I much admire it.

(Letter from Elizabeth Barrett Browning, 1859,
quoted in Smalley, 1969, p. 64)

We may say, on the whole, that Thackeray was written for men and women, and Trollope for women.

(*Literary World*, 1884)

But this prolific author, often dismissed in his own time as a writer for Mudie's and jeunes filles, gradually accepted as a creator of adult books for adult minds. . . . seems still in process of being discovered.

(Lionel Stevenson, 1964)

Our exploration of the role of gender in Victorian literary criticism takes a complex twist in the case of Anthony Trollope. As I have argued in previous chapters, gender figures prominently in the

66

reception of Reade and Brontë; Reade is praised and accorded prestige for the ways in which his writing is thought to express masculine stereotypes, while the ways in which Emily Brontë is thought to
diverge from conventions of femininity form one of the central critical preoccupations of the reviews of *Wuthering Heights*. In both cases
gender associations create a governing framework – an horizon of
expectations – through which critics can begin to formulate responses to the works. Unlike literary responses to Reade or Brontë, critical
reaction to Trollope does not at first glance seem structured around
preoccupations with gender.[1]

A closer examination of commentary on *Barchester Towers* and on
Trollope's later works reveals, however, that critics do employ gendered thinking to assess Trollope's works, and that their overall evaluations of his literary strengths and weaknesses are informed by a
gendered rhetoric of reception. As the opening quotations indicate,
Trollope has in turn, and sometimes even simultaneously, been seen
as an intensely masculine writer directing himself towards a male
audience, and as a popular writer focusing on young women's love
affairs and emotional confusions, writing therefore to a predominantly
female circulating library audience. Unlike Charles Reade or Emily
Brontë, who respectively conform to or deviate from conventional
expectations about gender and writing, Trollope is variously thought
to do both.[2]

In order to investigate this apparent paradox, this chapter will examine the role of gender in several aspects of critical discussion about
Trollope, including the relation between his social persona and his
writing, the subject-matter of his novels, his depiction of male and
female characters, his popularity, his prolific production of novels,
and the nature of his imagination and inspiration. This chapter will
argue that gender considerations influence how seriously Victorian
critics take Trollope and that the often pejorative connotations of femininity can also be applied to men in Victorian literary criticism.

There is evidence to suggest that from the 1860s to the end of the
nineteenth century the criteria used by Victorian reviewers to judge
novels became increasingly polarized according to gender, with "masculine" qualities in writing more highly valued, and "feminine" qualities denigrated accordingly. Gaye Tuchman, in *Edging Women Out*,
sees this unwritten critical code as evidence of men's desire to wrest
control of the economics of the literary marketplace from women. She
argues that it was women's success in the genre of novel-writing in
the 1840s and 1850s that gave men the provocation and desire to "edge

women out": "partly as a reaction to women's prominence as novel-ists, partly as a reaction against the . . . library-subscribers who crowned the 'queens of the circulating library,' and partly because of the clear economic opportunities that the novel offered writers, men began to define the high-culture novel as a male preserve" (1989, p. 47).

Tuchman's argument is supported by, among other things, the archives of the publishing house of Macmillan. Women submitted more novels than men in the 1850s and 1860s and were more likely than men to have novels accepted; by the end of the century men were more likely (and women less likely) to have novels published, even though men still submitted fewer novels (pp. 7–8). Tuchman's argu-ment views the quest for literary success by authors in the second half of the nineteenth century as a fight for power between men and women. My study of the decline of Trollope's reputation in this same period suggests that aesthetic criteria were determined not just by sex but also by gender. As a man, Trollope suffers from being associated with "feminine" literary qualities, which would suggest that the situation is more complicated than a straightforward battle between the sexes.

A survey of literary criticism of Trollope's novels from *Barchester Towers* onwards reveals that Trollope was held in highest critical esteem from the late 1850s through the mid-1860s; during this peri-od he was seen as a possible successor to the literary throne of Dickens and Thackeray, but increasingly, as the sixties progressed, Trollope's literary reputation as a serious artist began to decline. David Skilton summarizes the tone of critical commentary on Trollope in the sev-enties as one of condescension. Trollope, Skilton writes, "was no longer thought of as a next-to-great novelist. . . . He clearly retained a fairly large public, but mainly as an author of circulating library fiction" (1972, p. 32). Related to this loss of critical prestige, in my opinion, is the growing tension that emerges in the same period (1860s to 1870s) between admiration for the "masculine" style and persona that critics associate with the author of *Barchester Towers* and disparage-ment for the increasingly feminized associations made with his writ-ings.[3] As with Reade and Brontë, masculine associations have obvious correlations with perceptions of literary merit.

Trollope's career as a writer follows an extremely different pattern from that of Reade or Brontë. Charles Reade's successful career as a writer began with the publication of *It Is Never Too Late To Mend*, and the gendered compliments the critics bestowed upon this work radi-ated a residual glory on the several novels that succeeded it. *Wuthering Heights*, by Emily Brontë, is, of course, the only novel she produced;

the preoccupation with gender-appropriate writing that dominated its reception has become part of the Brontë legend. Just as *It Is Never Too Late To Mend* and *Wuthering Heights* were, for different reasons, the works that brought their authors to literary prominence, so, too, was *Barchester Towers* the novel that first catapulted Trollope into the literary arena. But for Trollope this novel was only the second in what was to be a lengthy Barchester series, and the intense productivity of Trollope from 1856 until his death in 1884 (he wrote 47 novels in all) demands that any investigation of patterns in Trollope's reception also consider critical commentary on his later work.

   Barchester Towers was published in 1857, and was, as Trollope states proudly in his *Autobiography*, "one of the novels which novel readers were called upon to read" (1883, p. 79). It was, in fact, Trollope's fifth novel; the first three had been unequivocally unsuccessful, and the fourth, *The Warden*, had received some, if fairly limited, critical attention.[4] (Probably one of the reasons why *The Warden* did not attract wider attention was the fact that it was not a three-decker.) The appearance of *Barchester Towers*, however, proved to be the turning point in Trollope's writing career, both in critical attention and in general popularity. As R. H. Super documents, 750 copies of *Barchester Towers* were published in 1857, of which 200 were bought by Mudie's, and these were followed by a one-volume edition in 1858 (1988, p. 80).[5]

   Barchester Towers was reviewed in the following journals: the *Westminster Review*, the *National Review*, *The Times*, the *Saturday Review*, the *Eclectic Review*, the *Examiner*, the *Leader*, the *Spectator*, and the *Athenaeum*. Reviewers were unanimous in singling out Trollope's novel as one of the season's most distinguished offerings. The *Examiner* gives it "unquestionable rank among the few really well-written tales that every season furnishes" (16 May 1857, p. 308), while the *Leader* "cannot but describe it as uncommonly graphic and clever" (23 May 1857, p. 497). The *National Review* describes *Barchester Towers* as "undeniably one of the cleverest and best-written novels which have been published of late years" (October 1858, p. 425), and the usually recalcitrant *Saturday Review* devotes an entire article to it, calling it "a very clever book", and admiring "its power and finish" (30 May 1857, p. 503). The *Leader* praises "the astonishing energy with which the author writes, the sharpness and concision of his style" (23 May 1857, p. 497).

   Barchester Towers was thus taken seriously by reviewers, seen as intelligent, powerful, "clever", and "well-written", and in a class apart from ordinary novels. The *Westminster Review* provides the most explicitly gendered assessment, and highlights the implicit gender connotations of terms used in other reviews. In its opinion, *Barchester Towers* is "decidedly the cleverest novel of the season, and one of the most masculine delineations of modern life . . . that we have seen for many a day" (October 1857, p. 326). The *Westminster Review* praises Trollope for having written a "novel that men can enjoy" and for his "caustic and vigorous" qualities (p. 327); it concludes by comparing *Barchester Towers* to Mrs Oliphant's *The Athelings*, which is "in construction and execution altogether feminine" (p. 327); it is perhaps unnecessary to add that Mrs Oliphant's novel suffers from the comparison. The 1857 reviews of *Barchester Towers* are thus reminiscent of the strongly gendered assessments of Reade's *It Is Never Too Late To Mend*, praised for its "vigour", which was thought to be located in the book's content and style; seen as atypical of conventional novels, contrasted, by the *Spectator*, with "the sentimental woes and drawingroom distresses which form the staple of so much of our circulating library fiction" (16 August 1856, p. 877), and juxtaposed, to its credit, with inferior works by women writers.

Critics focus on and seem to enjoy what Jane Nardin terms the conservative comedy of *Barchester Towers*: "*Barchester Towers'* comedy of errors begins when a woman tries to think for herself" (*He Knew*, 1989, p. 33). Nardin argues that "the narrator's tone is . . . consistently misogynistic . . . and there is a lot of rib-digging, antifeminist humour" (p. 39). Trollope's novelistic persona in this work is clearly that of an orthodox middle-class Victorian gentleman as far as sex roles are concerned, as the resolution of the romance between Eleanor and Arabin indicates:

> And now it remained to them each to enjoy the assurance of the other's love. And how great that luxury is. . . . And to a woman's heart how doubly delightful! When the ivy has found its tower, when the delicate creeper has found its strong wall, we know how the parasite plants grow and prosper. They were not created to stretch forth their branches alone, and endure without protection the summer's sun and the winter's storm. Alone they but spread themselves upon the ground, and cower unseen in the dingy shade. But when they have found their firm supporters, how wonderful is their beauty . . .   (vol. 2, pp. 239–40)

Many critics single out the characters of Mrs Proudie and Madeline Vesey-Neroni for attention, the characters who are the source of so much of the novel's humour, along with the despicable clergyman

Mr Slope. The *Westminster Review,* for example, is intrigued by the battle for power between the Bishop and Mrs Proudie, and is paternally anxious for Eleanor's dangerous independence to end in matrimony: "We are anxious for the widow, and long to get her havened out of her perilous widowhood in fast wedlock; man's great ambition to become a Bishop, and woman's wonderful art in ruling one, cannot fail to interest us exceedingly" (October 1857, p. 327). *The Times* also singles out for attention the conflict between the sexes, clearly identifying with the Bishop:

> Perhaps the scenes between the Bishop and Mrs. Proudie are a little overdrawn, but, although highly coloured, they are not the less amusing delineations of human misery, as experienced by a man who permits himself not only to be henpecked in his private relations, but also to be in his public capacity under female domination. The poor bishop is not only assailed by his wife in the privacy of his dressing-room, he cannot receive a visitor without her permission.   (13 August 1857, p. 5)

Critics seem attracted by the treatment of relations between the sexes and by the conservative nature of the humour.

In her book on Victorian novelists, Mrs Oliphant refers to both Trollope and Reade as "robust and manly figures", writers who "will always stand together in the front of the second rank of Victorian novelists" (1892, pp. 471–2). Leaving aside for the moment the vexed question of Trollope's rank among novelists, one of the more interesting aspects of criticism on Trollope is the way it tends to blur the boundaries between Trollope the man and Trollope the writer. Critics viewed Trollope's persona as extremely masculine, and as perfectly congruent with ideas about appropriate masculinity.[6] They frequently compared Trollope's lifestyle, attitudes, persona, or beliefs with the details of his work. This delicate line between Trollope's public image and his writing usually functioned to his advantage, giving him credibility and allowing reviewers to identify and sympathize with the writer as "one of us", an educated and somewhat conservative mid-century gentleman.

Time, for example, writes admiringly of the similarities between Trollope's own conversation and the dialogue in his novels, and between his style as a hunter and his style as a writer:

> As it is with the dialogue of Mr. Trollope's literary heroes and heroines, so it is with the conversation of Mr. Trollope himself. In each

there is the same definiteness and direction; the same Anglo-Saxon
simplicity. . . . As a writer . . . Mr. Trollope is precisely what he is,
or used to be, as a rider across country. He sees the exact place at
which he wants to arrive. He makes for it; and he determines to
reach it as directly as possible. There may be obstacles, but he sur-
mounts them.   (no. 1, 1879, p. 627)

David Cecil's remarks on Trollope, written in 1934, still echo Victorian
discussion of the author. Like so many Victorian critics, he praises
Trollope for being a "sensible man of the world": "Like the other mid-
Victorian gentlemen he enjoyed hunting and whist and a good glass
of wine, admired gentle, unaffected, modest women, industrious,
unaffected, manly men" (1934, p. 228).

Critics praised Trollope for his knowledge and experience of the
world, and such compliments are always explicitly or implicitly based
on gender. *Time*, for example, admires his "manly imagination" and
praises the way Trollope "exemplifies and enforces" his ideas "with
whatever suggests itself as suitable in the treasure-house of diversi-
fied knowledge and experience which he has assimilated" (no. 1, 1879,
p. 632). The *North British Review* is impressed by Trollope as an experienced "man of the world": "His books are the result of the experience of life, not of the studious contemplation of it. . . . While we read
them we are made to share . . . the experience of a man who in going
through his own daily business, has been brought in contact with an
immense variety of people; who has looked at so much of the world
as it came in his way to consider, with a great deal of keenness, kind-
ness, and humour" (June 1864, p. 370).

While such experience of the world is theoretically open to both
sexes, being a "man of the world" in Victorian society usually involved
being male. Trollope was thought to reap literary advantages from
his own experience as a Victorian gentleman. The *North British Review*,
for example, believed that Trollope's combination of knowledge of
the world with his subtlety allowed him to outshine all female
writers:

Mr. Trollope, with the delicate perception which he possesses, seizes
upon the distinctive features which underlie so much apparent uni-
formity, and creates, or rather portrays, a character which is not the
less amusing because it is perfectly commonplace. Some female
writers have possessed this peculiar subtlety in still greater per-
fection, but then it is accompanied in Mr. Trollope with a mascu-

line maturity and a knowledge of the world to which there is no kind of parallel in Miss Austen nor in any of her English sisters. (June 1864, p. 375)

The ease with which critics are able to identify and sympathize with Trollope reveals how his masculine persona enhances his literary credibility. The *Saturday Review* is disarmed by the similarities between Trollope's profile and that of its own readers and reviewers: "he always writes like a gentleman, and like an educated, observant, and kindly man" (26 March 1859, p. 368). The *North British Review* writes that Trollope "thoroughly understands, because he shares the thoughts and feelings of the majority of educated Englishmen" (June 1864, p. 370).

Occasionally, the intensity of Trollope's masculine image or persona creates a feeling of disjunction between the man and his work. As Juliet McMaster comments, "At social gatherings he was a bluff and blustering presence, and people were often astonished at the contrast between the delicacy of his novels and the aggressive assertiveness of their author: 'The books, full of gentleness, grace and refinement; the writer of them bluff, loud, stormy, and contentious,' wrote his friend W. P. Frith' " (quoted in McMaster, "Anthony Trollope", p. 304).

When critics comment specifically on Trollope's writing, their impression of Trollope the man casts a constant shadow over their observations. As David Skilton remarks, "in general he is socially approved by the critics, even the fastidious *Saturday* naming him as 'one of the few popular writers of the day who always write as a gentleman and a man of sense and principle should write'" (1972, p. 8). Writing "as a gentleman and a man of sense" is seen by most critics as one of Trollope's main talents, if not his central one. Henry James admires Trollope's "masculine" thought, stance, and judgement. Trollope "writes", James avers, "he feels, he judges like a man, talking plainly and frankly about many things, and is by no means destitute of a certain saving grace of coarseness" (1886, p. 99). James thus equates Trollope's straightforward lack of prudishness with masculinity.[7]

The clarity and plainness of Trollope's style are also complimented as a masculine trait. Geoffrey Tillotson, writing recently, states that Trollope's style is characterized by "a preference for monosyllables. It likes plain words" (1965, p. 56). It seems to be exactly this aspect of Trollope's style that strikes critics as masculine. *Time*, in 1879, expresses its enjoyment of the "definiteness and direction; the same Anglo-Saxon simplicity" (no. 1, 1879, p. 627) of Trollope's style. Paul Elmer More praises Trollope's "clear, manly, straightforward style" ("My Debt", p. 91).

The *North British Review* admires Trollope's plots, and believes that they conjure up the delights of boyhood confrontations. In an 1864 article it calls the plots "simply a new version of the old fighting stories of our boyhood transferred to a far more delicate atmosphere; and we watch the struggle between Mrs. Proudie and Archdeacon Grantly with very much the same kind of anxiety as that with which we used to regard the engagements of the Deerslayer with the bloody Mingoes" (June 1864, p. 378).

The posthumous appearance of Trollope's *An Autobiography* was greeted by Richard Holt Hutton in the *Spectator* within an explicitly gendered framework:

> The absolute frankness of *An Autobiography* is most characteristic of Mr. Trollope; and so is its unequalled – manliness we were going to say; – but we mean something both more and less than manliness, covering more than the daring of manliness and something less than the quietness or equanimity which we are accustomed to include in that term, so we may call it, its unequalled masculineness. ("Anthony Trollope's *Autobiography*", p. 1377)

And David Cecil's reassessment of Trollope admires the "masculine friendliness" of Trollope's "tone of voice", the "genial leisurely masculinity" of Trollope's "vital and vigorous" humour, and the strength of his satire, which is not weakened "by diluting it in sentimental rosewater" (1934, pp. 246–57).

Critics often attributed their enjoyment of Trollope, then, to his "masculine" qualities, and in many respects identification and discussion of Trollope's strengths revolved around Victorian ideologies of gender. The volatile nature of Trollope's reception, however, is stranger than the preceding discussion might imply. Despite critical perceptions of Trollope the man and Trollope the writer as intensely masculine, many critics, paradoxically, also felt that Trollope's writing had many feminine qualities. This perception grew stronger as the 1860s progressed. Occasionally such critics praised Trollope for the versatility and imagination that allowed him to exhibit supposedly feminine writing characteristics; more frequently, just as perceptions of masculine qualities in *Barchester Towers* raised his critical reputation, feminine associations with his later work are, as I will show, partly responsible for critical attacks on Trollope, ranging from a refusal to take him seriously as a leading and important writer, to an affectionate dismissal of him as entertaining but slight.

Occasionally critics praised Trollope's juxtaposition of "masculine" and "feminine" qualities, as in the following remark by the *Saturday Review* in 1882:

> He was in the best sense of the word a masculine man and writer, and yet he knew more of the feminine mind and nature than any author of his generation. . . . Among many signal merits of Mr.Trollope's genius was this – that he could handle at will and with equal success the masculine and the feminine nature and bent. (9 December 1882, p. 755)

And the *North British Review*, in the 1864 article quoted above, argues that Trollope's ability to combine the "delicate perception" and "subtlety" of feminine writers with masculine strengths puts him in a unique category, one clearly above the reach of women writers.

More usually, however, Trollope's "feminine" qualities caused him to be taken less seriously. As the preceding remarks from the *Saturday Review* and the *North British Review* indicate, Trollope's apparent knowledge of women and insight into their characters was widely remarked upon and seen as a feminine trait. The *Saturday Review*, praising his "extraordinary insight" into the "working of the feminine . . . mind" (9 December 1882, p. 755), recounts a story to this effect: during a dinner conversation, someone posed the following question to Trollope: "'Mr. Trollope, how do you know what we women say to each other when we get alone in our rooms?'" (p. 755). The *Edinburgh Review* seems perplexed at the apparent paradox in Trollope's ability to identify with young women in the creation of his numerous heroines: "Here we have a middle-aged or elderly gentleman worming himself into the hearts and confidences of young ladies, and identifying himself with the innermost workings of their minds; and a very remarkable phenomenon it is" (quoted in Helling, 1956, p. 81). Henry James, adopting a rather sinister predatorial image, also comments on Trollope's fondness for depicting young English women: "Trollope settled down steadily to the English girl; he took possession of her, and turned her inside out" (quoted in Helling, 1956, p. 82).

But this ambivalent admiration for the attention Trollope devoted to his heroines and the insight he seemed to have into their thoughts and feelings was also frequently the occasion for critical dismissals, as in the following comment in 1869, from the *Fortnightly Review*: "[W]e admit Mr. Trollope's power in describing young ladies in love and in doubt. He knows English girls by heart . . . as the prose laureate of English girls of the better class, why should not Mr. Trollope record something else beside flirtations that end well?" (1 February 1869, p. 198).

Unlike Reade, who chose "epic" plots based on theme and action rather than character analysis, Trollope was more attracted to romance-based plots and character. Burns describes Reade as "consciously abjuring the techniques of Trollope and the domestic novelists . . . in an effort to create epic characters equal to what he conceived to be his epic theme" (1961, p. 159). It is quite clear that for Reade, Trollope's "chronicles of small beer" cannot possibly measure up to his "epic themes", and we remember from *It Is Never Too Late To Mend* how Reade tends to conflate "small" with "old women and children of the pen" (pp. 76–8). Trollope himself was quite candid about the importance of the romantic plot to his fiction. In his lecture on novels, "On English Prose Fiction as a Rational Amusement", Trollope states boldly that novels "not only contain love stories, but they are written for the sake of the love stories" (Parrish, 1938, p. 109). As Park Honan stated recently, "Trollope's women remind us that he had immense sentimental energy" ("Trollope after a Century", p. 323).

Unfortunately for Trollope, being regarded as a "chronicler of young ladies' thoughts" was not conducive to being taken seriously as a novelist. Reade was not the only Victorian who held such a gender-determined hierarchy, as we remember from the reviews of *It Is Never Too Late To Mend*. The *Fortnightly Review*'s praise of Trollope's *Last Chronicle of Barset* reads like a response to such attacks on Trollope's work: "[In his] *Last Chronicle of Barset* [Mr Trollope] has given us glimpses of a certain tragic and poetic power that place him far above any chronicler of young ladies' thoughts" (1 February 1869, p. 190). The implication clearly is that the thoughts of women, young women especially, are by definition frivolous and silly rather than interesting or serious. And my earlier chapter on Reade showed how Reade's subject-matter was identified as intensely masculine, and was complimented accordingly. The *Spectator*, for example, argues that Reade transcends the stereotypes of the conventional novel in his treatment of the battle "'between good and evil'".[8]

One of the ways in which critics classified and evaluated Trollope was by defining his readership. The preceding discussion of Charles

Reade's readership demonstrated how he gained prestige from being read by men.[9] Discussion about the sex of Trollope's readership led inevitably to evaluative statements about his merit as a writer. *Barchester Towers* was greeted by the *Westminster Review* as "a novel that men can enjoy" (October 1857, p. 327), and Elizabeth Barrett Browning praised *The Three Clerks* as "a thoroughly man's book", describing how her husband who normally did not like novels was "held" by *Barchester Towers, Doctor Thorne*, and *The Three Clerks* (quoted in Smalley, 1969, p. 64). As Trollope became increasingly popular, however, critics began to categorize his audience as both male and female, and, in some cases, as predominantly female. *The Times*, for example, in an 1859 article, argues that Trollope is suitable both for "patrons of Mudies" and for "thoughtful men":

> To those who are in the habit of reading novels it is unnecessary to say that Mr. Trollope is one of the most amusing of authors; and to those who in general prefer blue-books, statistics, and telegrams, but now and then indulge in the enormity of romance, we may report . . . that he is a "safe man".   (quoted in Smalley, 1969, p. 109)

In a retrospective assessment of Trollope's readership, Michael Sadleir echoes this judgement, calling Trollope "at the same time . . . a novelist for the jeune fille and a most knowledgeable realist" (1927, p. 373).

Trollope himself, writing about the author's relationship to his readers, describes novel-readers in primarily female terms, describing how they receive instruction in the ways of the world from the novelist:

> The novelist creeps in closer than the schoolmaster . . . He is the chosen guide, the tutor whom the young pupil chooses for herself. She retires with him, suspecting no lesson . . . throwing herself head and heart into the narration . . . and there she is taught how she shall learn to love; how she shall receive the lover when he comes. . . .   (quoted in Helling, 1956, p. 109)[10]

Presumably we can take these remarks as indicative of Trollope's sense of his implied and actual reader. Regardless of Trollope's own assessment of his readership, his popularity as a writer, and thus his status as a circulating-library novelist, seems to be partly responsible for his reputation as a writer for young women.

The *Saturday Review*, for example, writes disparagingly of the popularity of *Framley Parsonage*'s serialization in *Cornhill Magazine*: "[T]he author of *Framley Parsonage* is a writer who is born to make the fortune of circulating libraries. At the beginning of every month the new number of his book has ranked almost as one of the delicacies of the season; and no London belle dared to pretend to consider herself literary who did not know the very latest intelligence about the state of Lucy Robart's heart and of Griselda Grantley's flounces" (4 May 1861, p. 452).[11] It is perhaps only a small step from this kind of gendered assessment of readership to the pronouncement of the *Literary World* in 1884 that while Thackeray is a writer for men, Trollope is a writer for women. Trollope's view of life is, according to this periodical, "nearer what we may call the female view", and thus, "we may say, on the whole, that Thackeray is written for men and women, and Trollope for women" (23 August 1884, p. 275). The *Literary World* goes on to praise Thackeray as "rooted in what is permanent on our nature" whereas Trollope's pictures are destined for only transient popularity.

Trollope's mass popularity and consequent association with circulating libraries constitute (along with his focus on romantic plots and interest in female characters) grounds for many Victorian critics to dismiss him as a serious writer, although it was common for such critics still to express their enjoyment of Trollope. In 1859 *The Times* places Trollope firmly in the category of circulating-library writer by virtue of his popularity: "If Mudie were asked who is the greatest of living men, he would without one moment's hesitation say Mr. Anthony Trollope. . . . Trollope is, in fact, the most fertile, the most popular, the most successful author – *that is to say, of the circulating library sort*" (Dallas, 23 May 1859, p. 12; my emphasis). For *The Times*, however, Trollope's association with the circulating library raises *its* prestige rather than lowering Trollope's: "These novels are healthy and manly, and so long as Mr. Anthony Trollope is the prince of the circulating library our readers may rest assured that it is a very useful, very pleasant, and very honourable institution" (p. 12). Trollope's continued association with Mudie's, however, eventually led to some critical dismissal. The pejorative associations with circulating-library readers made in the above excerpts from reviews of Reade indicate how being "the prince of the circulating library" was a somewhat dubious privilege.

Trollope was also criticized for being unimaginative or for having a mechanical kind of imagination that reproduces rather than creates.

He did receive praise for his ability to replicate Victorian society and life, but many Victorian critics saw this as essentially artless. The *Saturday Review*, for example, in 1861, states that "Mr. Trollope himself nowhere pretends to do more than to write down what he sees going on around him. He paints from the outside" (4 May 1861, p. 452). Trollope's reputation for superficiality of imagination, and a prolificacy of production that seemed incompatible with "true" genius or even artistry, had a derogatory influence on his literary reputation. Both accusations had certain feminine connotations or associations, as I will argue.

The *North British Review* (in 1864) and the *Fortnightly Review* (in 1869) reiterate the complaint of the *Saturday Review* about the apparent absence of imagination in Trollope's brand of realism. The *North British Review* suggests that Trollope disqualifies himself from the ranks of imaginative artists through his emphasis on realism: "he represents ordinary characters, and paints real life as it is, only omitting the poetry. The highest object of imaginative literature he neither attains nor aims at" (June 1864, p. 401). The *Fortnightly Review* argues that "common-place" life is incompatible with high literary art: "The genteel public of the day may demand portraits of themselves . . . but no amount of skill can make common-place men and common-place incidents and common-place feelings fit subjects of high or true literary art" (1 February 1869, p. 196).[12]

These remarks all stem from similar assumptions about the components and attributes of great art: high art should not rely too much on everyday life, but should transcend these particulars by suggesting universals or by dealing only with the heroic or extraordinary. Perhaps inevitably in the divisions and hierarchies of Victorian culture, rigidly schematized according to gender, such critiques and adjectives assume gender associations; the critical objections to Trollope cited above correspond closely to the kind of critical attacks levelled at women's writing. "Masculine" was identified with high culture, male readers, originality, power, and truth, whereas feminine was associated with popular culture, female readers, and stereotypically female qualities such as lack of originality, weakness of intellect, and feebleness of ideas.

In 1867 and 1868, Trollope conducted a literary experiment producing two novels, *Nina Balatka* and *Linda Tressel*, that he published anonymously. The *London Review* responded thus to *Linda Tressel* on 30 May 1868: "We are not aware that *Nina Balatka* was ever said to be the writing of a woman . . . but the appearance of *Linda Tressel* almost settles the point. The heroic fortitude, the simple frankness, and maidenly honour of *Nina Balatka* were the attributes of a creation which might have arisen in the mind of a male artist; but *Linda Tressel* seems to us altogether a woman's woman" (quoted in Smalley, 1969, p. 20). This interesting observation sheds some light on what was perceived as intrinsically yet paradoxically feminine in the character portrayals in Trollope's other novels.

The world of Trollope's novels was a very recognizable one for his readers, focusing as it did primarily on genteel middle-class Victorian relationships in society. And while domestic realism was clearly not the exclusive preserve of women writers, it was, as Elaine Showalter reminds us, seen as their most appropriate domain: "By the 1840s women writers had adopted a variety of popular genres, and were specializing in novels of fashionable life, education, religion, and community, which Vineta Colby subsumes under the heading 'domestic realism'" (1977, p. 20). Gaye Tuchman argues that women writers were associated "with the least-admired aspects of novels: the details of personal, emotional, and everyday life" ("When The Prevalent", p. 154).

Women writers were thought to specialize in domestic realism because it required less imaginative and intellectual effort or strength, allowing them to passively regurgitate the details of life they saw around them. Lack of imagination, as noted in the chapter on Brontë, was seen as one of the chief limitations of women writers for many Victorian critics. G. H. Lewes, in his essay "The Lady Novelists", also argues that women's writing is characterized by a close adherence to domestic experience rather than inspired by intellect or imagination: "The domestic experience which forms the bulk of women's knowledge finds an appropriate form in novels" (*Westminster Review*, 1852, p. 133).

It is apparent that the kinds of criticism directed towards Trollope's supposed lack of imagination and focus on domestic realism were also characteristic of criticisms aimed at women's writing. In my judgement, Trollope is taken less seriously as an artist because of his apparently "feminized" attributes as a writer in these respects. As Tuchman argues, "by 1870 men of letters were using the term high culture to set off novels they admired from those they deemed run-of-the-mill" (Tuchman and Fortin, 1989, p. 3). Tuchman analyses the readers' reports for the publishing house of Macmillan, run by Morley, and believes that the readers viewed "high-culture" in terms of gender:

As Morley and his successors tried to distinguish and define the high-culture novel through their in-house reviews, they insistently identified men with high culture and women with mass or popular culture, although they did not use these twentieth-century terms. They identified men with ideas capable of having an impact upon the mind – with activity and the production orientation associated with high culture. Women were identified with mass audiences, passive entertainment, and ... popular culture.   (p. 78)

Trollope, then, is condemned by many Victorian critics for choosing to focus on "common-place incidents and common-place feelings", for ignoring the "highest object of imaginative literature", for being uncomfortably close in popularity and subject-matter to female "circulating-library" novelists, although his skill and wide experience of life make him, for many critics, superior to such "second-rate" writers. An important testimony to these kinds of associations is the *Saturday Review*'s conflation of feminized content, commercial popularity, imaginative weakness, and artistic inferiority in the 1863 critique of *Rachel Ray*: "There is a brisk market for descriptions of the inner life of young women, and Mr. Trollope is the chief agent in supplying the market. . . . Mr. Trollope . . . has taught himself to turn out a brick that does almost without straw, and is a very good saleable brick of its kind" (quoted in Skilton, 1972, p. 54).

Trollope's precarious position as a serious Victorian writer was also endangered by his productivity. His ability to write so many books, one after the other, was seen as suspicious, tantamount to a rejection of high aesthetic seriousness and to an adoption of a money-motivated and formulaic approach. From 1857 to 1869, twenty reviews of different Trollope works appeared in the *Athenaeum*, twenty-four in the *Saturday Review*, and twenty-four in the *Spectator* (Skilton, 1972, p. 12). Of course other Victorian writers such as Dickens, Mrs Oliphant, or Charlotte Yonge were also prolific, but Trollope is unusual, unique even, not only for the sheer quantity of novels he wrote, but for his own outspoken and gleeful pride in his production. As he put it in his *Autobiography*:

And so I end the record of my literary performances, – which I think are more in amount than the works of any other living English author. If any English authors not living have written more . . . I do not know who they are. I find that . . . have published much more than twice as much as Carlyle. I have also published considerably more than Voltaire, even including his letters. . . . I am still living and may add to the pile. . . . It will not, I am sure, be thought that, in making my boast as to quantity, I have endeavoured to lay claim to any literary excellence. . . . But I do lay claim to whatever merit should be accorded to me for persevering diligence in my profession. (pp. 253–5)

Although men, such as G. P. R. James and G. W. M. Reynolds, as well as women wrote prolifically and for commercial reasons, women in general were thought to be more susceptible to rapid and unskilled writing, a prejudice that goes back to the eighteenth-century idea of "scribbling women". W. R. Greg, in his essay "False Morality of Lady Novelists", states that "there are vast numbers of lady-novelists for much the same reason that there are vast numbers of seamstresses": "Every educated lady can handle a pen tant bien que mal: all such, therefore, take to writing – and to novel-writing – as the kind which requires least special qualification and the least severe study, and also as the only kind which will sell" (quoted in Ewbank, 1966, p. 11). Lewes protests in an 1865 essay against the "presumptuous facility" of "indolent novelists", and implies that women novelists are especially guilty (McMaster, "Anthony Trollope", p. 361). E. S. Dallas felt that "women have a talent for personal discourse and familiar narrative, which, when properly controlled, is a great gift, although too frequently it degenerates into a social nuisance" (quoted in Showalter, 1977, p. 82). Showalter argues that women's writing was seen as effortless, an extension of their natural role and instinct: "Such an approach [i.e., that of Dallas] was particularly attractive because it implied that women's writing was as artless and effortless as birdsong, and there-fore not in competition with the more rational male eloquence" (p. 82).

Trollope was vulnerable to similar accusations because of his enor-mous productivity. Many critics felt that the sheer volume and rapid-ity of his literary production meant that the works had to be produced "naturally", without undue intellectual exertion. His notorious state-ments about writing in his *Autobiography* only served to accentuate existing distrust and disregard for his status as a literary figure.[13] Trollope was perhaps more vocal about the quantity of his work and the financial rewards that followed than any other Victorian figure; James Payn writes that "[H]e took almost a savage pleasure in demol-ishing the theory of 'inspiration,' which has caused the world to deny his 'genius'" (1884, p. 167). Trollope was thus dangerously vulnera-

ble to the kinds of critical attacks and associations normally connected with the productivity and literary status of women writers.
McMaster attributes negative and ambivalent responses to Trollope
to the rate of his literary production: "Trollope's enormous productivity has had much to do with a patronizing dismissal of his work
by some critics and a rather apologetic attitude adopted even by his
admirers" ("Anthony Trollope", p. 317).

Victorian critics were preoccupied with classifying Trollope as a
major or second-rate writer. Despite their initial enthusiasm for
Barchester Towers and its immediate successors in the late 1850s and
early 1860s, and despite their own enjoyment of Trollope's work, many
had reservations about his status as a leading novelist who would
rank with Dickens or Thackeray. Skilton attributes part of the critical
ambivalence to a degree of insecurity about what the "rules" were for
excellence in the relatively new genre of novel. Skilton notes that "We
see the reviewers confronted by the problem of whether or not to
regard him as a great novelist, and of how to establish in the first place
what constitutes greatness in a genre in which they are still not at
home, critically speaking" (1972, p. xiii). (Dickens and Thackeray were
often taken as the two "masters" against whom other contenders were
measured [resurrecting the Richardson/Fielding opposition of the
previous century], and of course such a preconception or standard
tended to influence critical vision and judgement somewhat
unfairly, making it harder to see a novelist in terms of his or her unique
strengths.)

The Times's obituary of Trollope had no reservation about placing
him in the second rank of novelists, along with Austen and Gaskell
who wrote "realistic studies of English domestic life" (quoted in
MacDonald, 1987, p. 113). The *Saturday Review*, however, perhaps
remembering their previous partiality to Trollope, rose to his defence,
objecting vehemently to critics who associated him with second-ranked
authors like Austen: "it is only the stupid critic that has placed Jane
Austen and Trollope together in the second rank" (quoted in Fielding,
"Trollope", p. 434).[14]

John Olmsted and Jeffrey Welch suggest that critical ambivalence
towards Trollope really began in the 1860s, and argue that the most
interesting aspect of Trollope's critical reputation has been the general reader's refusal to be influenced by the often negative remarks
of the critics: "Trollope's readers have for the most part been going it
alone since the 1860s when writers for the *Athenaeum* and the *Saturday
Review*, first began to express their irritation at Trollope's 'supersti-

tious adherence to facts' and at what Henry James called 'the inveteracy with which he just eludes being really serious'" (1978, p. xi).

It is not coincidental that both of the obituaries mentioned above juxtapose Trollope with Jane Austen. It was, in fact, a critical common-place to compare Trollope to Austen. As Smalley states, "both stopped short of the depth of vision or the high seriousness that were essential to art of a more elevated sort. Both were, however, wonderfully amusing" (1969, p. 14). Smalley's summary conveys the sense that domestic realism was seen as somehow incompatible with serious art, as well as the way in which Trollope's popularity was actually detrimental to his stature as an artist. Smalley goes on to imply a similar point when he states that Victorian critics regarded Trollope as "a popular novelist delightful to read" rather than as a "genius" (p. 26).

Implicit in the idea that Trollope was "popular" and that he was "delightful to read" is the reservation that he was too accessible to the ordinary novel-reader to be taken very seriously. Leslie Stephen's dismissal of Trollope in 1901 is particularly telling in this respect: "We can see plainly enough what we must renounce in order to enjoy Trollope. We must cease to bother ourselves about art. . . . We must not desire brilliant epigrams suggesting familiarity with aesthetic doctrines or theories of the universe. A brilliant modern novelist is not only clever, but writes for clever readers" (p. 160). Michael Sadleir, in 1927, makes an equally revealing observation with retrospective insight: "The initial obstacle to a sober-minded definition of Trollope's novels is that they provide a sensual rather than an intellectual experience" (1927, p. 366). Again, I would argue that perceptions like these have implicit gender associations – clever, educated, and intellectual were adjectives more commonly associated with male writers and readers in Victorian culture, and even though Stephen and Sadleir's comments are from the early twentieth century, they sum up the nebulous qualities of Trollope's work and image that complicated the assessment and ranking of Trollope by Victorian critics from the 1860s until his death in 1884.

Frederic Harrison's comparison of Trollope with Austen in 1895 explicitly feminizes Trollope:

Now Trollope reproduces for us that simplicity, unity, and ease of Jane Austen, whose facile grace flows on like the sprightly talk of a charming woman, mistress of herself and sure of her hearers. This uniform ease, of course, goes with the absence of all the greatest

1. Charles Reade: 'Something Like a Novelist' from *Once a Week*, 20 January 1872

2. Charles Reade at his writing table, by Charles Mercier

3. Charlotte Yonge's writing desk in her room at Elderfield

4. Charlotte Yonge aged twenty, by George Richmond, R. A.

5.   Group of contemporary prose writers (standing, from left) George MacDonald,
     J. A. Froude, Wilkie Collins, Anthony Trollope. (Seated) W. M. Thackeray,
     Lord Macaulay, Edward Bulwer-Lytton, Thomas Carlyle, Charles Dickens

qualities of style; absence of any passion, poetry, mystery, or subtlety. He never rises, it is true, to the level of the great masters of
language. But, for the ordinary incidents of life amongst well-bred
and well-to-do men and women of the world, the form of Trollope's
tales is almost as well adapted as the form of Jane Austen.
("Anthony Trollope's Place", p. 208)

These remarks demonstrate the artlessness so many nineteenth-
century critics associated with women's writing, the identification of
domestic subject-matter as somehow incompatible with the "great
masters", and the way Trollope's reputation suffers from being associated with "the sprightly talk" and "facile grace" of a "charming
woman". Brigid Brophy, writing as late as 1968, reiterates the
Trollope/Austen comparison, feminizing Trollope even more strongly than Harrison: "Indeed Trollope is that nice, maundering spinster
lady with a poke bonnet and a taste for cottagey gardens whom superficial readers thought they had got hold of when they had in fact got
hold of the morally sabre-toothed Jane Austen" (Brophy et al., 1968,
p. 64).

Trollope's so-called "masculine" characteristics were largely responsible for the critical approval he did receive, for *Barchester Towers* for
example, and the "feminine" characteristics of his writing (his subject-matter, his interest in and insight into female characters, his imagination or lack thereof, his productivity, his popularity, his readership)
are partly responsible for his critical dismissal. If we juxtapose the
critical receptions of Trollope and Reade, the gendered framework of
reaction becomes even harder to ignore. In the middle and latter part
of his career, Trollope was often associated with the less prestigious
feminine qualities and connotations; as I have shown, critical ambivalence began creeping in during the mid 1860s, and was fairly solidly
in place from, and after, 1870.

The timing of Trollope's critical fall from grace coincides, then, with
the rise of a critical aesthetic that increasingly desired to distinguish
"high art" from "popular art", often along gender lines. Tuchman, as
we recall, argues that "[b]y 1870 men of letters were using the term
high culture to set off novels they admired from those they deemed
run-of-the-mill" (Tuchman and Fortin, 1989, p. 3). And in 1880 the
Athenaeum laments that "Mr Trollope is not an artist according to the
modern school of high art" (quoted in Skilton, 1972, p. 33). As we have
seen, the criteria defining "high art" rigorously excluded the
feminized qualities so commonly applied to Trollope from the late

1860s onwards, and these gender connotations played a major, even a central role in Trollope being "edged out".

The volatility of Trollope's reputation has never been satisfactorily accounted for, though critics such as Skilton, Smalley, Olmsted and Welch provide comprehensive surveys of its bizarre twists and turns. Ruth ApRoberts attributes this critical failure to "come to grips with his work" to the inappropriate application of "old theories" of art, such as modernist premises and "new critical" frameworks: "Of all English novelists Trollope seems to be the perfect example of the kind least served by our old theories; and for this very reason, to come to grips with his work may help us towards a new and more workable theory" (1971, p. 11). Contemporary twentieth-century critics overlook the issue of gender in the decline of Trollope's reputation, probably assuming that Trollope's sex guarantees him safety from any sexual double standard that might exist. Ironically though, my argument does not contradict but supplements or complicates conventional accounts of Trollope's fall from "high art", since the very reasons most commonly used to account for this decline – Trollope's productivity and lack of superior imagination, and changing literary tastes – themselves have gender connotations which have been ignored in discussions of Trollope. While it would be overstating the case to claim that associations with gender constitute the sole cause of the decline in Trollope's reputation, a "new more workable theory" that would help us understand Trollope should, I think, take into account the previously invisible and overlooked relation of nineteenth-century gender associations with ideas of literary value and high art, as applied to Trollope's novels. Being a "Queen" of the Victorian circulating library was problematic for any writer when popular and high art began to diverge, but particularly problematic if the author happened to be male.

5

"The Angel in the Circulating Library": Gender and the Reception of Charlotte Yonge's *The Heir of Redclyffe*

When *The Heir of Redclyffe* appeared anonymously in 1853, it received little immediate critical attention. By the summer of 1854, however, Yonge's novel had become one of the best-selling novels of the century. Although *The Heir of Redclyffe* was not widely reviewed in 1853, reviewers made up for this omission in 1854 when their discussion of Yonge's follow-up novel, *Heartsease*, included sustained retrospective consideration of *The Heir of Redclyffe*.[1]

The Heir of Redclyffe tells the story of the life and death of an appealingly wild yet virtuous young Byronic hero, Sir Guy Morville, the Heir of Redclyffe, who struggles with his hereditary temper; other characters include the docile Amy, who marries Guy and is widowed during their honeymoon, and Guy's self-righteous cousin Philip Morville, who envies Guy's wealth and social standing and does his best to complicate Guy's relations with Amy's family, though ostensibly his actions are motivated by his disapproval of Guy's headstrong and passionate disposition. Inspired by Malory's Galahad, Guy eventually triumphs over his temper, and loses his life trying to nurse Philip through an Italian "plague". Guy's death-bed scene inspired readers to tears. Jo, in the English edition of Louisa May Alcott's *Little Women*, cries over *The Heir of Redclyffe*; an English bishop found his wife crying over Guy's death. Tillotson calls Guy's death "one of the most famous and least gratuitous of Victorian fictional deaths" ("*The Heir*", p. 50).

Guy's battle with his temper and ensuing spiritual transformation

87

is the thematic core of the novel and is responsible for much of its pathos and power. Guy's innate goodness and sensitivity are emphasized throughout. He is reluctant, for example, to take his horse to Oxford with him, for fear that the groom might have his morals corrupted by life in the city! The following scene represents Yonge's treatment of Guy's inner struggle; it describes his furious reaction to a letter from his guardian, Amy's father, that, prompted by allegations from his jealous cousin Philip, accuses him of gambling. After reading this letter, Guy's face turns "a burning, glowing red, the features almost convulsed, the large veins in the forehead and temples swollen with the blood that rushed through them; and if ever his eyes flashed with the dark lightning of Sir Hugh's [his Byronic ancestor] it was then" (p. 173). Guy rushes outside, overcome with violent "indignation and pride" (p. 174). Anger and desire for vengeance "swept over him, and swayed him by turns, with the dreadful intensity belonging to a nature formed for violent passions, which had broken down, in the sudden shock, all the barriers imposed on them by a long course of self-restraint" (p. 174). After indulging in his fury at great length and plotting vengeance on Philip, Guy raises his head to see the sun setting "in a flood of gold" (p. 175). This sight moves him and reminds him of his "good angel" and "true and better self", and he then struggles with the "hereditary demon of the Morvilles". He forces himself to pray:

> "Forgive us our trespasses, as we forgive them that trespass against us." Coldly and hardly were they [these lines] spoken at first; again he pronounced them, again, again – each time the voice was softer, each time they came more from the heart. At last the remembrance of greater wrongs, and worse revilings came upon him; his eyes filled with tears, the most subduing and healing of all thoughts – that of the great Example – became present to him; the foe was driven back. . . . He looked up, and saw that the last remnant of the sun's disk was just disappearing beneath the horizon. The victory was won!   (p. 176)

(The kinds of religious emphasis and emotionalism that we see in this passage were perceived by the reviewers as intrinsically feminine, as will be further discussed below.)

Whereas initial reviewers of *Wuthering Heights* assumed unanimously that Ellis Bell was male, reviewers of *The Heir of Redclyffe* believed that the anonymous author was female. Just as Charles Reade's *It Is Never Too Late To Mend* was complimented by critics for its robust masculinity of content and tone, Yonge's novel was seen as intrinsically and delightfully consistent with reviewers' assumptions about appropriate feminine writing. The critic in *The Christian Remembrancer* believed Charlotte Yonge was the epitome of decorous femininity, "amiable, high-minded, profoundly religious as she shows herself to be" (no. 26, 1853, p. 35). Both Reade and Yonge were praised for conforming to what reviewers considered appropriate gender ideals.

A fervent disciple of John Keble and a member of the Anglo-Catholic Oxford Movement, Yonge's religious perspective infused her work but seldom produced an indigestible preaching effect. Charlotte Yonge's mission to "make goodness attractive", the almost exclusively domestic settings of her books, and her habit of donating all monetary proceeds of the book to charity were among the elements that made her appear to conform closely to the Victorian notion of ideal femininity. According to the tenets of Victorian literary criticism, if a woman was to be a novelist, her writing should form an extension of the domestic "angel in the hearth" role, and Yonge's literary persona coincided closely with this idealized view of womanhood. This chapter will explore how the proximity between Yonge's writing and novelistic persona and Victorian stereotypes of femininity conditioned and shaped Victorian critical reaction to *The Heir of Redclyffe* and was partly, perhaps largely, responsible for the book's enormous popularity.

Ironically, the disjunction between nineteenth- and twentieth-century conceptions of appropriate feminine behaviour makes Yonge's ideologies difficult to accept in the twentieth century and seems responsible for the silence of contemporary feminist critics who, probably disgusted by Yonge's anti-feminism, tend to ignore her altogether. As Edith Sichel put it in the *Monthly Review* as early as 1901, "she is never perfect outside the hearth, and the hearth is not very popular just now. No more is the British Gentlewoman, but if ever a temple were built for her, Miss Yonge should figure as its goddess" ("Charlotte", p. 95).

Georgina Battiscombe calls *The Heir of Redclyffe* "one of the most popular novels of the century" (*Charlotte*, 1943, p. 73) and describes its "immediate and phenomenal success" (*Charlotte*, p. 93).[2] The vast audience transfixed by the book caused it to "share the season's success with *Villette* and *Ruth*" (Tillotson, "*The Heir*", p. 49). Most nineteenth- and twentieth-century commentators on Yonge stress the remarkably wide audience of *The Heir of Redclyffe*; its readers ranged from school-girls to the soldiers of the Crimean War, where it was apparently the book most in demand. Barbara Dunlap describes the novel as "the novel of the Crimean War period" and states that it "helped inspire the ideals of a generation" ("Charlotte", p. 314).

Fervent admirers of *The Heir of Redclyffe* included Tennyson, William Morris, Edward Burne-Jones, Charles Kingsley, and D. G. Rossetti. Tennyson was known to stay up all night reading Yonge by candlelight.[3] Canon Dixon argues that Yonge's novel was an important influence on the emerging Pre-Raphaelite movement: "it was the first book that seemed greatly to influence William Morris and also Burne-Jones" (quoted in Bailey, "Charlotte", p. 191). The emotional sincerity and use of colour and detail in the description of Guy's wedding helps explain what might have attracted the Pre-Raphaelites to the novel: "It was a showery day, with gleams of vivid sunshine, and one of these suddenly broke forth, casting a stream of colour from a martyr's figure in the south window, so as to shed a golden glory on the wave of brown hair over Guy's forehead, then passing on and tinting the bride's white veil with a deep glowing shade of crimson and purple" (p. 298).[4] Bishops and statesmen enjoyed the novel; as John Sutherland explains, "it was found universally moving, even by the Victorian intelligentsia" ("Charlotte", *The Longman Companion*, p. 686).[5]

As mentioned above, Guy's death, occurring after he had risked his life trying to nurse his cousin Philip through a "plague", is regarded as the most moving scene of the novel. Although it is hard to get a full sense of its effect when taken out of context, the following excerpt should give an indication of the scene's emotional power:

He smiled and said, "Is no one here but you?" "No one." "My own sweet wife, my Verena, as you have always been. We have been very happy together." "Indeed we have," said she, a look of suffering crossing her face, as she thought of their unclouded happiness. "It will not be long before we meet again." . . . There was something in his perfect happiness that would not let her grieve. . . . He dozed and woke, said a few tranquil words, and listened to some prayer, psalm, or verse, then slept again, apparently without suffering, except when he tried to take the cordials. . . . He strove to swallow them . . . but at last he came to, "It is no use; I cannot." Then she knew all hope was gone. . . . At last he opened his eyes. "Amy!" he said, as if bewildered or in pain. "Here, dearest!" "I don't see." At that moment the sun was rising, and the light streamed in at the open window, and over the bed; but it was "another dawn than ours" that he beheld, as his most beautiful of smiles beamed over his face, and he said, "Glory in the Highest!" . . . She read the Commendatory Prayer . . . even as she said "Amen" she perceived it was over. The soul was with Him with whom dwell the spirits of just men made perfect; and there lay the earthly part with a smile on the face. She closed the dark fringed eyelids – saw him look more beautiful than in sleep – then laying her face down on the bed she knelt on.   (pp. 362–4)

In the mid-nineteenth century, Guy's death scene was thought to be the most emotionally powerful moment of a novel that was thought to be generally moving; even today, out of textual and historical context, the scene retains its emotional sincerity and mythic quality.

Initially the scarcity of reviews of Charlotte Yonge's *The Heir of Redclyffe* seems surprising, particularly bearing in mind comments such as those of Amy Cruse that Yonge's novel "had a reception such as has been given to no other book in the English language" (1935, p. 50).[6] It became clear that Cruse must have been commenting on popular rather than critical reception. Even though most critics expressed admiration for *The Heir of Redclyffe* and its successor, *Heartsease*, their response was still less ecstatic than that of the reading public.[7] With *The Heir of Redclyffe*, critics respond to a pre-existing public enthusiasm and popularity rather than creating such an audience or market through their critical commentary, and they therefore comment on *The Heir of Redclyffe* in their reviews of Yonge's subsequent novel, *Heartsease*, in 1854. Wide popularity, then, precedes critical notice in the case of *The Heir of Redclyffe*, and the two different types of "reception" need to be distinguished and accounted for. (In 1853 the only two references to *The Heir of Redclyffe* appear to have been the article previously referred to in *The Christian Remembrancer*, and a cursory mention in the *Gentleman's Magazine*. In January of 1854, *The Times*, probably aware at that point of *The Heir of Redclyffe*'s commercial success, devoted two columns to a serious review). When we consider that, unlike Reade's *It Is Never Too Late To Mend*, or Trollope's *Barchester Towers*, *The Heir of Redclyffe* had been preceded by several works for children rather than by a successful or even a noticed novel, and that unlike *Wuthering Heights*, it did not, at first glance, have the benefit of eccentric singularity or the recent fame of "Currer Bell", the lack of critical attention is not surprising.

Reviews of Charlotte Yonge's work invariably approach and conceptualize the author through two basic categories, frames which have persisted to the present day: Yonge as a woman novelist in the tradition of female writers, and Yonge as a religious or didactic novelist. Reviewers' tendencies to categorize Yonge are also evident in the titles of the articles or reviews. Of the 1850s reviews, at least four explicitly place Yonge in contexts of women authors, with titles like "The Lady Novelists of Great Britain" and "Memoranda about our Lady Novelists". Others have titles such as "Religious Novelists" or "Ethical and Dogmatic Fiction", betraying the preconceptions brought to bear on Yonge by those particular reviewers.

These two frames often overlap, since associations with ideal femininity tend, in this period, to have moral and religious implications.[8] The *London Quarterly*, for example, conflates pure morality with "ladylike" writing: Yonge's "moral tone is pure and high throughout; [there is] not a word that any lady might blush to read or write" (July 1858, p. 495). The *North American Review* also juxtaposes and parallels "ladylike delicacy" with "devout" characteristics: "The ladylike delicacy of mind . . . uprightness, and devout and elevated tone of feeling are the same in both" (January 1855, p. 458). *Fraser's Magazine* follows the same pattern, but takes it further by implicitly equating the demeanour and tone of *The Heir of Redclyffe* with Christianity: "[the novel] is perfectly quiet in movement, refined and graceful, it is . . . based upon a solid foundation of Christian principle" (November 1854, p. 491). Perhaps the most explicit juxtaposition of decorous femininity with devout Christianity appears in the *Prospective Review*'s speculation on the identity of the anonymous author of *The Heir of Redclyffe*: "We had at first some transient doubts as to whether the writer was a lady or a clergyman" (no. X, 1854, p. 460).[9]

Once reviewers identify Yonge as a woman writer, they proceed to place her securely within the context and tradition of female novelists. Possessing the knowledge of the writer's sex immediately allows reviewers to conceptualize the scope and nature of the author's accomplishments, creating the comfortable feeling of control that so eluded reviewers of *Wuthering Heights* and caused them so much frustration. The *North American Review* begins its review of *The Heir of Redclyffe* by assessing it in relation to women's writing in general: "No large share of the triumphs of the pen has hitherto belonged to woman. . . . That this fact is owing to natural incapacity in the sex, we do not say, and no one knows. Uncultivated and unenriched, as well as naturally sterile brains have very probably had much to do with it" (January 1855, p. 439). Yonge, however, forms one of the few, the exception who do merit a larger "share of the triumphs of the pen".

Jeaffreson's 1858 work, *Novels and Novelists from Elizabeth to Victoria*, has a lengthy entry on Yonge. He too situates Yonge as a woman writer and judges her according to how she "has excelled . . . her rivals" (p. 407). According to Jeaffreson, "she [Yonge] well deserves the £1000 which publishers are ready to give her for a tale" because her writing talents are "seldom to be found in any but very superior women" (p. 407).

When reviewers compare Yonge with specific female novelists, they usually juxtapose her with Jane Austen. The *Prospective Review* "ascribe[s] to this author no small share of the talent of Miss Austen" (no. X, 1854, p. 467). The *Christian Remembrancer* is more self-aware of this labelling tendency in literary criticism: "any female writer who composes dull stories without incident" is compared to "Miss Austen" (no. 26, 1853, p. 33). Yonge, they declare, is more talented and thus more like Austen than "any other of her so-called school. But because she has genius, that is, because she is original, she belongs to no school but her own" (p. 33). Despite declaring that a juxtaposition between Austen and Yonge would be inappropriate as Yonge is "original", the *Christian Remembrancer* goes on to discuss what Austen taught women writers in general and Yonge in particular, thus revealing that even when Victorian reviewers were self-consciously aware of the limitations of their gender-based frames, they were still, to varying extents, prisoners of such preconceptions.

Essentially, reviewers agree that what Austen teaches Yonge and other women writers is how to maximize and use to best effect "naturally" feminine talents in writing, and how to avoid inappropriate attempts to mimic masculine qualities in writing. As the *Christian Remembrancer* puts it, "Miss Austen taught her countrywomen where to look for materials of fiction, and in what style of writing the finest qualities of female intellect, delicate observation, refined description, easy and graceful conversation, simple and pathetic tenderness, might find their widest scope and legitimate development" (p. 35).

The *Gentleman's Magazine, Fraser's Magazine*, the *North American Review*, and Jeaffreson all identify Yonge's literary strengths as typical of women writers: her talent in depicting character, the elegance and beauty of her style and content, and her skill at portraying domestic life and advocating moral responsibilities and roles. According to *Fraser's*, Yonge's ability to portray character is her distinguishing quality: "In common with Miss Austen, the gifted author of *Heartsease* is chiefly remarkable for truthful delineations of character" (November 1854, p. 490). The *Gentleman's Magazine* agrees that character portrayal is the main strength of women writers: "as far as they [women writers] go . . . they are admirable portrayers of character and situation" (July 1853, p. 19).

For Jeaffreson, Yonge's main talent lies in her ability to preach moral lessons: "to be able to address the young and gentle truthfully and with solemnity, on the most sacred subjects of their affections and hopes and eternal interests . . . is a high endowment" (p. 407). And the *North American Review* agrees that Yonge, like other superior women writers, has "the inspired art at once to charm, to soothe, and to hallow" (January 1855, p. 441). The most appropriate kind of fiction to exert such effects is, for the *North American Review*, domestic fiction, and it is not surprising that this is seen as the most legitimate field for women writers: "In one most fascinating department of literature, that of the novel of domestic life, we think the gentler sex if not unequalled, quite unsurpassed" (p. 442).

The Heir of Redclyffe both conformed to and transcended the category of domestic novel; it was an exceptional example of the genre in the minds of the reviewers. When *The Heir of Redclyffe* was criticized, criticism fell along the lines of conventionally defined shortcomings of women writers in general and domestic novels by women writers in particular. Such deficiencies included a certain narrowness of scope, and an inability to portray male characters and conversation.

Yonge was also criticized, as early as the late 1850s, for being too prolific, a characteristic that many reviewers saw as typical of women writers. The *Dublin Review* laments that "Miss Yonge's works have followed each other with marvelous celerity, and as might therefore be expected, fall off in power and finish. . . . *Heartsease* was decidedly inferior to *The Heir of Redclyffe*" (December 1858, p. 318). Jeaffreson states that "of late there has been a cry that Miss Yonge writes too much and too fast; and certainly her pen has during the six years ending at the close of 1856 been very prolific" (p. 407). Such accusations only intensified as Yonge's career continued, and as she eventually became even more productive than her rival Mrs Oliphant. Barbara Dunlap, writing of Yonge's overall career, states that "her enormous output of over 200 books has tended to be held against her" ("Charlotte", p. 312). As I argued in my discussion of Trollope's reputation in the preceding chapter, women writers were thought to be particularly susceptible to producing rapid and unskilled writing.[10]

The *Prospective Review*, in an 1854 article, finds internal evidence and deficiencies that suggest the author's sex; the religious component constitutes the firmest evidence. An apparent absence of profundity and intellectual rigour in the presentation of religious issues causes the reviewer to speculate on whether the author is female or a clergyman: "But the sacerdotal element is so very feebly and so unquarrelsomely presented and is obviously so superficial an enamel superinduced upon the fundamental religion of the writer, that our doubts soon vanished" (no. X, 1854, p. 460). Implicit in this assessment is the commonly held Victorian critical belief that women writers lack intellectual rigor. The *Gentleman's Magazine* couches the deficiencies of women writers in terms of physical weakness or vulnerability: women writers "cannot . . . fetch up materials from the haunts into which a Dickens or Bulwer may penetrate. They may in vain try to grapple with the more complicated difficulties of many a man's position and career" (July 1853, p. 19).

Yonge's male characters are often thought to be weak; this criticism is in line with conventional beliefs about women writers' lack of worldly experience and artistic imagination. According to the *Prospective Review*, "all the male characters – ably as they are delineated – are drawn in the aspects in which they present themselves to women. There is the masculine side of men's conversation with women, but no purely masculine talk" (no. X, 1854, p. 460). *Fraser's* expresses its admiration for the depiction of the hero Guy Morville, but finds the portrayal of Guy's cousin, Philip Morville, inferior, and typical of women's inability to "judge for men": "it is . . . very difficult for a woman to present us with a perfectly truthful and consistent picture of male character. Philip Morville is an instance of this; he puzzles and dissatisfies us from first to last" (p. 502). The *North British Review* and the *Prospective Review* both feel somewhat stifled by the atmosphere of *The Heir of Redclyffe*. The *North British Review* holds that Yonge "wants a wider sympathy with the varieties of human character, and with the manifold interests of life" (November 1856, p. 117). The *Prospective Review* complains that Yonge should "exhibit the career of her characters, not get them to sit quietly for their likeness" (no. X, 1854, p. 463). It criticizes Yonge and other female domestic novelists for too "closely 'hugging the land' in their small cruises on the ocean of imagination . . . they delineate narrow specimens of humanity; they lose the freedom and breadth of scale belonging to the greater power that can transmute its experience" (p. 472). Implicit in remarks like this last one is a sense that the experience of reading domestic novels is, for many reviewers, like being forced to inhabit the middle-class world from the perspective of a Victorian woman – the resulting feeling is a claustrophobic irritation, particularly strong, perhaps, if the

imaginative power of the novel is strong enough to cause the reviewer to identify with the world presented.[11]

After the reviewers' original impulse to situate Charlotte Yonge in
the context of women writers as a group had been satisfied, they then
turned their attention to *The Heir of Redclyffe* itself. Here too, gender
plays a principal role in shaping thought, though less blatantly: the
adjectives, for example, used to praise *The Heir of Redclyffe* could easily be transposed to apply to a perfect and conventional specimen of
Victorian womanhood.[12]

Probably the most frequently used adjective, whether applied to
The Heir of Redclyffe as a whole, or to scenes from it, is "beautiful". In
1854, the *Gentleman's Magazine* calls *The Heir of Redclyffe* "a very beautiful novel" (November 1854, p. 443). The *Christian Remembrancer* calls
The Heir of Redclyffe "a beautiful . . . tale" (no. 26, 1853, p. 34), and finds
Guy "one of the most beautiful and elevating characters to be met
with in fiction" (p. 48). The *Dublin Review* states that "there are passages [in *The Heir of Redclyffe*] of extreme beauty" (December 1858,
p. 316). Conflated with the idea of beauty are the qualities of grace-
fulness, refinement, elegance, morality, and tenderness, all characteristics normally associated with ideals of Victorian femininity. The
London Quarterly, for example, believes that "a love of quiet and home
is instilled in the course of the narrative" (July 1858, p. 496). Jeaffreson
labels Yonge "a writer of elegant stories, inculcating a healthy morality and true womanly sentiments" (p. 407). And *Fraser's* writes
admiringly that *The Heir of Redclyffe* is "refined and graceful"
(November 1854, p. 491). In the above respects, then, *The Heir of
Redclyffe's* image clearly conforms to approved Victorian notions of
stereotypical femininity.

Often juxtaposed with admiring references to the feminine qualities described above, however, are fulsome compliments about Yonge's
power and genius. At a first glance, the juxtaposition of "genius" with
"graceful", or "power" with "pretty", seems contradictory to the point
of paradox, bearing in mind the double standard in literary criticism
discussed in previous chapters. *Fraser's*, for example, terms *The Heir
of Redclyffe* both "quiet" and "vigorous", "refined" and "animated"
(November 1854, p. 491). The *Gentleman's Magazine*, in 1854, states
that *The Heir of Redclyffe* contains "many whole scenes of extraordinary beauty and power" (November 1854, p. 442). The *Dublin Review*
asserts that *The Heir of Redclyffe* "bears evidence indeed of much genius
. . . [with] passages of extreme beauty" (December 1858, p. 316). And
London Quarterly explicitly attributes the novel's "delicacy" and

"power" to "a great delicacy and refinement which makes them [Yonge's novels] admissible to the female circle, to a power of mental analysis which gives them an air of consummate judgment" (July 1858, p. 513).

Critics found it possible to identify and admire Yonge's "power" and "genius" precisely because her work so strongly coincided with their preconceptions about femininity. In other words, because Yonge's novel conforms so closely to critics' expectations about appropriate female behaviour and feminine spheres, critics identify the novel's strengths as a legitimate extension of the feminine role and are consequently disarmed into an unthreatened recognition of the novel's merits. Yonge's talent and work appear to fit unpretentiously into the appropriate area for women's literary endeavours, unlike *Wuthering Heights*, for example, which provoked very different reactions from critics. The similarity between the gender schemas of the reader and the depictions of gender roles in *The Heir of Redclyffe* produces interactive readers. Since readers find their preconceptions about appropriate female writing confirmed, they are not forced into an antagonistic relationship with the text, as they were in the case of *Wuthering Heights*. Instead, there is the degree of consensus between reader and work that Stanley Fish identifies as crucial for response to occur ("Literature in the Reader", p. 88). Readers of *The Heir of Redclyffe* can relate to the world presented in the novel and assimilate it to their own structure of thinking.

Interestingly, critics tend to focus their comments on the effects *The Heir of Redclyffe* has on its readers, rather than on the work's intrinsic literary qualities, perhaps partly in response to the novel's religious elements. Critics commonly, as in the following review in *Fraser's Magazine*, reveal an intensely emotional response to the work in general and to the characters in particular: "Above all, she succeeds in interesting us so much in her protégés, that when at last we bid them farewell, it is ever hereafter to recall them to our affectionate remembrance, as friends whom we have known and loved on earth, and whom we hope one day to meet in heaven" (November 1854, p. 491). Such reactions persist into the twentieth century: in 1901 Edith Sichel calls Yonge's "chief gift . . . not a literary one" but rather a "moral gift – the faculty of intimacy" ("Charlotte", p. 89). And in 1934, Sarah Bailey terms Yonge's strong point "her success in drawing characters whom we get to know and love" ("Charlotte", p. 191). This kind of focus on the audience/reader and concentration on the emotional and didactic effects of the book seems to lend itself to idealizing the book

as an "angel in the circulating library", to seeing it as the most appropriate, and least threatening kind of writing for a woman to produce
– women's writing at its best.

   Two articles, one in *Blackwood's Magazine* and one in *The Times*,
further explain and support my analysis of why *The Heir of Redclyffe*
was found exceptional, yet feminine, brilliant, yet not unsettling.
Blackwood's article, "Modern Novelists Great and Small", written by
Mrs Oliphant in 1855, distinguishes between first-rate or great novels written by men and "second-rank" novels written by women: "Nor
does it seldom happen that a storyteller of this second rank", characterized by "minds of a lower range and scantier experience", "finds
a straight road and a speedy entrance to the natural *heart* which has
but admired and wondered at the master minstrel's loftier tale; . . .
women who rarely or never find their way to the loftiest class, have
a natural right and claim to rank foremost in the second" (May 1855,
p. 555; emphasis added). Oliphant is not referring specifically to
Yonge, but her assessment of the relation between gender, rank, and
literary appeal sheds light on the apparent paradox identified above
in the reception of *The Heir of Redclyffe*.

   Oliphant's analysis is also strangely similar to an equally telling
article in *The Times* in 1854, in this case an actual review of *The Heir of
Redclyffe*. After combining praise of Yonge's novel with criticism of
its limitations, *The Times* concludes the following:

> *The Heir of Redclyffe* is a very beautiful and moving book, and will
> charm more and do infinitely more good than works of far stronger
> intellect and higher artistic excellence. If it is not admired, it will be
> loved, which is, any day, the better fortune of the two. The form
> and character of Guy, and the picture of his reconciliation with
> Philip, and his early death will live in all hearts, and perhaps wake
> in some new affections and impulses for good. Never, perhaps, did
> the beauty of holiness appear more beautiful or more winning than
> in this pure and excellent creation. People will feel more about it
> than many will confess; and we are mistaken if it does not help to
> raise the tone of English fiction.   (5 January 1854, p. 9)

The Times's article is indeed extremely positive about *The Heir of
Redclyffe*, but its reaction is expressed in intensely gendered terms –
The Heir of Redclyffe will be "loved" rather than "admired"; it is "beautiful" and "moving" rather than "strong", "intelligent", or "excellent";
thus *The Times* actually draws attention to the binary oppositions at

work. The structure of gendered oppositions used seems at first to coincide with what Elaine Showalter calls the critical double standard (1977, p. 90). The discussion of the reception of Reade, Emily Brontë, and Trollope in earlier chapters confirms the existence of such a critical double standard, and indicates, not surprisingly, that the literary qualities associated with men are normally elevated over their feminine counterparts. But in the case of the reception of *The Heir of Redclyffe*, a paradox emerges – the gendered stratification of adjectives is intact, but the hierarchy is reversed. In the words of *The Times*, *The Heir of Redclyffe* may be more likely to be "loved" than "admired", but being "loved" is fundamentally, in this particular case, seen as more important and significant.

If we juxtapose particular representative mid-Victorian comments about the appropriate role of women with particular critical reactions to *The Heir of Redclyffe*, the degree of parallelism becomes apparent. Peter Gaskell makes the following comment about woman's moral influence:

The moral influence of woman upon man's character and domestic happiness is mainly attributable to her natural and instinctive habits. Her love, her tenderness, her affectionate solicitude for his comfort and enjoyment, her devotedness . . . exercise a most ennobling impression upon his nature, and do more towards making him a good husband, a good father, and a useful citizen than all the dogmas of political economy.   (quoted in Poovey, 1988, p. 8)

The Christian Remembrancer makes a similar point about the moral influence of *The Heir of Redclyffe*:

It is difficult to speak [of *The Heir of Redclyffe*] in terms which will not, to those who have not yet read it, appear exaggerated and impossible. It is not that *The Heir of Redclyffe* is a faultless work. . . . But it is a book of unmistakable genius and real literary power; a book to make men pause and think, to lift them out of themselves and above the world, and make them . . . the wiser and the better for their reading. . . . [It is] more affecting and far more practically useful than the run of moral treatises or public exhortation.
(no. 267, 1853, p. 47)

The Heir of Redclyffe is again paralleled with woman's role if we juxtapose Coventry Patmore's "Angel in the House" with another review of Yonge. Patmore's "Angel in the House, written in 1855 and 1856, creates the character of Honoria, whom Poovey describes thus: "Naturally self-sacrificing and self-regulating, this domestic deity radiated morality because her substance was love, not self-interest or ambition" (1988, p. 8). The *North American Review* writes admiringly that Yonge's "style is unstudied, even to carelessness. Its perfect freedom from pretension, and from all parade of originality is among the most remarkable things about it" (January 1855, p. 446). Like Honoria, Yonge – the Angel in the Circulating Library – triumphs through her apparent lack of self-interest and ambition. Paradoxically, the freedom from "all parade of originality" is, by inversion, one of the distinguishing aspects of Yonge's work that causes it to be perceived as remarkable or a work of genius. In all four of the above examples it becomes apparent how *The Heir of Redclyffe* is feminized, functioning in the public eye as a metonymical representation of the ideal woman, and like her, achieving transcendence through a spiritual path that short-circuits structures of temporal power, value, judgement, or hierarchy.

Reviewers of *The Heir of Redclyffe* reacted to the work in a way that can best be accounted for by the ways in which the novel affirmed the reader's identity, and more specifically, society's beliefs about gender, along with readers' gender schemas. Poovey, commenting on how texts reproduced ideology in mid-Victorian England, asserts that "[p]art of the work that texts perform is the reproduction of ideology; texts give the values and structures of values that constitute ideology body – that is, they embody them for and in the subjects who read. In this sense, reading, or more precisely interpretation – is a historically and culturally specific activity; it is part of a public institution" (1988, p. 17). Hans Robert Jauss argues that commercial success "presupposes a book which expresses what the group expects, a book which presents the group with its own image" (*Toward*, 1982, p. 26). As I have demonstrated, the ways in which Charlotte Yonge's *The Heir of Redclyffe* reproduced ideology for its contemporary readers, embodying structures of gender, allowed the novel to function as an Angel in the Circulating Library, something not "to be written or judged by common rules" (*North American Review*, January 1855, p. 449), something that transcends and inverts customary hierarchies of gender in critical standards. As Houghton explains in his discussion on "woman worship" in *The Victorian Frame of Mind*, if women conformed to and excelled in their domestic role and did not compete in the public male world, they could be idealized spiritually and seen as divine priestesses; similarly, by conforming to Victorian ideas about appropriate writing for women, Yonge is exalted by critics, and gender ideology is confirmed.

An analysis of the shifts in the literary reputation of Charlotte Yonge and *The Heir of Redclyffe* demonstrates just how historically and culturally specific interpretation and evaluation really are. Henry James, for example, had a profound admiration for Charlotte Yonge. Writing of *The Heir of Redclyffe*, he argued that the novel revealed "a first rate mind . . . a mind which is the master and not the slave of its material", and he characterized Yonge as "almost a genius" (quoted in Tillotson, *"The Heir"*, p. 51). And Gordon Haight reveals that Lewes bought Yonge's *The Daisy Chain* while on holiday in Italy, to read out loud to George Eliot after "Anthony Trollope had warmly recommended it" (1968, p. 344). From this height, however, Yonge's reputation had perhaps reached its nadir by the end of the nineteenth century. Richard Ellmann describes a visit Oscar Wilde made to a man in prison who was waiting to be hanged. Wilde asked the man if he read, and after being told that he was currently reading *The Heir of Redclyffe*, "Wilde left the cells with his party, and then could not resist a comment: 'My heart was turned by the eyes of the doomed man, but if he reads *The Heir of Redclyffe* it's perhaps as well to let the law take its course'" (1988, p. 202). In 1901 *Literature* commented that "there probably never was a trained critic who ranked Miss Yonge's work very high or derived acute pleasure from its perusal" (quoted in Cooper, *"Charlotte"*, p. 853).

What the above remarks indicate, however, is a split in the popular and critical reception of Yonge, and they reveal the increasingly gendered hierarchy of literary criticism that we saw emerging for Trollope in this same period. From the middle to late 1860s, the pattern and content of critical reviews reveals a decline in the general critical esteem in which Yonge was held. Articles in periodicals became few and far between, and those that existed, such as an 1865 *Reader* article and an 1866 *Saturday Review* article, tended to be derogatory.[13] However, Yonge remained popular with the general public. In 1876 *The Heir of Redclyffe* entered its 22nd edition and in 1912 Macmillan issued a complete reprint of all Yonge's works. And critics did not reject Yonge unanimously. Edward Cooper, for example, in a 1901 article in the *Fortnightly Review*, calls the critics who think Yonge irrelevant to the present age "absolutely wrong" (January–June 1901, p. 857). Interestingly though, what Cooper focuses on is not so much Yonge's literary merit but more the emotional effect she has on her reader, echoing commentary from the 1850s: "A thousand grown-up folk yesterday, today, and for years to come have gone and will go to Charlotte Yonge's books for pure love of studying such serene faith and high ideals as live in them. . . . Most of us today know rather intimately what it means to be tired in mind, soul, and body. . . . It is in these moods that literature like *The Daisy Chain* is a necessity" (p. 856).

In the 1940s Yonge's reputation and popularity underwent a revival, perhaps partly due to the nostalgic longing for security and escapism created by the disorienting experience of the Second World War. At that time about six of her novels were still in print. In 1945 Mrs Susan Hicks Beach actually wrote a "sequel" to *The Heir of Redclyffe*. A 1945 *Punch* article, describing the sequel, refers to "that sustained interest in the novels of Charlotte Yonge which a *Times Literary Supplement* of 1943 stigmatized as 'deplorable'" (H.P.E., "Twenty", p. 105); it refuses, however, to align itself with *The Times* and praises the "sincere and moving piety" of the original (p. 105). Yonge's admirers in the 1940s included intellectuals such as C. S. Lewis, and we can sense how strong the vogue was for Yonge's writing by the intensity with which Q. D. Leavis, in a 1945 *Scrutiny* article attemps to protect the canon from Yonge. Leavis is appalled by "claims for this writer as a serious artist", that had recently been made, and finds it her duty to "investigate" these claims "before the canon of English literature finds itself permanently burdened with one of the prolific fiction-writers whom time alone has already expelled" (1965, p. 153). Leavis ridicules Yonge's religious views, with undeniably humorous results: "the most blessed life for a man is to give up the natural field for his abilities in order to become a South Seas missionary, and for a woman to renounce a possible husband in order to devote herself to her relatives, even if they are only imbecile grandparents – self-sacrifice is an end in itself" (p. 157). Furthermore, Leavis attacks Yonge for being "schoolgirlish" (p. 154).

From the 1950s until the present day, Yonge's reputation has increasingly faded. A new edition of *The Heir of Redclyffe* appeared in 1964, but the novel is currently out of print. Occasionally claims surface for her as a serious writer. In 1953, for a BBC talk on the 100th anniversary of its publication, Tillotson called *The Heir of Redclyffe* a "classic"; in 1977 Robert Lee Wolff wrote that "she has never been wholly forgotten and she is perpetually being rediscovered with new appreciation" (1977, p. 117). Only two of her novels are currently in print, through the feminist press Virago.[14] Literary criticism has little to say about Yonge these days.

Jauss would argue that the decline in Yonge's reputation can be attributed to a change in the "horizon of expectations" and an "altered aesthetic norm" that causes the "audience [to] experience formerly successful works as outmoded, and [to] withdraw its appreciation" (*Toward*, 1982, p. 27). Changes in aesthetic norms and horizons of expectation involved Yonge's status as a quintessentially Victorian writer as well as changing ideas about gender roles; these factors are, of course, related. Gender continued to play a crucial role in the reception of Yonge, though it functioned differently from in the 1850s.

I believe there are two central and related reasons that account both for Yonge's loss of favour and for her continued appeal to some readers. Yonge is positioned in such a way that she seems quintessentially Victorian: she was born in 1823 and died in 1901, dates that coincide almost exactly with the birth and death of Queen Victoria (1819–1901); she was one of the most popular of Victorian novelists, and, by later modernist critical standards, the mere fact of such popularity makes her somewhat suspect as a serious novelist; she was the most prolific of all Victorian novelists (writing more even than Mrs Oliphant) during a time when novelists were known, and later scorned, for being prolific; she was an extremely didactic novelist, and again later scorned for having didactic aims; she was an intensely earnest writer, and Oscar Wilde displayed late nineteenth-century amusement and contempt for this Victorian trait.

The Heir of Redclyffe, as Yonge's most famous and largest selling work, is also positioned as the novel that most centrally represents Yonge. Consequently, when things Victorian fell into disfavour, and modernist principles were applied to the "loose baggy monsters" of Victorian prose, Yonge in general, and *The Heir of Redclyffe* in particular, seemed likely candidates for the critical guillotine. Moreover, the extremity of Yonge's attachment to and promotion of stereotypical Victorian ideas about femininity functioned in a similar way. In *The Heir of Redclyffe*, for example, there are two main female characters: Amy, who, as we will see from the excerpt below, epitomized the angelic child-like domestic role of Victorian women, and the headstrong and independent Laura, who marries Philip without her father's permission and is punished by suffering from depression for the rest of her life. The following extract from the novel, taken from the middle of the book, after Guy and Amy become engaged and before they go to Italy for the fatal honeymoon, provides a concrete example of what readers are reacting to when it comes to gender roles:

"Guy," said Amy, looking up, with the gentle resolution that had lately grown on her, "you must not take me for more than I am worth, and I should like to tell you fairly . . . I know, and you know, too, that I am a foolish little thing; I have been silly little Amy always; you and Charlie have helped me to all the sense I have, and I don't think I could ever be a clever, strong-minded woman, such as one admires." "Heaven forbid!" ejaculated Guy . . . "But," continued Amy, "I believe I do really wish to be good, and I know you have helped me to wish it much more, and I have been trying to learn to bear things, and so" – out came something, very like a sunny smile, though some tears followed – "so if you do like such a silly little thing, it can't be helped, and we will try to make the best of her. Only don't say any more about my being happier without you; for one thing I am very sure of, Guy, I had rather bear anything with you, than know you were bearing it alone. I am only afraid of being foolish and weak, and making things worse for you." (pp. 264–5)

It is perhaps not surprising that such portrayals of ideal femininity would grow increasingly unpalatable as ideas about women changed over the late nineteenth and throughout the twentieth centuries. Jacques Leenhardt demonstrates that readers are most comfortable with material close to their own preconceptions and stereotypes: "sweet, foolish little Amy" who is said to cry over 300 times in the course of the novel bears little relation to today's heroines.

A 1940s reader of Yonge, Hester Chapman, expressed her ambivalent mixture of irritation and fascination in the following comment about *The Daisy Chain*: "at the end they [the characters] stand solid, massed, as in a school photograph, staring you straight in the face; however much they may have annoyed you (and they are as a rule extremely irritating) you cannot forget or confuse them" ("Books", p. 123). Implicit in this comparison of the characters to a school photograph is the mixture of nostalgia, distance, attraction, and revulsion the writer feels about Yonge, much as one might feel on examination of an old school photograph. Even though the characters are annoying, they are still compelling to the point of being unforgettable.

Making generalizations about twentieth-century readers and their reactions may seem perilous when one considers the vast differences between pre-First World War readers, readers in the 1950s, and contemporary readers who have been exposed to the post-1960s feminist movement. Commentary from all three of these periods, though, in different ways and to different degrees, discusses the alien nature of Yonge's portrayal of gender roles. Up until the 1960s, however, such commentary seems more widespread and more passionate, implying perhaps that readers in the early to mid-nineteenth century were still faced with the persistence of Yonge's ideas about women. Contemporary readers tend more to ignore Yonge than to attack her, presumably because they no longer have the same need to reject her.

The clash between the overtly expressed depiction of gender in Yonge's works and the changed gender schema of post-nineteenth-century readers seems likely to block the kind of interaction that would produce understanding, let alone appreciation. Elizabeth Flynn would describe the resulting readers as dominant, readers whose preconceptions conflict with the text in such a way that the text is held at a distance, controlled, and limited in its power. Hester Chapman's reactions, however, could best be characterized as a mixture of dominant and interactive reading, with the reader moving rapidly from fascination and absorption to irritation and distance. The fact that occasional interactive reading occurs is even more irritating and threatening when the reader does not wish to identify with gender schema that she finds threatening.

If, as Norman Holland suggests, "all of us, as we read, use the literary work to symbolize and finally to replicate ourselves" ("Unity", p. 124), then our desire is thwarted if our schemas are such that they do not allow us to "replicate" ourselves, or worse still, if they create a disturbing and undesirable replication. David Bleich's argument that we judge as good work that which is psychologically bearable and does not make us defensive ("The Determination") also applies to readers' difficulties with Yonge in the twentieth century – clearly the gender roles and the emotionality and religiosity in Yonge's work are liable to make readers defensive.

As early as 1901, Edith Sichel, in *The Monthly Review*, states that "the girls of today cannot see themselves in Miss Yonge and that is their chief demand from literature" ("Charlotte", p. 95). In other words, Sichel's "girls of today", like all readers in Holland's view, seek to "symbolize" and "replicate" themselves in their reading, with schizophrenic results in reading Yonge. Similarly, Hester Chapman argues in 1943 that Yonge's characters cannot be separated from the Victorian age. She, however, believes that they still have an appeal, albeit a disturbing one, perhaps leading to the fractured sensation described above: "They [Yonge's characters] have nothing to do with today or tomorrow. They stand, not for all time, but for the investigation of

those who like to be for a moment enclosed in a self-contained vio-
lently agitated microcosm" ("Books", p. 123).

Another factor in the deterioration of Charlotte Yonge's literary
reputation is her association with women readers in general and with
young women readers in particular, causing her to become doubly
marginalized. Although, as I explained above, Yonge was admired
and read by both men and women in the Victorian age, and by "intellectual" men at that, by the turn of the century comments like the following one by Sichel were ubiquitous: "it is impossible to imagine
many men reading Miss Yonge. There is an intemperate tameness
about her – at once her charm and her defect – which forbids our asso-
ciating mankind with her. It would be as if we dreamed of them taking high tea in perpetuo" ("Charlotte", pp. 92–3).

Nina Baym's and Jane Tompkins's work on American literature
investigates the canonical invisibility of American nineteenth-
century popular writers, and many of their insights apply to Yonge.
Baym, for example, argues that literary prejudices existed against
women writers, which included automatic biases against popularity
with women readers and preoccupations with women's lives and concerns (*Women's* , 198, p. 14). Similarly, and this comment is particularly relevant to *The Heir of Redclyffe*, our contemporary criticisms of
sentimentality in popular nineteenth-century novels by women are
themselves "culture-bound" criticisms that "refuse to assert to the
work's conventions" (p. 24). In *Sensational Designs*, Tompkins argues
that modernist critical principles tend to be incompatible with the
writing of nineteenth-century popular women writers and that apply-
ing different criteria would result in different evaluations (1985,
p. xvii). She suggests that we should not view literary texts as
"attempts to achieve a timeless, universal ideal of truth and formal
coherence", but instead think about their function "expressing and
shaping the social context that produced them" (p. 200). Looked at
thus, *The Heir of Redclyffe* is clearly worthy of study, a fascinating work
that responds to contemporary Victorian views and concerns about
gender, religion, and leading a spiritual life in middle-class Victorian
society, rather than a sentimental and irrelevant propaganda vehicle
for antediluvian gender stereotypes. Jauss also believes that "the
aesthetic judgement of the present world favors a canon of works that
correspond to modern taste, but would unjustly evaluate all other
works only because their function in their time is no longer evident"
(*Toward*, 1982, p. 30). Yonge has, in my view, been "unjustly" neglected
and evaluated for precisely these reasons.

Most hard to reconcile, in the case of Charlotte Yonge, is the puzzling fact that when critics do mention her, it tends to be with respect – Barbara Dunlap, Robert Lee Wolff, Kathleen Tillotson, and John Sutherland, for example – and yet this respect does not translate into sustained or serious critical attention. Yonge, and more specifically, even *The Heir of Redclyffe*, seem unpalatable to contemporary taste to the point of being taboo. I tend to agree with the many nineteenth-century critics and the few twentieth-century critics who believe the novel approaches brilliance, and think that, regrettably, Yonge has fallen between both patriarchal/sexist and feminist critical agendas. Because, as I argued above, she was a popular and prolific Victorian woman writer with a reputation for writing for women and children, she is usually ignored by mainstream critics for reasons suggested by Baym and Tompkins. But of equal importance, because Yonge's ideas and depiction of gender roles seem so impossible to translate as covert rebellion, Yonge has also been neglected by contemporary feminist critics and has not therefore participated in the revival of so many, often less talented, Victorian novelists. In these ways, preconceptions about gender roles have been crucial in determining interpretation and evaluation of Charlotte Yonge from the 1850s to the present: in the 1850s *The Heir of Redclyffe* offered readers a mirror in which they saw themselves confirmed in the idealized roles they aspired to; twentieth-century readers find the reflection more like that presented by a distorting mirror at a fun-fair or amusement park.

Conclusion

This analysis of Victorian "horizons of expectations" concretely demonstrates how criteria used to determine literary value were, in the Victorian period anyway, definitely not the "universal" and "transhistorical" gender-neutral criteria so beloved of upholders of the Western literary canon. In *Sensational Designs* Jane Tompkins argues that "great literature does not exert its force over and against time, but changes with the changing currents of social and political life" (1985, p. 192). As Jauss puts it, "A literary work is not an object that stands by itself and that offers the same view to each reader in each period" (*Toward*, 1982, p. 21). Canons, Paul Lauter reminds us, are "the products of historically specific conflicts over culture and values" (168).

From the Victorian age to the present, the horizon of expectations for the critical reader and reviewer has been continually characterized by peristently strong and influential preconceptions about sex and gender, though an analysis of how such schema influence the interpretation and evaluation of literature has appeared only relatively recently, with the advent of feminist criticism. Feminist reader-response and reception studies to date have tended to focus on issues of sex, pointing out the obvious under-representation of women in literary histories, questioning the ways in which women are represented by the canonical male writers, exploring the effects of such representations on women readers, and analyzing the differences in the ways that men and women read and interpret texts. Such approaches have distinguished, then, between male and female writers and between male and female readers.

This study suggests that in the Victorian period literary value was not simply an effect of the author's sexual identity. Certainly there were particular qualities that Victorian reviewers associated with men and with women; certainly there existed a critical hierarchy which valued the characteristics identified with men's writing over those connected with women. However, in the case of the four writers considered, literary reputations were formed less by the author's sexual identity than by the way their works conformed to or transgressed from the gendered framework of reviewers' expectations (and female reviewers were often more rigorous in enforcing gender conformity than their male peers, as we saw in Chapter 1).

Reade's *It Is Never Too Late To Mend* and Trollope's *Barchester Towers* both received acclaim for what reviewers perceived as their palpably masculine qualities, and both novels were described as ideal for intelligent male readers who did not often read fiction. In the process of being praised for their "vigour" and "power", both novels were juxtaposed, to their credit, with inferior works by women. As Trollope's career continued, however, his writing acquired "feminine" characteristics, rendering him vulnerable to the kinds of critical attacks normally reserved for women writers. His attraction to romance-based plots, his focus on character rather than action, his interest in and insight into female characters, his imagination (or lack thereof), his productivity, his popularity, and his readership led him to be perceived as intrinsically less masculine – and less significant – than Reade. Indeed, Trollope was increasingly seen as merely a circulating-library novelist, while Reade's work, as G. H. Lewes averred, was a bit too good for "that unfastidious class of readers subscribing to circulating libraries" (*The Leader*, 23 August 1856, p. 810). By 1884, the *Literary World* described Trollope flatly as a writer for women, in comparison now with Thackeray, a man's writer. Thackeray, the *Literary World* contended, was destined for permanent popularity; Trollope was a transient popular fad.

Turning now to the female novelists, we see that when *Wuthering Heights* was thought to be written by a man, the book was shocking, but at the same time it was appreciated for its "masculine" qualities: power, originality, and all the ways it differentiated itself from "effeminate" works. With the provision of the new biographical context in Charlotte Brontë's "Preface", preconceptions about women writers formed the particular interpretive horizon within which *Wuthering Heights* was subsequently viewed, and the critics' attempts to classify the work became tortured as they struggled to fit Brontë's powerful, vigorous, and forceful – that is, "masculine" – writing into the same category with the refined, moral, and tender-hearted narratives women were supposed to write. Recall George Eliot's bitter observation in "Silly Novels by Lady Novelists" that "no sooner does a woman show that she has genius or effective talent, than she receives the tribute of being moderately praised and severely criticized . . . if ever she reaches excellence, critical enthusiasm drops to the freezing point" (Nadel, *Victorian Fiction*, 1980, p. 400).

Charlotte Yonge's *The Heir of Redclyffe*, on the other hand, though also written anonymously, enchanted reviewers, who were able to place it confidently and comfortably within the context and tradition of female writers. Whereas *Wuthering Heights* transgressed the conventions of women's domestic novels to a monstrous degree, the "beauty" and "gentleness" of *The Heir of Redclyffe* ratified gendered ideologies to such an extent that its critics idealized the book and its authoress. Thus Yonge managed to effect a triumph of sorts over the critical double standard. Remember, for example, *The Times* remarking that "*The Heir of Redclyffe* is a very beautiful and moving book, and will charm more and do infinitely more good than works of far stronger intellect and higher artistic excellence. If it is not admired, it will be loved, which is, any day, the better fortune of the two" (5 January 1854, p. 9). In Jauss's terms, *The Heir of Redclyffe*

> can be characterized by an aesthetics of reception as not demanding any horizonal changes, but rather as precisely fulfilling the expectations prescribed by a ruling standard of taste, in that it satisfies the desire for the reproduction of the familiarly beautiful; confirms familiar sentiments; sanctions wishful notions; makes unusual experiences enjoyable as "sensations"; or even raise[s] moral problems, but only to "solve" them in an edifying manner as predecided questions. (*Toward*, 1982, p. 25).

Currently, we read and valorize *Wuthering Heights* and Trollope's novels, the works that troubled the gendered categories of Victorian reviewers, whereas the two Victorian best-sellers, Reade's *It Is Never Too Late To Mend* and Yonge's *The Heir of Redclyffe* that epitomized Victorian gender roles are no longer read. It would be overly simplistic to conclude that the only reason we overlook these two writers is because their portrayals of men and women are outmoded; a period's horizon of expectations is informed by a complex amalgam of material factors and ideological presuppositions. Nevertheless, imagining survey courses in which Reade and Yonge replace Trollope and Emily Brontë reveals the "horizonal" distance that separates us from the Victorians; it also highlights the crucial role that gendered ideologies play in the successful reception of literary works: it is, I think, in particular the intensely patriarchal gender roles of Reade and Yonge that don't allow the contemporary reader to engage with their fictional worlds.

Contemporary formations and re-formations of the canon are of course contingent upon late twentieth-century assumptions about gender, writing, and literary value. Tompkins argues that we currently operate within a modernist framework for literary merit that is not conducive to appreciating the sentimentality or emotionalism (or the historically specific role behind the latter) characteristic of nineteenth-century American popular fiction by women. Recently critics have begun investigating the gender biases of modernism, arguing that the abhorence of emotion and the disdain for the popular reader that we find in modernist critical manifestos are connected with an association between women and these characteristics. And the reluctance until recent years to take novels such as Fanny Burney's *Evelina* seriously because it doesn't deal with "serious subjects" shows us how we still tend, like Trollope's critics, to associate domestic subjects and discussions of love and romance with triviality and with women readers and writers.

A recent study, for example, *Reviewing the Reviews. A Woman's Place on the Book Page*, written and edited by a British group, "Women in Publishing", argues that women writers (and readers) do not receive equal treatment in the book review pages of leading British journals. The book was researched in 1985 by a group of women in publishing who decided to conduct a systematic study of reviews of women writers to see if and how women writers were treated differently from men in British book reviews. Throughout 1985, 28 publications were examined closely and 12 issues of each journal were surveyed; in total, over 5000 book reviews were considered.

The publications investigated by the "Women in Publishing" study included the *London Review of Books*, *The Times Literary Supplement*, and *The Times Higher Education Supplement*. The issues covered by the survey included: the relative percentage of reviews devoted to books by women authors, the relative length of reviews of men's versus women's writing and the relative page space given to each, the percentage of the time men as opposed to women writers were given the leading article or top spot, the location of the review, the percentage of the reviewers who were male and female, and finally, the influence of reviews on book buyers and libraries.

As the authors of the "Women in Publishing" study note, the results of their investigation produce "a statistical portrait that is extraordinary for its clearly defined overall patterns of sex bias on most publications" (1987, p. 38). Focusing on the findings of three journals in particular, *The Times Literary Supplement*, the *London Review of Books*, and *The Times Higher Education Supplement*, we see that only 19 per cent, 17 per cent, and 9.5 per cent, respectively, of the books reviewed were written by women authors. Similarly, reviews of women's books were invariably shorter than reviews of books by men: in the *London Review of Books*, for example, the average length of reviews for women's books was 59.37 inches, compared with 72.07 inches for men's books. And the *London Review of Books* gave men the leading article 100 per cent of the time, with *The Times Literary Supplement* and *The Times Higher Education Supplement* giving male writers the top spot 92 per cent of the time. The study reveals that women reviewers form a distinct minority (27 per cent in *The Times Literary Supplement*, 24 per cent in the *London Review*, and 9 per cent in *The Times Higher Education Supplement*).

Reviewing the Reviews concludes that in the 1980s in England, books by women "are not subject to the same criteria for evaluation as books by men" (p. 49). They suggest that since publishers are more likely to get comprehensive review coverage for "women's titles" in women's magazines rather than in the general press, the tendency is to send fewer books by women to the national press, exacerbating the ways in which, while ostensibly aimed at a general readership, the national press is in practice more directed to a male readership (p. 48).

The focus of the "Women in Publishing" study is clearly statistical; does this simplify the problem? Perhaps what matters is not so much, or not only, the issue of what percentage of total reviewers the women reviewers form, but how they, along with their male peers, collude with, investigate, or resist the biases of what is clearly very much still a patriarchal literary culture.

In my analysis of the work of Victorian female reviewers, such as Geraldine Jewsbury, Margaret Oliphant, Elizabeth Rigby, and George Eliot, in Chapter 1, I argued that the desire to be taken seriously as part of the patriarchal literary establishment, combined with the often anonymous use of first person plural, and the "dominant discourse" tendency of each journal, made the voices of female critics often indistinguishable from those of their male peers – that a kind of chameleon-like merging took place. I suggested that it was therefore more productive to focus on the ways in which cultural preconceptions about gender affected interpretation than to fixate too specifically on the impact of the sex of the individual reviewer.

In *Reviewing the Reviews* we see the persistence of the essentialism of Victorian gender categories, although there are a few interesting incidents where they are reversed. The Victorian assumption that whereas men were fully able to understand women, women's sheltered experience and delicate imaginations restricted their comprehension of men, seems to be interestingly reversed in contemporary reviews in the frequent choice of women reviewers to review books by women authors. Women are thought, by virtue of their sex, to be more credibly legitimate and authoritative feminists than men are. The persistence of the essentialism of Victorian gender categories, whether reversed or not, is troubling. Judith Butler's recent exploration of contemporary feminism suggests some of the pitfalls inherent in such a structural mindset:

> Is the construction of the category of women as a coherent and stable subject an unwitting regulation and reification of gender relations? And is not such a reification precisely contrary to feminist aims? . . . If a stable notion of gender no longer proves to be the foundational premise of feminist politics, perhaps a new sort of feminist politics is now desirable to contest the very reifications of gender identity, one that will take the variable construction of identity as both a methodological and normative prerequisite . . . if not a political goal.   (Butler, 1989, p. 5)

The "Women in Publishing" survey portrays a literary world still rigidly organized according to binary and reified notions of sex and gender. On 16 of the 28 publications, female reviewers are mostly assigned books by women. The authors of the study raise the question of whether this same-sex book allocation is retrogressive, forming a kind of literary ghetto for women, or whether it is progressive, showing an understanding of the different life experiences men and women bring to their approach to literature based on sex. In either case, however, whether writing reviews of women's books for the "women's page" or "women's section", or writing for part of the general publication, women reviewers are clearly presumed to have added interpretive and evaluative authority based on their sex, a somewhat essentialist premise, perhaps.

The results of the "Women in Publishing" survey imply that contemporary women reviewers often write self-consciously as women readers, as opposed to being spokespeople for mainstream literary culture, or at least that the editors who assign reviews assume that this is the case. More information is clearly needed to extend these comparisons. It would be useful, for example, to learn how and if women writing in different journals internalize or resist the patriarchal/"dominant discourse" position of the journal. It would be interesting to analyze how writing in the women's page or section affects the voice of the review. The question should perhaps also be raised as to whether the contemporary linkage of women reviewers with books by women authors is dangerously essentialist, in some ways more sinister than the assumption of Victorian critics such as Geraldine Jewsbury or George Eliot that they spoke for the literary culture and that the anonymous voice of their reviews liberated them from reviewing self-consciously as women.

Interestingly, many continuities between Victorian and contemporary reviewing exist when it comes to the issue of whether articles and pages devoted exclusively to women writers are a positive or negative factor for women authors and readers. We remember, for example, that George Eliot loathed being categorized among and reviewed with other women authors and wished to differentiate herself from authors like Mrs Mulock, who was "a writer who is read only by novel-readers pure and simple, never by people of high culture" (quoted in Tuchman, "When the Prevalent", p. 155). A letter of complaint to the *Guardian* newspaper by Gaby Weiner in 1986 asked why a section of the newspaper should be entitled "Women Writers" as if women were a sub-group, and why Marilyn French and Emma Tennant should be reviewed in the other section: "'Why were they left out of the women's section? Or is it the case that when women writers become successful they become discernable from other women writers and so qualify for honorary membership of the male literary elite?'" quoted in *Reviewing the Reviews*, 1987, p. 59). These questions are reminiscent of George Eliot's stance in her essay "Silly Novels by Lady Novelists", where she clearly feels the need to disassociate herself from the mainstream of women writers in order to be taken seriously as part of the literary elite.

Then, as now, reviews have to frame the literary work in order to label and contextualize it, and then, as now, definition of the type of work along gender lines, along with comparison and juxtaposition to "similar" works, is used as a helpful, simplifying reviewing device.

We have seen how in Victorian literary reviews it was an advantage for writers to conform to the reviewers' gendered framework of expectations. It still seems an advantage for women writers, feminist ones in particular, to conform unthreateningly to contemporary ideals of what is attractive in femininity. A crudely extreme example of this is evident in a 1981 review of Kate Swift and Casey Miller's *Handbook of Non-Sexist Writing*, by Auberon Waugh in the *Daily Mail*:

> From the photograph supplied of Ms. Casey Miller and Kate Swift, I should judge that neither was sexually very attractive. . . . A sense

of grievance can often bring out the worst in people, and there is no reason to extend our sympathy where the motives of these disgruntled feminist agitators is simply to make a nuisance of themselves. This would appear to be the inspiration behind Swift and Miller's *Handbook of Non-Sexist Writing.* (quoted in *Reviewing the Reviews*, p. 3)

As the authors of *Reviewing the Reviews* state later in their discussion of the recent treatment in reviews of contemporary women writers, "reviewers seem incapable of distinguishing between the way a female author writes and the way she looks" (p. 82). Jeffrey Barnard, for example, in the *Spectator*, wrote the following equally shocking comment about the appearance of "loony" feminists: "It isn't difficult to despise loony feminists like Andrea Dworkin, but I promise you that it has nothing to do with the fact that they are all physically repulsive to a man" (quoted in *Reviewing the Reviews*, p. 81).

One of the interesting twists in the intersections of gender ideology and literary criticism since nineteenth-century book reviewing is the way in which the term "feminist" shapes the content and context of the review by immediately channelling a book and its author into a category with its own preconceived schema and pre-determined structuring shape of reviewer expectations, a third category with preconceptions and expectations distinct from those applied to other writing by women or by men. Feminism is often perceived as less threatening if its proponents conform to societal stereotypes of feminine roles and appearance, as we see in the *Reviewing the Reviews* comments on a 1984 review of Margaret Forster's *Significant Sisters: The Grassroots of Active Feminism, 1839–1939* in *Femail on Sunday*:

The female reviewer was so concerned to present feminism in a non-threatening light that she bent over backwards to apply the adjectives "beautiful" and "gorgeous" to as many sisters as was remotely possible. Having announced at the start of the review that "Feminism is a dirty word. It causes a ripple of shock in mixed company . . . she concludes with the following paean to Forster's social campaigners: "So next time you are tempted to reject the term 'feminist,' think of these eight women whose feminism was indistinguishable from their femininity." (*Reviewing the Reviews*, p. 80).

Margaret Forster's *Significant Sisters*, for example, her first explicitly feminist study, was criticized for being insufficiently feminist, was reviewed at less length than her previous "mainstream" biographies, and was given to female reviewers to review. Because, in the words of the "Women in Publishing" study, Forster's work was "labelled 'feminist history' ", it somehow missed being taken as seriously as conventional history and yet at the same time failed to be taken seriously as a "true" feminist work in the tradition of Betty Friedan or Germaine Greer (p. 79). In this situation we can see a parallel with the reception history of Charlotte Yonge in the twentieth century. As I argued in Chapter 5, Victorian women writers considered suitable candidates for literary exhumation and revisitation are usually those whose ideology can be viewed as consistent with current feminist ideas, or those who, at the least, can be read as subversive in their adherence to Victorian gender conventions. And of course Yonge's work does not qualify in either category.

The ways in which reviewers are disarmed by tidy conformity to society's fairly rigid images of what is acceptable and appealing in femininity and masculinity are remarkably and distinctly reminiscent of the intensely conventional gender schemas of Victorian reviewers, as are the ways in which a framework of gendered ideology shapes the interpretive and evaluative position of the literary review. (We do need to bear in mind, of course, that *Reviewing the Reviews* was written in England in the 1980s – it is possible that the gendered ideology might be less extreme ten years later, though my own reading of recent English book reviews suggests a similar framework of expectations, as will be discussed below. It is obviously also important to remember that *Reviewing the Reviews* was researched in England and that its conclusions should not necessarily therefore be extrapolated to America.)

Contemporary reviewers, like their Victorian counterparts, have firmly fixed ideas about what constitutes women's versus men's writing. We remember how George Eliot was thought, in Victorian literary reviews, to write, in both her content and style, like a man, and how the reception of Emily Brontë's *Wuthering Heights* was complicated by an ambivalence to the so-called "masculine" attributes of her writing. The "Women in Publishing" study reports a fascinatingly parallel situation in the reception of American feminist Andrea Dworkin's work:

Ironically, the American feminist publisher, Daughters, accused her of writing "like a man" – a sentiment echoed by several British reviewers. Stanley Reynolds, in a 1982 edition of *Punch*, described her as the "Leon Trotsky of the sex war" and went on to pay her a back-handed compliment when he stated: "She writes with an aggressive manner, like a man, except that no man writes with such utter conviction these days.' " (p. 84)

Apparent in these comments, apart from the lingeringly essentialist concept that it is possible to classify writing as male or female, is a certain (if ambivalent) respectful admiration for the forceful power of Dworkin's ideological fervour, a power that is still classified, as in the Victorian reviews of *Wuthering Heights*, as a masculine quality.

A recent review from the British magazine *Time Out* on the back cover of Fay Weldon's *Growing Rich* (1992), makes it clear how automatically books and writers are still liable to be pigeonholed according to the writer's sex: "Prolific and provocative, Fay Weldon shines brightest in the league table of British women novelists". The classification of Weldon's work in the category of writing by women novelists, the implicit hierarchy evident in the term "league table", and the juxtaposition of "prolific" with women's writing are all interestingly parallel to the content, structure, and even the language of the Victorian literary review.

Another telling legacy or continuity between the gender politics of contemporary literary reviewing and those of the Victorian period is the way in which the prejudice against "domestic" novels lingers, in large part now, as then, because of their association with the disparaged connotations of women and femininity. In the March 1994 issue of *Mirabella*, Adam Begley's review of Canadian novelist Carol Shields has the following title: "Small Wonder. Carol Shields is a really big writer. But you have to look closely" ("Small Wonder", p. 66). Begley goes on to argue that Shields is a talented writer who considers "small things that matter" (p. 66). He summarizes the reception of a 1992 novel by Shields, *The Republic of Love*, thus: "*The Republic of Love* (1992), a most user-friendly romantic comedy, was widely praised for its 'high I.Q.' and somehow damned at the same time, the reviews littered with diminishing adjectives like 'cozy' and 'sweet'" (*Mirabella*, March 1994, p. 66).

Similarly, British novelist Margaret Forster's defensiveness about the patriarchal literary establishment's tendency to denigrate domestic novels is extremely reminiscent of the gendered hierarchies in Victorian (and later) commentary on the content and focus of Anthony Trollope's novels discussed in Chapter 4. *Reviewing the Reviews* explains that Forster "no longer heeds the sneers of authors like Anthony

Burgess who scorn the domestic novel, and she now firmly believes that 'what goes on in peoples' heads is nothing to be ashamed of writing about. . . . You can discover worlds in them, you don't need to span continents '"   (1987, p. 81).

In assessing the similarities and differences between Victorian and contemporary literary reviews and their treatment of sex and gender, it becomes evident that whether or not the review is located in the "women's section" or "women's page", the gendered division and hierarchy in the classification, interpretation, and evaluation of literature is still distinctly prominent, even primary. The discussion of attitudes towards contemporary writing genres in relation to gender makes it clear that we still, as Virginia Woolf so eloquently explained in *A Room of One's Own*, privilege and elevate concerns we associate with men over those we associate with women:

> And since a novel has this correspondence to real life, its values are to some extent those of real life. But it is obvious that the values of women differ very often from the values which have been made by the other sex. . . . Yet it is the masculine values that prevail. Speaking crudely, football and sport are "important"; the worship of fashion, the buying of clothes "trivial". And these values are inevitably transferred from life to fiction. This is an important book, the critic assumes, because it deals with war. This is an insignificant book because it deals with the feelings of women in a drawing room.   (Woolf, 1989, p. 74)

The comments cited above about Shields's stature as a novelist writing about domestic and romantic concerns and about Weldon's position in the category of "women novelists" demonstrate without a doubt that "league tables" based on societal ideology about sex and gender are still firmly in place. The relative status and social acceptability of detective or mystery novels in comparison with the romantic novels directed almost exclusively to women is yet further testimony to this fact. Many fairly highbrow or intellectually oriented bookstores which stock such genres as mystery novels, for example, tend to shun romantic best-sellers with their erotically charged cover illustrations.

In *Gender Trouble: Feminism and the Subversion of Identity*, Judith Butler argues persuasively that conventionally essentialist feminism often "constrains the very 'subjects' that it hopes to represent and liberate" (1989, p. 148):

> I have tried to suggest that the identity categories often presumed to be foundational to feminist politics, that is deemed necessary in order to mobilize feminism as an identity politics, simultaneously work to limit and constrain in advance the very cultural possibilities that feminism is supposed to open up. The tacit constraints that produce culturally intelligible "sex" ought to be understood as generative political structures rather than naturalized foundations. (1989, p. 147)

Clearly, *Reviewing the Reviews* makes an important contribution to our efforts to understand the role and situation of women as writers, readers, and reviewers in the contemporary literary marketplace and in contemporary literary journalism. At the same time, however, the sharpness of its focus on "culturally intelligible 'sex'" and the kind of feminist interrogation it enacts and represents does seem vulnerable to charges of reductive over-simplification. I would argue that in our consideration of sex and gender in the contemporary review, as in my exploration of their role in Victorian literary society, it is helpful to move beyond a single-minded focus on whether writers and readers are male or female and to consider also the complicated and fascinating ways in which our cultural constructions of gender fashion our often unconscious ways of looking at the world and at literature and relate to the political underpinnings and agendas of the society that shapes the thinking of women and men.

While this study focuses on the construction of literary reputations rather than on canons *per se*, it does show how hierarchical ideas about the relative merits of men's and women's writing, whether conscious or unconscious, explicit or implicit, play a role in establishing a body of texts considered worthy of serious study, to be read by intelligent readers. And analyzing the critical context of a work's reception reveals the importance of the literary review in the creation of a literary reputation, and the contribution the contemporary review makes in an ongoing attempt to establish an historical ground for interpretations.

Appendix
Victorian Periodicals: Reputation, Readership, and Circulation

Of all the periodicals, *The Athenaeum* is the one that receives most praise today for the significance and fairness of its critical commentary. Casey states that it normally reviewed novels within three weeks of their publication dates, and that it "reviewed a higher percentage of the novels which everyone was reviewing and presumably reading than either of the other weeklies" (1990, p. 11). Marchand argues that it was fairer than others: "The prejudices of the journal are not, in the main, party prejudices, but human prejudices, affected by the whole intellectual atmosphere of the period" (1941, p. 230).

READERSHIP OF VICTORIAN PERIODICALS

This issue of who constituted the readership of Victorian journals is an important and complicated one, with interesting implications for a feminist criticism. Ellegard states that "scarcely any direct information of the characteristics of the readers of each periodical exists" (1957, p. 9). Contemporary Victorian writers often hypothesized or made generalizations about the periodical-reading public. Newman, for example, in *The Idea of a University* in 1852 expressed satisfaction at the increase of awareness and knowledge that journals provided, arguing that this was "a graceful accomplishment, and a suitable, nay, in this day a necessary accomplishment, in the case of educated men" (quoted in Houghton "Periodical literature", p. 8). Newman claimed that "the extreme influence of periodical publications at this day" was due to their ability to "teach the multitude of men what to think and what to say" (quoted in Houghton, p. 8). Another critic made a similar point in the *Literary Gazette* in May 1860, stating that people who might have "read nothing beyond a trashy novel or political journal . . . may now . . . become fairly acquainted with the leading subjects in science and general literature; and though review-reading will never produce a scholar . . . it may make an intelligent and well-informed man" (quoted in Houghton, p. 8). One of the questions that arises from these comments is whether "men", as in "intelligent" or "educated" men, is actually being used as a generic pronoun, or whether it implicitly excludes women. The answer to this question depends partly on whether one believes the Victorian ideal of womanhood included being "well-informed" and "educated" in these definitions. Then, too, different journals constructed different ideal readers; some were just more explicit than others about the readers they anticipated or sought. Kellett's point that each journal self-consciously constructed its own personality, outlook, and policy is also relevant to its readership.

Margaret Beetham, writing about periodicals in general, argues that the very nature of periodicals entails creating, defining, and projecting an identity for the reader: "Maintaining a regular readership means offering readers a recognizable position in successive numbers, that is creating a consistent 'reader' within the text. The reader is addressed as an individual but is positioned as a member of certain overlapping sets of social groups, class, gender, region, age, political persuasion or religious denomination" (1989, p. 99). Although there is little to no direct information on the readership of Victorian periodicals (apart from what they say themselves in their prospectus or advertisements), we can get a good idea of a journal's readership by looking at its price, size, tone, and contents. Circulation is also hard to determine exactly, though several scholars make educated guesses (mainly Richard Altick and Ellegard), based on such factors as stamp returns. Ellegard states that "it was apparently not considered good form to reveal circulation figures to the outside world" (1957, p. 8). In general we can make guesses based on facts like the following: Mudie had over 50,000 subscribers in the 1850s and carried 23 journals (Blake, 1989, p. 5); the gross potential British reading public in 1852 stood at between five and six million (Altick, *Writers* , p. 144); monthly magazines tended to have wider circulation than quarterlies, as the public was intrigued by lighter and more frequent reading matter, but the circulation of quarterlies was steadier, as that of monthlies depended on the popularity of what novel they were carrying on any particular month (Ellegard, 1957, p. 9).

Altick's *Writers, Readers and Occasions* and *The English Common Reader*, along with Ellegard's *The Readership of the Periodical Press in Mid-Victorian England* give the most authoritative and detailed statistics for the circulation of individual Victorian periodicals. Ellegard bases his figures on a manipulation of the stamp returns for journals, but some later critics, including J. Donn Vann, dispute the accuracy of his findings. Circulation figures do not equal number of readers: even apart from their use in circulating libraries, journals usually had at least several readers. Blake and Shattock give the following circulation figures per issue for 1860, based, I think, on an interpretation of Ellegard: the *Edinburgh Review* 7000, the *Quarterly Review* 8000, the *Westminster Review* 4000, the *North British Review* 2000, *Blackwood's Edinburgh Magazine* 10,000, and *Fraser's Magazine* 8000. *Cornhill* is widely reported to have had an average of 90,000 subscribers per issue in its first two years. Altick claims that in 1856 the *Athenaeum* had 2,100 subscribers per issue.

Some periodicals helpfully declare the identity of their anticipated reader, though some do so more obviously than others. A quick perusal of the respectable quarterlies, together with Ellegard's research, makes it evident that they were aimed at highly educated middle-to upper-class readers. The *Quarterly* was clearly conservative in its political stance, while the other three main quarterlies were less so; the *Westminster* took a Reformer position. The most likely place to find an explicit declaration of intended readership is in the prospectus of a journal. The *Pall Mall Gazette*, for example, declared itself "by gentlemen for gentlemen". In 1882 Charles Peabody described its tone thus: "Its tone has from the first been aristocratic, the tone of the club window, of the smoking room, of the House of Commons and of the drawing room" (quoted in Robertson Scott, 1950, p. 126). There is no mistaking the gender of the anticipated reader in this declaration. The *Saturday Review* had a similar position and was explicitly geared to university-educated men with classical educations; it was often quite rude about people who lacked these "advantages". Thackeray struck a different tone in his prospectus for the *Cornhill*: writers would "tell what they know, pretty briefly and good-humouredly" and not "in a manner too obviously didactic. . . . We shall suppose the ladies and children always present" (quoted in Griest, 1970, p. 140). We can presume, then, that there were more women readers of the *Cornhill* than of the other two journals mentioned above. *Chambers's Journal* explicitly included women and children (interesting juxtaposition again!) in its prospectus: "With the ladies of the 'new school,' and all my young countrywomen in their teens, I hope to be on agreeable terms. . . . I will also inform them of a thousand useful little receipts of housewifery, calculated to make them capital wives" (quoted in Griest, 1970, pp. 60–1).

WOMEN'S PERIODICALS

There were several extremely successful women's journals in the mid-Victorian period, and many contained reviews. Some of the more prominent ones include *The Lady's Magazine, Eliza Cook's Journal, The New Monthly Belle Assemblée* (established in 1847), *The Lady's Newspaper and Pictorial Times* (established in 1847), and *The Englishwoman's Domestic Magazine* (1852–79). These journals tended to perpetuate the Victorian ideal of domestic femininity, however, and material that was to any degree intellectual was often thought to be inappropriate for women. *The Lady's Newspaper and Pictorial Times* complained about this limiting stance in 1847: "in works professedly published for feminine perusal, no attempt has been made to consult also the intellectual capacity of women, or to advance in any way the cultivation of her mind. A series of frivolous articles, alike destitute of genius in their conception, or of talent in their execution, were expected to meet with a grateful reception from the taste and discernment of those to whom they were offered" (quoted in White, 1979, p. 43). Some women's magazines did better in this respect than others, and it is important to remember that women, to varying degrees, formed part of the readership of the journals for general consumption. Cynthia White states that "no periodicals which espoused the women's cause survived for more than a year" (p. 47). The following quotation from *The Ladies' Treasury* seems representative of many other women's journals: this journal was intended to "illustrate and uphold each dear, domestic virtue, child of home", with nothing to "enervate or bewilder the pure female mind" (quoted in White, 1979, p. 47).

Notes

Notes to the Introduction

1. For full citation see Bibliography for Chapter 3.
2. For full citation see Bibliography for Chapter 4.
3. For full citation see bibliography for Chapter 4.
4. Publishers usually printed a small and expensive first edition which sold mainly to circulating libraries like Mudie's (founded in 1842). This system eliminated much of the financial risk for the publishers, who were able to predict the approximate number of books the library would order, but the expense of the books put them out of the reach of all of the working class and most of the middle classes.
5. Mudie's Circulating Library was the most frequented and prominent lending library in mid-Victorian England, and a central institution. Borrowing books from Mudie was how Victorians tended to read novels; Mudie had over 50,000 subscribers in the 1850s.
6. The *Victorian Periodicals Review*, sponsored by the Research Society for Victorian Periodicals, was started in 1968, and deals with the editorial and publishing history of Victorian periodicals; it appears four times a year. The Modern Language Association published two collections of essays entitled *Victorian Periodicals: A Guide to Research*, volume 1 in 1978 and volume 2 in 1989, edited by J. Donn Vann and Rosemary T. VanArsdel. See also Merle Bevington, *The Saturday Review 1855–1868: Representative Educated Opinion in Victorian England* (New York: Columbia University Press, 1941); Ellen Miller Casey, "Weekly Reviews of Fiction: The *Athenaeum* vs. the *Spectator* and the *Saturday Review*", *Victorian Periodicals Review*, 23.1 (1990) 8–12; Joanne Shattock and Michael Wolff (eds), *The Victorian Periodical Press: Samplings and Soundings* (Leicester: Leicester University Press, 1982).
7. See especially *Gender and Reading: Essays on Readers, Texts, and Contexts*, ed. Elizabeth A. Flynn and Patrocinio P. Schweickart (Baltimore: Johns Hopkins University Press, 1986); other useful works include Susan Suleiman and Inge Crosman, (eds), *The Reader in the Text* (Princeton: Princeton University Press, 1980); Jane Tompkins (ed.), *Reader-Response Criticism* (Baltimore and

London, 1980); Michael Steig, *Stories of Reading: Subjectivity and Literary Understanding* (Baltimore: Johns Hopkins University Press, 1989); Janice Radway, *Reading the Romance: Women, Patriarchy, and Popular Literature* (Chapel Hill: University of North Carolina Press, 1984).

8. See, for example, Richard Altick, *The English Common Reader* (Chicago: University of Chicago Press, 1957); Amy Cruse, *The Victorians and their Books* (London: Allen & Unwin, 1935); Deirdre David, *Intellectual Women and Victorian Patriarchy* (London: Macmillan, 1987); Carl Dawson, *Victorian Noon: English Literature in 1850* (Baltimore: Johns Hopkins University Press, 1979); Royal Gettman, *A Victorian Publisher: A Study of the Bentley Papers* (Cambridge: Cambridge University Press, 1965); Guinevere Griest, *Mudie's Circulating Library and the Victorian Novel* (Bloomington: Indiana University Press, 1970); Elizabeth Helsinger, Robin Lauterbach Sheets, and William Veeder (eds), *The Woman Question: Society and Literature in Britain and America, 1837–1883* (Chicago: Chicago University Press, 1983); John Sutherland, *Victorian Novelists and Publishers* (Chicago: Chicago University Press, 1976).

9. Other recent studies include Christine Battersby's *Gender and Genius: Towards a Feminist Aesthetics* (although not specifically a Victorian study) (Bloomington: Indiana University Press, 1989); Mary Poovey, *Uneven Developments: The Ideological Work of Gender in Mid-Victorian England* (Chicago: University of Chicago Press, 1988); Robyn Warhol, *Gendered Interventions: Narrative Discourse in the Victorian Novel* (New Jersey: Rutgers University Press, 1989). See Kate Flint's impressively comprehensive *The Woman Reader 1837–1914* (Oxford, 1993) for a full discussion of the woman reader in Victorian England; since Flint's work appeared after this book was completed, I was unable to engage with its interesting arguments.

Notes to Chapter 1: Reviewing and Writing: Sex and Gender

1. By importance I mean the effect on educated opinion, in cultural and literary contexts, as well as the numbers of readers. My main source for information about readership is Allvar Ellegard's *The Readership of the Periodical Press in Mid-Victorian Britain.*

2. Elizabeth Rigby's notorious hostile review of *Jane Eyre* (*Quarterly Review*, December 1848) is also affected by considerations of class; she links what she perceives as the feminist tendencies of *Jane Eyre* with the social uprisings of 1848.

3. People like Harriet Martineau, who fought for female education, tended to justify it by claiming that it made women better in their domestic realm. In her essay "Household Education", Martineau claims that "the most ignorant women I have known have been the worst housekeepers; and . . . the most learned women I have known have been among the best" (Yates, 1985, p. 94). "[T]he more she [woman] becomes a reasoning creature, the more reasonable, disciplined and docile she will be" (Yates, p. 97).

4. In an 1865 essay, G. H. Lewes makes a similar argument about the "presumptuous facility" of "indolent novelists" (Nadel, *Victorian Fiction*, 1980, p. 361), and their tendency to write without ideas; one wonders about the mutual influence of Lewes and Eliot.

5. The *Saturday Review*'s dislike for Dickens was exacerbated by their political differences.

6. For full reference see bibliography for Chapter 3.

7. See the discussion of Trollope in Chapter 4 for examples of this tendency.

8. For example, Mudie bought 1,962 of the 3,864 novels Bentley sold by subscription in 1864.

9. See Elizabeth Segel's essay "'As the Twig is Bent . . . ': Gender and Childhood Reading", in *Gender and Reading: Essays on Readers, Texts, and Contexts* (Baltimore: Johns Hopkins University Press, 1986), pp. 165–86. Segel discusses how the polarization of gender roles in mid-Victorian England led to a division of childrens' reading into girls' and boys' books; see also Judith Rowbotham's *Good Girls make Good Wives: Guidance for Girls in Victorian Fiction* (Oxford: Basil Blackwell, 1989).

Notes to Chapter 2: The "Virile Creator" versus the "Twaddlers Tame and Soft"

1. As the 1856 *Bentley's Miscellany* review put it, "the sources from whence the fearful and too true pictures of abuses of prison discipline are derived are known to all. The humane but weak theorist, Captain O' Connor; Mr. Williams, the 'shallow and

slender' justice; the brutal Hawes, the efficient chaplain, are all real personages" (p. 292). Reade was taken to task by some critics, notably Fitzjames Stephen in an 1857 *Edinburgh Review* article, for exaggerating the facts and scapegoating someone who had already been punished.

2. One of his friends, John Hollingshead, enjoyed observing Reade write letters: "It was a great source of amusement to me to watch him writing letters in the 'morning room' of that club [Garrick]. The more placid and benevolent he looked the more violent was his language. His favourite terms were 'skunk' and 'pirate'" (Hollingshead, 1898, p. 145).

3. For the purposes of this study my discussion of the role of gender in Victorian literary criticism is predicated on nineteenth-century middle-class gender norms. The dominant polarized gender stereotypes are distinctly middle-class. For more information on this area, see Gareth Stedman Jones's *Languages of Class: Studies in English Working Class History, 1832–1982* (Cambridge: Cambridge University Press, 1983).

4. Walter Besant, an admirer of Reade's, hoped that "by means of literae humaniores women will recover the critical faculty, learn what is meant by style", and that "in twenty years or so the women novelists will write like Reade rather than like their predecessors of the present generation" ("Charles Reade", p. 200).

5. From the later dates of more explicitly gendered association with readership, we can perhaps conclude that Reade's reputation as a writer for men gathered momentum as the century progressed.

6. Tuchman states that between 1840 and 1879 women submitted more novels to Macmillan than men did, and were more likely to be accepted (*Edging*, 1989, pp. 7–8), and that "solid data seem to support the assumption that many male writers masqueraded as women in the novel's heyday . . . . through the 1870s cultural expectations were that novel writing was largely a female occupation" (*Edging*, 1989, pp. 53–4).

7. See, for example, "Charles Reade's Opinion of Himself and His Opinion of George Eliot", *Bookman*, XV, November 1903, p. 254.

8. George Eliot was, in fact, generally reviewed as an eccentrically brilliant anomaly to customary ideas about the relation between gender and writing. Ironically, Eliot herself refers to most writing by women as "feeble imitation" of writing by men (quoted in Helsinger et al., 1983, vol. 3, p. 59). Perhaps Reade accuses Eliot of exactly this "feeble imitation", using strongly gendered

terms and hierarchies, in order to bolster up his own fragile sense of self and superiority, which were so intrinsically connected with his own sense of himself as masculine.

9. As recently as 1931, Malcolm Elwin states that Eliot "made a model of Reade", and "had the idea of a medieval story from him ... whether she intended to imitate or not, she was branded as an imitator, and, as such, suffered not only at the hands of contemporary critics, but also at those of later generations, like Swinburne, Besant, and Oscar Wilde" (1931, pp. 157–8).

10. *Once a Week* juxtaposes the following two scenes, from Reade's *Hard Cash* (vol. iii, p. 294, 1863) and Eliot's *Felix Holt* (vol. iii, p. 228, 1866) respectively in order to prove plagiarism, but, as should be evident from the passages, does not make a convincing case: Reade: "'Julia Dodd entered the box, and a sunbeam seemed to fill the court. She knew what to do: her left hand was gloved, but her right hand was bare. She kissed the book and gave her evidence in her clear, mellow, melting voice: gave it reverently and modestly, for to her the court was a church'" (quoted in *Once a Week*, 20 January 1872, p. 83). Eliot: "'There was no blush upon her face: she stood, divested of all personal considerations, whether of vanity or shyness. Her clear voice sounded as it might have done if she had been making a confession of faith. She began and went on without query or interruption. Every face looked grave and respectful'" (quoted in *Once a Week*, p. 83).

11. There is in fact a rumour that the author of this *Once a Week* article was none other than Charles Reade himself! See *Bookman*, November 1903, vol. XVIII.

12. When *It Is Never Too Late To Mend* was turned into a play in 1865, the audience rioted, shocked by the graphic representations of violence that functioned as a substitute for Reade's overbearing style. The *Reader* described the scene thus: "the murmurs of disapprobation amongst the members of the stalls grew ominous, and at length, burst out into a cry of eager and decisive condemnation. An old critic ... rose and declared it 'was revolting, and ... mere brutality and one-sided politics.' Of course, this immediately set the house in a flame ... " (14 October 1865, p. 438). The play was subsequently revised, and proved both successful and profitable.

13. Reade's language and use of typography were also perceived as

forceful or puerile, depending on the perspective of the individual critic. The *Literary Gazette* was impressed by the way "the ideas and events . . . are conscious of being born full armed like Minerva – ready clothed in forcible and appropriate phrase" (23 August 1856, p. 607). Eliot was annoyed at Reade's eccentric typography: "the most amazing foible in a writer of so much power as Mr. Reade, is his reliance on the magic of typography . . . we find Mr. Reade endeavouring to impress us with the Titanic character of modern events by suddenly bursting into capitals at the mention of "THIS GIGANTIC AGE!" ("Three Novels", p. 315). The *Saturday Review* lamented that "we could not have believed a man of education capable of descending to such trifling" (16 August 1856, p. 360).

14. The daughter of his publisher, John Blackwood, expressed surprise on first meeting him, in the late 1870s, because he seemed so different from his virile and "fire-eating" persona: "The heroic ideas we had somehow associated with him . . . were not quite reconcilable with his appearance and manners, which showed nothing of a fire-eating description. On the contrary, we saw a very quiet-looking elderly gentleman, with a particularly soft voice and courteous manners, whose approach was rendered still more quiet by his wearing cloth boots" (Oliphant and Porter, pp. 219–20). One could, of course, construct a psycho-biographical argument around this anecdote, and suggest that Reade's literary persona was an unconscious attempt to compensate for failures to conform to masculine stereotypes in his everyday life; Reade never married, for example.

15. However, the riot that occurred during the performance of the dramatic version of Reade's novel indicates the extent to which the audience reacted strongly against what they perceived as the sickening domination of the realism that functioned as the corollary of Reade's overbearing style.

Notes to Chapter 3: The Unveiling of Ellis Bell

1. Showalter's description of how the sexual double standard affected men is as follows: "Male writers had most of the desirable qualities: power, breadth, distinctness, clarity, learning, abstract

intelligence, shrewdness, experience, humor, knowledge of every-one's character, and open-mindedness" (1977, p. 90).

2. For Marxist studies, see Terry Eagleton's 1975 *Myths of Power: A Marxist Study of the Brontës*; and Peter Miles's 1990 *Wuthering Heights*. Recent feminist studies include Naomi Jacobs's 1986 *Journal of Narrative Technique* article, "Gender and Layered Narrative in *Wuthering Heights* and *The Tenant of Wildfell Hall*", Patricia Yaeger's 1988 *Genre* article, "Violence in the Sitting Room: *Wuthering Heights* and the Woman's Novel"; Michael Macovski's 1987 *English Literary History* (*ELH*) article, "*Wuthering Heights* and the Rhetoric of Interpretation"; Beth Newman's 1990 *Publications of the Modern Language Association of America* (*PMLA*) article, "'The Situation of the Looker-On': Gender, Narration, and Gaze in *Wuthering Heights*"; and Irene Tayler's 1990 *Holy Ghosts: The Male Muses of Emily and Charlotte Brontë*. Recent biographies include Edward Chitham's *A Life of Charlotte Brontë* (1987), Katherine Frank's *A Chainless Soul: A Life of Emily Brontë* (1990), and Lyn Pykett's *Emily Brontë* (1989).

3. The *North British Review*, for example, was not alone in allowing its disapproval of *Wuthering Heights* to contaminate its opinion of *Jane Eyre*, already perceived as somewhat shocking, under the popular impression that the two Bell authors were one and the same: "But there are more latent objections to the tendency of this powerful book [*Jane Eyre*], which we are apt to overlook on a first perusal, and of the perniciousness of which we can only judge when we have seen them developed in other works [*Wuthering Heights*] professedly proceeding from the same source" (vol. XI, August 1849, pp. 475–93). This point will be discussed further below.

4. See *On Deconstruction: Theory and Criticism after Structuralism* (Ithaca: Cornell University Press, 1982).

5. Apart from declaring that "the vast majority of women who rush into print write badly" (11 November 1865, p. 602), the *Saturday Review* declares that women writers are overly sentimental, have difficulty constructing plots, lack the necessary classical training and knowledge of the world, and basing characters on personal experience, are usually unable to transcend "petty" drawing-room observations about heroes and heroines (p. 602). An 1850 *Leader* article urges women to resist the temptations of author-ship: "This is the 'march of mind' but where, oh where are the dumplings! Does it never strike these delightful creatures that

their little fingers were made to be kissed and not inked? Women's proper sphere of activity is elsewhere. Are there no husbands, lovers, brothers, friends to coddle and console? Are there no stockings to darn, no purses to make, no braces to embroider? My idea of a perfect woman is one who can write but won't" (quoted in Ewbank, 1966, p. 9).

6. See Showalter's "The Female Tradition", in *A Literature of their Own*.

7. Marxists, of course, such as Eagleton and Miles, take issue with the implications of such statements.

8. Alone among the four novels surveyed in this study, *Wuthering Heights* was seen as original to the point of being unique, and it was extremely rare for reviewers to place it in any literary historical context or to comment on any precursors. The 1847 *Athenaeum* compares the "dreariness" or somberness of *Wuthering Heights* to the works of eighteenth-century novelist Charlotte Smith; the 1848 *Examiner*, as noted in the chapter, remarks that "the only book which occurs to us as resembling *Wuthering Heights* is a novel of the late Mr. Hooton's – a work of very great talent; in which the hero is a tramper or beggar ... which, notwithstanding its defects, we remember thinking better in its peculiar kind than anything that had been produced since the days of Fielding" (8 January 1848, p. 2). The *Britannia* comments only that the work is "strangely original" (15 January 1848, p. 42). The *Eclectic Review* of 1851 states that the characters of *Wuthering Heights* have "little more power to move our sympathies than the romances of the middle ages, or the ghost stories which made our granddames tremble" (February 1851, p. 227). We may, perhaps, detect in this last allusion a veiled reference to gothic novels as possible predecessors, but it is far from explicit. And the *New Monthly Magazine* states that "our novel reading experience does not enable us to refer to any thing to be compared with the personages we are introduced to at this desolate spot" (January 1848, p. 140). *Britannia* compares *Wuthering Heights* to "German tales". In the articles and reviews surveyed, there were no other apparent references to Gothic novels, Scott, or any other literary precursors.

9. David Bleich's "Gender Interests in Reading and Language" (in Schweickart and Flynn) suggests that modern male readers still "get a handle" on *Wuthering Heights* through Emily Brontë's biographies and through considering the author as a woman, whereas female readers tend to immerse themselves in the world

of the text, often identifying with characters. Bleich's suggestions about gender and reading correspond with Flynn's characterization of male readers as tending towards the "dominant" pole and female readers as tending more towards an "interactive" reading approach.

10. Part of the attention that *Wuthering Heights* received can be attributed to the recent successful appearance of *Jane Eyre* under a similar pen-name. Many of the reviews of *Wuthering Heights* comment on the similarity of the pen-names and of the style and content of the two books, and it is arguable that the reviewers' preconceptions about *Jane Eyre* were at least partly responsible for their decision to review *Wuthering Heights* at all, and for the subsequent direction and focus of the reviews. Ten of my thirteen 1847 and 1848 reviews compare *Jane Eyre* with *Wuthering Heights*.

11. Showalter discusses the tendency among Victorian reviewers to assume women's writing was autobiographical, on the basis of their ideas about women's limited intellectual energy and creativity (1977, pp. 89–90).

12. Rigby's article appeared in the *Quarterly Review* in December 1848; Gaskell's *Life of Charlotte Brontë*, and Margaret Oliphant's *Women Novelists of Queen Victoria's Reign* (London: Hurst and Blackett, 1897) discuss the contemporary reception of *Jane Eyre*.

13. Note, for example, the following remarks about Charlotte Brontë's correspondence with Mr Williams, the reader for Messrs Smith and Elder: "Upon its [*Wuthering Heights's*] publication . . . we find Charlotte . . . half apologizing for the contrast between the 'refined' poetry of 'Ellis Bell' and the prose of *Wuthering Heights* – a prose which she says 'breaks forth in scenes which shock more than they attract' " (Law, 1923, p. 112).

14. Simpson quotes from this review in his biography of Emily Brontë, but explains that its origin and authorship cannot be determined (1929, pp. 172–4).

15. In Chapter 14 of *Biographia Literaria*, Coleridge portrays supernatural narrative as a symbol of the author's psychological state.

16. It seems possible that the criteria applied to evaluations of Victorian poetry were even more rigidly marked according to gender than the criteria applied to evaluations of Victorian fiction, given the Romantic legacy of the poet as hero, prophet, and social commentator inherited by the Victorians.

17. Inga-Stina Ewbank elaborates upon this point (1966, p. 38), as does Showalter (pp. 89–90). See also Chapter 1 for further

discussion of gender and literary criticism.

18. The following quotation from an 1865 edition of the *Saturday Review* clearly states Victorian assumptions about the relation between female innocence and female literary talent: "In knowledge of the world women stand at a similar disadvantage. That they should be as fitted for literary work as the opposite sex, in respect of their knowledge of the various shades of character and life, is neither possible nor desirable. Half their function in life would be gone if they lost that fine gloss of innocence and delicacy which perhaps is incompatible with a profounder experience of the world. It is their business and ought to be their pleasure, to preserve intact some of the finer ideals and illusions of the race" (11 November 1865, p. 602).

19. The 1848 *Economist* review, the *Quarterly Review* article by Elizabeth Rigby, and the 1850 *Leader* review all take this position.

20. But not all 1850 reviewers concentrated exclusively on the biographical background to *Wuthering Heights*: both the *Leader* and the *Eclectic Review* comment on the novel as a serious work of art. The *Leader* finds "a want of air and light in the picture", but "cannot deny its truth: sombre, rude, brutal, yet true" (December 1850, p. 953). The *Eclectic Review* admits that "the work has considerable merit. . . . Such a company we never saw grouped before; and we hope never to meet with its like again" (February 1851, p. 227).

21. It is interesting to note how the reviewer from the *Leader* adopts Charlotte's tone from the "Biographical Notice" in commenting on Emily's passively obedient submission to an external dictatorial inspiration.

22. Some twentieth-century critics respond to this apparent paradox by minimizing the artistic merit of *Wuthering Heights*; one example is the frustrated-spinster line of criticism, where Keighley Snowden thinks the novel is simply "the cry of 'woman wailing for her demon lover'" (Watson, 1949, p. 259). See Melvin Watson's and Carol Ohmann's essays for further details on twentieth-century reception.

23. None of the reviewers seem to imagine that part of Emily's "experience" and part of the inspiration for *Wuthering Heights* could have stemmed from her reading.

24. This debate also explains the constant stress so many reviewers and critics placed on Emily Brontë's (and Catherine's) "sexless

purity" – see A. Mary Robinson, Alice Law, David Cecil, and Elizabeth Gaskell's letters for examples of this.

25. A recent article by N. M. Jacobs, "Gender and Layered Narrative", argues that Emily Brontë was parodying the masculine aspects of her own personality and of the male public world through the portrayal of Lockwood: "male impersonations [were] necessary as a way to silence the dominant culture by stealing its voice, to exorcise the demon of conventional consciousness and male power by holding it up to ridicule" ("Gender", p. 208).

26. It is indeed possible that exposure to Branwell Brontë's behaviour could have familiarized his sisters with "coarse expressions". Heathcliff is sometimes thought to be a representation of Branwell.

27. See the quotations opening this chapter for details.

28. Somerset Maugham, for example, in his 1948 *Great Novelists and their Novels*, argued that "it is much more the sort of book that her scapegrace brother Branwell might have written and a number of people have been able to persuade themselves that he had either in whole or in part in fact done so" (1948, p. 127). Maugham also follows the then typical pattern of finding fault with the artistic crafting of *Wuthering Heights*: "the whole book is very badly written in the pseudo-literary manner that the amateur is apt to affect" (p. 129).

29. Sanger's work can also be seen as a harbinger of the "New Critical" school, which focuses on the work of art, rather than biographical material.

Notes to Chapter 4: "Something Both More and Less than Manliness"

1. Gender is not something that contemporary twentieth-century critics tend to take into account or consider important when they write about Trollope's literary reputation. Jane Nardin's *He Knew She Was Right: The Independent Woman in the Novels of Anthony Trollope* is the only explicitly feminist work I am aware of in this field, and it is devoted to textual study rather than to reception considerations.

2. Reade was born in 1814; Trollope was born in 1815. Reade died in 1884; Trollope died in 1882. *It Is Never Too Late To Mend*, Reade's

first widely reviewed novel, was published in 1856; *Barchester Towers*, Trollope's first widely reviewed novel, was published in 1857. Although my principal reason for choosing these two male novelists for this study was the contrast in the way Reade's writing embodied male-gendered stereotypes and Trollope's writing deviated from them, the similarity of the dates seemed to make for a more interestingly parallel historical context. (The two men were in fact fairly close friends for much of their lives, but had a notorious feud after a disagreement over copyright of Trollope's *Ralph the Heir*, which Reade produced as a play while Trollope was holidaying unawares in Australia.)

3. This chapter argues that gender associations contributed to the deterioration of Trollope's critical reputation. Contemporary twentieth-century critics do not address the issue of gender in this respect; they attribute Trollope's loss of literary prestige to changing literary tastes, to the incompatibility of his productivity with the idea of romantic genius, and to the sense that his subject-matter and his treatment of it were not indicative of superior imagination or profundity, but the gendered connotations of these aesthetic criteria are not discussed. See Susan Peck Macdonald's *Anthony Trollope*; Donald Smalley's Introduction in *Anthony Trollope: The Critical Heritage*, and Olmsted and Welch's Introduction in *The Reputation of Trollope: An Annotated Bibliography*, for surveys of the decline of Trollope's reputation. For a general discussion of changes in aesthetic and literary critical ideals from the middle to the late nineteenth century, Stang's *The Theory of the Novel in England* is a helpful source; David Skilton's *Anthony Trollope and his Contemporaries* discusses how Victorian literary critical conventions about imagination, subject-matter, and character depiction affected Trollope's reception and reputation.

4. Trollope's first four novels were as follows: *The Macdermots of Ballycloran* (1847), *The Kellys and the O'Kellys* (1848), *La Vendée* (1850), and *The Warden* (1855).

5. In 1858, Mudie advertised fifty books, but bought most copies of the following four novels: Charles Kingsley's *Two Years Ago* (1200 copies); Charles Reade's *It Is Never Too Late To Mend* (1000 copies); Charlotte Yonge's *Dynevor Terrace* (1000 copies); and 900 copies of Charlotte Yonge's *Heartsease* (Haight, vol. II, p. 467). Compared with such numbers, Mudie's order for 200 copies of *Barchester Towers* may seem paltry, but when we remember that the four books above were Mudie's top orders for a year, and

that *Barchester Towers* was really the first novel of Trollope's that attracted wide critical notice, 200 seems like a respectable number.

6. Such comments are extremely common in reviews of Trollope; a few examples are E. S. Dallas's article in *The Times*, 23 May 1859; the June 1864 article in *North British Review*, and the *Saturday Review* article of 1882. *The Times* calls Trollope's writing style "healthy and manly", and "cordially sympathizes" with his "manly aversion to melodramatic art" (p. 12). The *North British Review* finds that "the whole tone and habit of mind implied in these [Trollope's] novels is that of a man of activity and business, rather than of a man of letters" (p. 370). The *Saturday Review* says that he was "a masculine man and writer" (p. 755).

7. Trollope's disagreements with his publisher over the supposed vulgarity of *Barchester Towers*'s language ("fat stomach" was changed to "deep chest", and "foul breath" was eliminated by Longman's objection) are well known, and are documented with much mischief and wit in the *Autobiography*. In a letter in 1856, Trollope responded thus to Longman's accusations of "indecency" in *Barchester Towers*: "[N]othing would be more painful to me than to be considered an indecent writer. . . . I do not think that I can in utter ignorance have committed a volume of indecencies" (*The Letters of Anthony Trollope*, p. 47). In a letter of 1860 to George Smith Trollope declared ruefully that he would "never forget a terrible and killing correspondence which I had with W. Longman because I would make a clergyman kiss a lady whom he proposed to marry – He, the clergyman I mean; not he W. Longman" (*Letters*, p. 117).

8. In its review of *It Is Never Too Late To Mend*, the *Spectator* praises Reade's "battle between good and evil" in the following way: "It might once have been a question whether a subject of such stern practical importance [discussion of the criminal and prison discipline] involving so much that is saddening and even revolting to the heart and to the taste, and demanding for its treatment any qualities rather than one-sided sentimentality, is well adapted to give that pleasure which readers look for at the hands of the novelist. But . . . nothing but genius and true earnestness . . . are required to move the heart of mankind to fervid sympathy with the real, vulgar, everyday suffering of their brethren, far more strongly and truly than with the sentimental woes and drawingroom distresses which form the staple of so much of our

circulating library fiction" (16 August 1856, p. 877).

9. See Chapter 2 for more details.

10. This passage proceeds to mention male readers, but devotes more primacy and space to their female counterparts.

11. The sustained and ambivalent attention dedicated to Trollope by the *Saturday Review* is one of the more interesting aspects of Trollope's reception history. Trollope identified the *Saturday Review* in his *Autobiography* as one of the three most important British periodicals for contemporary literary criticism; the other two were *The Times* and the *Spectator*. The particular stance, approach, and readership of the *Saturday Review* was described in Chapter 1 as self-consciously representing University-educated men, and in fact the *Saturday Review* often interpreted its position as a call to arms to defend elite literary culture against popular invasions; the gender implications of its profile were also discussed in Chapter 1. As a result, the tone and content of the *Saturday Review*'s literary criticism is often more predictable and constant than that of other Victorian periodicals. The *Saturday Review* found itself in an uncomfortable predicament over Trollope, however: it identified with Trollope as a fellow middle-to-upper-class educated Victorian man, but objected to his heretical lapse into behaviour and characteristics which did not accord with its high-culture position, and which, as I argue, had become feminized. Consequently the many *Saturday Review* articles on Trollope show some sign of emotional intensity and conflict, and sometimes contradict each other, as is evident from the excerpts quoted in this chapter, particularly if Trollope's obituary is compared with the journal's earlier commentary on his work.

12. The second chapter of David Skilton's *Anthony Trollope and His Contemporaries*, "Critical Concerns of the Sixties: Tragedy and Imagination", situates criticism of Trollope's supposed lack of imagination in the context of the 1860s: "The better and more favourable of Trollope's contemporary critics . . . found various ways of accounting for why he fell short of artistic greatness. All their explanations amount in effect to the diagnosis that he lacked 'imagination,' that his subjects were mundane, his treatment of them plain, and that in short he was an 'observer' or 'photographer' rather than an inventive artist" (1962, p. 45).

13. A. L. Rowse's essay "Trollope's *Autobiography*" in *Trollope Centenary Essays* (edited by John Halperin), provides more back-

ground on how Trollope's *Autobiography* affected his reputation.

14. As K. J. Fielding explains in "Trollope and the *Saturday Review*", the *Saturday Review* "liked Trollope because, as they say, he wrote in 'the style of a gentleman'" (p. 431). Fielding goes on to state that "the *Saturday Review* did enjoy Trollope in spite of their apparently hostile criticism, which was sometimes actually hostile" (p. 432). Skilton sees the *Saturday Review* as leaning more towards the critical side of ambivalence, primarily because of Trollope's popularity: "Conscious of their social and intellectual superiority, the university men on the *Saturday* felt a deep scorn for any popular phenomenon, in literature, religion, dress or politics" (p. 53). Skilton summarizes the *Saturday's* attack on the 1866 *The Belton Estates* thus: "Trollope, says the reviewer, is like an artist who year after year submits to the Royal Academy a painting of a donkey between two bundles of hay. He has published no fewer than three novels in the past twelve months, all concerning someone who is hesitating between two loves, and the only difference between them is that the 'expression of the donkey's eye may vary a little' " (p. 56).

Notes to Chapter 5: "The Angel in the Circulating Library"

1. The only periodical to devote a whole article to *The Heir of Redclyffe* in 1853 was the *Christian Remembrancer*; it was enormously impressed and labelled the novel "a book of unmistakable genius and real literary power" (no. 26, 1853, p. 35).

2. Evidently, *The Heir of Redclyffe* was also rapturously received in America. An 1855 article from the *North American Review* refers to the "sensation" that the novel caused, and estimates that the readers consisted of "at least sixteen thousand weepers and wailers; for the man, woman, or child who could read it with dry eyes is yet undiscovered. . . . Not individuals merely, but households . . . plunged into mourning. . . . The soldier, the divine, the seamstress, the lawyer, the grocer-boy, the belle, and the hair-dresser . . . joined in full cry, according to their different modes of lachrymation" (January 1855, p. 445).

3. In 1901, Edith Sichel recounts an anecdote from Francis Palgrave's *Life of Tennyson*: "Palgrave records how one night, in a Devonshire inn, he shared a room with him [Tennyson], and how the poet

lay in his bed with a candle persistently reading a book of Miss Yonge's, which he had already taken out by day 'at every disengaged moment, while rambling over the moor.' 'I see land!' cried Tennyson at last. 'Mr.____ is going to be confirmed' " (Sichel, "Charlotte", p. 89).

4. Guy's favourite hero was Sir Galahad, and an artist, seeing Guy in church, "was very much struck" with Guy's face and asked if he could use him as a model for a sketch of Sir Galahad kneeling to adore the Holy Grail; it is well known that the Pre-Raphaelites, especially Dante Gabriel Rossetti, were intensely drawn to Malory's *Morte D'Arthur* – Houghton calls it "the handbook of the Pre-Raphaelite painters" (*Victorian Poetry*, 1959, p. 569) – and it seems likely that *The Heir of Redclyffe* influenced Pre-Raphaelite attitudes to the Middle Ages in general and Malory in particular.

5. Several books and articles try to analyze the appeal of *The Heir of Redclyffe*. Georgina Battiscombe, in the 1943 work *Charlotte Mary Yonge*, is one of several commentators who argue that *The Heir of Redclyffe* hit a popular nerve because it reconciled romanticism with goodness and everyday Victorian life. The following sources provide more detailed and sustained analyses: Edward H. Cooper, "Charlotte Mary Yonge", *Fortnightly Review* (1901); "Charlotte Mary Yonge", *The Church Quarterly Review* (1904); Hester W. Chapman, "Charlotte Mary Yonge", *New Statesman and Nation* (1943); Margaret Mare and Alicia Percival, *Victorian Best-Seller: The World of Charlotte Yonge* (1948); John Sutherland, "Charlotte Mary Yonge", *The Longman Companion to Victorian Fiction* (1988).

6. The absence of bibliographical material on Charlotte Yonge complicated my search for relevant reviews and articles. A collection of essays dedicated to Yonge that appeared in the 1960s listed only one mid-Victorian critical commentary, an article from 1861, and the usual reference sources that provide information, such as *Poole's Index to Victorian Periodicals* and *Allibone's Guide to English Literature*, provided at best elliptical, incomplete, and scanty references. Even a reference work dedicated to listing nineteenth-century book reviews did not provide any nineteenth-century reviews of *The Heir of Redclyffe*, though it did list reviews for some of her later works. Consequently, a comprehensive manual search through a large number of Victorian periodicals became necessary; the number of reviews and articles considered in this chapter should therefore be an accurate reflection of the body of Victorian criticism on Yonge.

7. Remarks from both Yonge and Charles Kingsley about *Heartsease* suggest some split between popular and critical reaction to the novel. In an 1855 letter, for example, Yonge writes "of the wonderful debut of Violet [*Heartsease*]. I only wonder whether she will thrive as well when the critics have set their claws on her" (quoted in Romanes, 1908, p. 75). And Kingsley, writing to compliment the publisher of *Heartsease*, thought "it the most delightful and wholesome novel I ever read. . . . I don't wonder at the immense sale of the book, though at the same time it speaks much for the public taste that it has been so well received. . . . Never mind what the *Times* or anyone else says" (quoted in Battiscombe, 1943, p. 87).

8. Walter Houghton and Richard Altick both discuss the quasi-religious connotations of ideal femininity in Victorian England. In his discussion of "woman worship" in *The Victorian Frame of Mind*, Houghton describes a mystical image of "Woman" in Kingsley's *Yeast*: "Woman was portrayed walking across a desert, the half-rising sun at her back and a cross in her right hand, 'emblem of self-sacrifice.' In the foreground were scattered groups of men. As they caught sight of this 'new and divine ideal of her sex,' 'the scholar dropt his book, the miser his gold, the savage his weapons . . .' " (1956, p. 350). This drawing is named "Triumph of Woman". Altick, in *Victorian People and Ideas*, discusses "the Victorian conception of the female as a priestess dedicated to preserving the home as a refuge from the abrasive outside world. Convention dictated a rigorously stereotyped personality. . . . The woman of the well-off middle class . . . was . . . The Angel in the House, to borrow the title of Coventry Patmore's hugely popular versified praise of domestic sainthood and the mystical, non-fleshly institution of marriage" (1973, p. 53).

9. Arguably, religious issues coloured *The Heir of Redclyffe*'s critical reception almost as much as gender considerations. Reviewers categorized and judged the novel as a religious work in at least four journals – the *London Quarterly*, the *Dublin Review*, the *Christian Remembrancer*, and the *National Review*. Reviewers in these periodicals judged Charlotte Yonge not primarily according to how she conformed to their expectations about writing and gender, but according to how closely she conformed to their ideas about the relation between religion, ethics, and the writing of novels. The *London Quarterly*, for example, was alarmed that *The Heir of Redclyffe* might awake a "spurious" religious feeling which

could be better channelled elsewhere, and protested against the "diversion of our sympathy to imaginary woes, when the stern ills of life darken around us on every side" (July 1858, p. 495). The *London Quarterly* also protested against what it perceives as the novel's Catholic tendencies: "The words are from the formularies of the Church of England; but the tendency of the teaching is that of the Church of Rome" (p. 500). The *Dublin Review*, on the other hand, is offended by Yonge's supposed "enmity against the Catholic religion . . . . [Yonge] uses the weapon of insinuation rather than direct attack. . . . Alas! She injures her own mind far more than she injures the Church of Christ" (December 1858, p. 320).

10. Contemporary Victorian critics such as W. R. Greg, G. H. Lewes, and E. S. Dallas all protested about the tendency of women novelists to write too much and too fast.

11. No reviewer seems conscious of the irony of this reaction.

12. Charlotte Yonge's own self-effacing persona as an author, humble, demure, religiously rather than commercially motivated, perhaps added to the gendered reputation of her works, although probably not until more became known about the author after the initial success of *The Heir of Redclyffe*. Yonge's father made it clear to Charlotte that he would approve of her work only if she wrote didactic novels and gave the profits to charity, thus preceding but foreshadowing the kinds of expectations many reviewers brought to their analyses of works by women authors. As Showalter explains, "[B]y doing good and taking no pay she was safely confined in a female and subordinate role within the family, and remained dependent upon her father" (1977, p. 57). Consequently, part of the profits of *The Heir of Redclyffe* were given to Bishop Selwyn of New Zealand for his missionary work, who declared "I suppose I am joint heir with the Heir of Redclyffe" (Battiscombe, 1943, p. 91). Yonge was extremely dependent on her father and John Keble for editing and approving her work, and her novels and subsequent anti-feminist treatise *Womankind* clearly reveal her ideas about women's mental and moral inferiority. A 1934 *Cornhill Magazine* article by S. Bailey states, for example, that "Miss Yonge . . . was no feminist . . . and in one of her novels she says that 'a woman's turn of thought is commonly moulded by the masculine intellect, which, under one form or another, becomes the master of her soul'" ("Charlotte", p. 189).

13. The anonymous 1904 *Church Quarterly Review* describes a

critical 1866 *Saturday Review* article about Yonge, but does not provide detailed bibliographical information.

14. The two novels published by Virago, *The Daisy Chain* and *The Clever Woman of the Family*, highlight Yonge's views about appropriate gender roles more markedly even than *The Heir of Redclyffe*; one can perhaps surmise that these two books were therefore chosen as literary curiosities – the title of the latter might appear appealing to contemporary readers, but the actual book seeks to demonstrate that being a "clever woman" leads to anarchy and death.

Works Cited and Consulted

PRIMARY SOURCES

Brontë, Charlotte, "Biographical Notice of Ellis and Acton Bell" (1850), in Brontë, *Wuthering Heights*, pp. 3–8.
——, "Editor's Preface to the New Edition of *Wuthering Heights*" (1850), in Brontë, *Wuthering Heights*, pp. 9–12.
Brontë, Emily, *Wuthering Heights* (1847), ed. William M. Sale, 2nd edn (New York: Norton, 1972).
Reade, Charles, *It Is Never Too Late To Mend* (1856; Boston, Mass.: the Grolier Society, 1943).
——, *Readiana: Comments on Current Events* (London: Chatto and Windus, 1883).
Trollope, Anthony, *Autobiography* (1883; Gloucester: Alan Sutton, 1987).
——, *Barchester Towers* (1857), ed. Michael Sadleir and Frederick Page (Oxford: Oxford University Press, 1989).
——, *The Letters of Anthony Trollope*, 2 vols, ed. N. John Hall (Stanford, Cal.: Stanford University Press, 1983).
——, *The Warden*, ed. N. John Hall (Oxford: Oxford University Press, 1989).
Yonge, Charlotte, *Heartsease* (London: John W. Parker, 1854).
——, *The Heir of Redclyffe* (1853; London: Macmillan, 1914).

PRIMARY BIBLIOGRAPHY FOR CHAPTER 2 (CHARLES READE)

Anonymous reviews and articles are listed alphabetically by title of periodical:

Rev. of *It Is Never Too Late To Mend* by Charles Reade, *Athenaeum*, 1502 (9 August 1856), pp. 990–1.
"Charles Reade's *It Is Never Too Late To Mend*", *Bentley's Miscellany*, 40 (September 1856), pp. 292–6.
"Charles Reade's Novels", *Blackwood's Edinburgh Magazine*, LXIX (October 1869), pp. 488–514 (American edn).
"Charles Reade's Opinion of Himself and his Opinion of George Eliot", *Bookman*, XVIII (November 1903) pp. 252–60.

"Mr. Coleman's Charles Reade", *Bookman*, October 1903, pp. 155–7.

Rev. of *It Is Never Too Late To Mend* by Charles Reade, *Critic*, 15 August 1856, pp. 395–6.

"Charles Reade", *Dublin University Magazine*, 91 (June 1878), pp. 673–9.

Rev. of *It Is Never Too Late To Mend* by Charles Reade, *Examiner*, (23 August 1856), pp. 533–4.

Rev. of *It Is Never Too Late To Mend* by Charles Reade, *Literary Gazette*, 23 August 1856, pp. 607–8.

"Charles Reade", *London Review*, 30 November 1861.

"Mr. Charles Reade's Novels: *The Cloister and the Hearth*", *National Review*, 14, XXVII (January 1862), pp. 134–49.

"Charles Reade", *Once a Week*, 26 (20 Januaury 1872), pp. 80–7.

"Charles Reade", *Punch*, 19 April 1884, 181.

"*It Is Never Too Late To Mend*", *Reader*, 14 October 1865, p. 438.

Rev. of *It Is Never Too Late To Mend* by Charles Reade, *Saturday Review*, II (16 August 1856), pp. 360–1.

"Reade's *It Is Never Too Late To Mend*", *Spectator*, XXIX (16 August 1856), pp. 877–8.

"The Works of Charles Reade", *Spectator*, 55, 2 (15 July 1882), p. 928.

Reviews and articles arranged alphabetically by author:

Besant, Walter, "Charles Reade", *Gentleman's Magazine*, 29 August 1882), pp. 198–214.

Eliot, George, "Three Novels", rev. of *It Is Never Too Late To Mend* by Charles Reade, *Westminster Review*, CXXX (October 1856), pp. 311–19 (American edn); LXVI, pp. 571–8 (English edn).

Hornung, E. W., "Charles Reade", *London Mercury*, IV, 19, pp. 150–63.

Lewes, G. H., "Charles Reade's New Novel", rev. of *It Is Never Too Late To Mend* by Charles Reade, *Leader*, 7 (23 August 1856), pp. 809–10.

Lord, W. F. "Reade's Novels", *Nineteenth Century*, LIV (August 1903), pp. 275–284.

Orwell, George, "Charles Reade", in his *The Collected Essays, Journals and Letters of George Orwell: My Country Right or Left, 1940–1943*, vol. II, ed. Sonia Orwell and Ian Angus (London: Secker and Warburg, 1968), pp. 34–7.

Ouida (M. L. Ramée), "Charles Reade", *Gentleman's Magazine*, 29 (August 1882), pp. 494–7.

Stephen, Fitzjames, "The License of Modern Novelists", *Edinburgh Review*, CVI, 215 (July 1857), pp. 64–81.

Swinburne, A. C., "Charles Reade", *Nineteenth Century*, XVI, 92 (October 1884), pp. 550–67.

PRIMARY BIBLIOGRAPHY FOR CHAPTER 3

Anonymous reviews and articles, alphabetically by title of periodical:

Rev. of *Wuthering Heights*, *Athenaeum*, 25 December 1847, pp. 1324–5.

Rev. of *Wuthering Heights*, *Athenaeum*, 28 December 1850, pp. 1368–9.

Rev. of *Wuthering Heights*, *Britannia*, 9 (15 January 1848), pp. 42–3.

"Patrick Branwell Brontë and *Wuthering Heights*", *Brontë Society Transactions* , 7 (1927), pp. 97–102.

Rev. of *Wuthering Heights*, *Douglas Jerrold's Weekly Newspaper*, 15 January 1848, p. 77.

Rev. of *Wuthering Heights*, *The Economist*, 29 January 1848, p. 126.

Rev. of *Wuthering Heights*, *The Economist*, 9 (1851), p. 15.

Rev. of *Wuthering Heights*, *Eclectic Review*, 5th series, February 1851, pp. 222–7.

"The Three Sisters", *English Woman's Journal*, IV (Febuary 1860), pp. 338–50, 413–22.

Rev. of *Wuthering Heights*, *Examiner*, 8 January 1848, pp. 21–2.

Rev. of *Wuthering Heights*, *Examiner*, 21 December 1850, p. 815.

"Notice of *Wuthering Heights*", *Godey's Lady Book*, 37 (July 1848), p. 57.

"Who Wrote *Wuthering Heights*?", *Halifax Guardian*, 15 June 1867, pp. 98–102.

"Notice of *Wuthering Heights*", *John Bull*, 1 January 1848, p. 12.

Rev. of *Wuthering Heights*, *Literary Register*, 15 (Febuary 1848), pp. 138–40.

Rev. of *Wuthering Heights*, *Literary World*, 3, 65 (29 April 1848), p. 243.

Rev. of *Wuthering Heights*, *The New Monthly Magazine*, 82 (January 1848): 140.

Rev. of *Wuthering Heights*, *North British Review*, XI (August 1849), pp. 475–93.

Rev. of *Wuthering Heights*, *Peterson's Magazine*, 13 (June 1848), p. 229.

"Authoresses", *Saturday Review*, November 11, 1865, pp. 601–3.

"A Review of *Wuthering Heights*", in Charles Simpson, *Emily Brontë* (London: Country Life, 1929).

"Notice of *Wuthering Heights*", *Spectator*, 18 December 1847, 1217.
"Books of the Month", *Union Magazine of Literature and Art*, 2 (June 1848), p. 287.

Reviews and articles arranged alphabetically by author:

Chorley, H. F., "Review of *Wuthering Heights* and *Agnes Grey*", *Athenaeum*, 25 December 1847, pp. 324–5.
Dobell, Sydney, "A Review of Work by Currer Bell, including *Wuthering Heights*", *Palladium*, September 1850, pp. 161–75; rpt. in *Brontë Society Transactions*, 5 (1918), pp. 210–38.
Lewes, G. H. "The Lady Novelists", *Westminster Review*, n.s., II (1852), pp. 129–41.
——, "Review of *Wuthering Heights*", *Leader*, December 1850, 953.
Rigby, Elizabeth, "A Review of *Jane Eyre* with Comments on *Wuthering Heights*", *Quarterly Review*, 84 (1848), pp. 153–85.
Smith, George Barnet, "The Brontës", *Cornhill Magazine*, 28 (July 1873), pp. 54–71.
Vaisey, the Honorable Mr Justice, "*Wuthering Heights*: A Note on its Authorship", *Brontë Society Transactions*, 11 (1946), pp. 14–15.
Williams, Alexander Malcolm, "Emily Brontë", *Temple Bar*, 98 (July 1893), p. 431.

PRIMARY BIBLIOGRAPHY FOR CHAPTER 4

Anonymous reviews and articles, alphabetically by title of periodical:

Rev. of *Barchester Towers*, *Athenaeum*, 1544 (30 May 1857), pp. 689–90.
Rev. of *Barchester Towers*, *Eclectic Review*, July 1857, pp. 54–9.
Rev. of *Barchester Towers*, *Examiner*, 16 May 1857, p. 308.
"Mr. Anthony Trollope's Novel", *Fortnightly Review*, 5, 26 (1 February 1869), pp. 188–98.
Rev. of *Barchester Towers*, *Leader*, 23 May 1857, 497.
[G. H. Lewes] "Charles Reade's New Novel", *Leader*, 7 (23 August 1856), 809–10.
"About Novels", *Literary World*, 15 (23 August 1884), p. 275.
"Anthony Trollope", *Nation*, 18 (12 March 1874), pp. 174–5.
"Mr. Trollope's Novels", *National Review*, 7 (October 1858), pp. 416–35.

"Mr. Trollope's Novels", *North British Review*, 40 (June 1864), pp. 369–401.

"Anthony Trollope on Female Character", *Pall Mall Gazette*, 6 (27 July 1867), p. 373.

Rev. of *Barchester Towers*, *Saturday Review*, 3, (30 May 1857), pp. 503–4.

Rev. of *The Bertrams*, *Saturday Review*, 7 (26 March 1859), pp. 368–9.

"Framley Parsonage", *Saturday Review*, 9 (4 May 1861), pp. 451–2.

"Mr. Trollope on Novels", *Saturday Review*, 36 (22 November 1873), pp. 656–7.

"Mr. Anthony Trollope", *Saturday Review*, 54 (9 December 1882), pp. 755–756.

Rev. of *Barchester Towers*, *Spectator*, 30 (16 May 1857), pp. 525–6.

"Reade's *It Is Never Too Late To Mend*", *Spectator*, 29 (16 August 1856), pp. 877–8.

"A Novelist of the Day", *Time: A Monthly Magazine*, 1 (1879), pp. 626–632.

[E. S. Dallas] "Mr. Anthony Trollope", *The Times*, 23 May 1859, p. 12.

"New Novels", *The Times* ,13 August 1857, p. 5.

"Contemporary Literature: Belles Lettres", *Westminster Review*, 68 (October 1857), pp. 326–7.

[G. H. Lewes] "The Lady Novelists", *Westminster Review*, n.s., II (1852), pp. 129–141.

PRIMARY BIBLIOGRAPHY FOR CHAPTER 5

Reviews and articles from the 1850s and 1860s, alphabetically by title of periodical or work:

"Modern Novelists – Great and Small", Margaret Oliphant, *Blackwood's Magazine*, 77 (May 1855), pp. 554–62.

"Miss Yonge's Novels", *Christian Remembrancer*, 26 (1853), pp. 33–63.

"Miss Sewell and Miss Yonge", *Dublin Review*, XLV (December 1858), pp. 313–29.

"*Heartsease; or, The Brother's Wife*", *Fraser's Magazine*, 50 (November 1854), pp. 489–503.

"Memoranda about our Lady Novelists", *Gentleman's Magazine*, November 1854, pp. 442–4.

"The Lady Novelists of Great Britain", *Gentleman's Magazine*, 1 (July 1853), pp. 18–24.

"Novels by the Author of *The Heir of Redclyffe*", *London Quarterly and Holborn Review*, July 1858, pp. 484–513.

"Ethical and Dogmatic Fiction: Miss Yonge", *National Review*, 23 (January 1861), pp. 211–29.

Rev. of *The Heir of Redclyffe* and *Heartsease*, *North American Review*, CLXVI (January 1855), pp. 439–59.

"Religious Novels", *North British Review*, XXVI, 51 (November 1856), pp. 112–22.

"The Author of *Heartsease* and Modern Schools of Fiction", *Prospective Review; A Quarterly Journal of Theology and Literature*, X (1854), pp. 460–82.

Rev. of *The Clever Woman of The Family*, *Reader*, 27 May 1865, p. 296.

"*Heartsease*", *Spectator*, 4 November 1854, pp. 1157–8.

"*The Heir of Redclyffe*", *The Times*, 5 January 1854, p. 9.

Twentieth–century articles about Charlotte Yonge, listed by author, or title of periodical when anonymous:

Anon.,"Charlotte Mary Yonge", *Church Quarterly Review*, CXIV, (January 1904), pp. 337–60.

Bailey, Sarah, "Charlotte Mary Yonge", *Cornhill Magazine*, August 1934, pp. 188–98.

Chapman, Hester, "Books in General", *New Statesman and Nation*, 21 August 1943, p. 123.

Cooper, Edward H., "Charlotte Mary Yonge", *Fortnightly Review*, LXIX n.s. (January–June 1901) pp. 852–8.

Dunlap, Barbara J., "Charlotte Mary Yonge", *Dictionary of Literary Biography*, vol. 18, pp. 308–25.

H.P.E., "Twenty Years After", *Punch*, 31 January 1945, p. 105.

Escott, T. H. S., "The Young Idea, 'Twixt Square and Thwackum", *Fortnightly Review*, XCII, n.s. (July–December 1912), pp. 675–89.

Leavis, Q. D., "Charlotte Yonge and 'Christian Discrimination' ", *Scrutiny*, XII, 2 (Spring 1944), pp. 152–60.

Sichel, Edith, "Charlotte Yonge as a Chronicler", *Monthly Review* (May 1901), pp. 88–97.

SECONDARY SOURCES

Adams, Hazard and Leroy Searle (eds), *Critical Theory since 1965* (Tallahassee: University Presses of Florida, 1986).

Allot, Miriam, *The Brontës: The Critical Heritage* (London: Routledge and Kegan Paul, 1974).

Althusser. L., *Lenin and Philosophy, and Other Essays* (London: New Left Books, 1971).

Altick, Richard, *The English Common Reader: A Social History of the Mass Reading Public 1800–1900* (Chicago: University of Chicago Press, 1957).

_____, *Victorian People and Ideas* (New York: Norton, 1973).

_____, *Writers, Readers and Occasions* (Columbus: Ohio State University Press, 1989).

ApRoberts, Ruth, *The Moral Trollope* (Athens, Ohio: Ohio University Press, 1971).

Archer, William, *English Dramatists of Today* (London: Sampson Low, 1882).

Armstrong, Nancy, *Desire and Domestic Fiction: A Political History of the Novel* (New York: Oxford University Press, 1987).

_____, "*Emily Brontë In and Out of her Time*", *Genre*, 15 (1982), pp. 243–64.

_____, "The Rise of Feminine Authority in the Novel," *Novel: A Forum on Fiction*, 15 (1982), pp. 127–45.

Ashton, Rosemary (ed.), *George Eliot: Selected Critical Writings* (Oxford: Oxford University Press, 1992).

Avery, Gillian, *Nineteenth-Century Children* (London: Hodder & Stoughton, 1965).

Baldridge, Cates, "Voyeuristic Rebellion: Lockwood's Dream and the Reader of *Wuthering Heights*", *Studies in the Novel*, 20 (1988), pp. 274–87.

Bankcroft, Marie, *The Bancrofts: Recollections of Sixty Years* (London: Benjamin Blom, 1909).

Battersby, Christine, *Gender and Genius: Towards a Feminist Aesthetics* (Bloomington: Indiana University Press, 1989).

Battiscombe, Georgina, et al., *A Chaplet for Charlotte Yonge* (London: Cresset Press, 1965).

_____, *Charlotte Mary Yonge* (London: Constable, 1943).

Baym, Nina, "Melodramas of Beset Manhood: How Theories of American Fiction Exclude Women Authors", *American Quarterly*, 33 (1981), pp. 123–39.

_____, *Novels, Readers, and Reviewers: Responses to Fiction in Antebellum*

America (Ithaca: Cornell University Press, 1984).

——, *Women's Fiction: A Guide to Novels by and about Women in America 1820–1870* (Ithaca: Cornell University Press, 1978).

Beetham, Margaret, "Open and Closed: The Periodicals as Publishing Genre", *Victorian Periodicals Review*, XXII, 3 (Fall 1989), pp. 96–100.

Begley, Adam, "Small Wonder", *Mirabella*, 58 (March 1994), p. 66.

Bennett, Tony, *Formation and Marxism* (London: Methuen, 1979).

Bevington, Merle Mowbray, *The Saturday Review 1855–1868: Representative Educated Opinion in Victorian England* (New York: Columbia University Press, 1941).

Blake, Andrew, *Reading Victorian Fiction. The Cultural Context and Ideological Content of the Nineteenth-Century Novel* (London: Macmillan, 1989).

Bleich, David, "Gender Interests in Reading and Language", in E. Flynn and P. Schweickart (eds), *Gender and Reading: Essays on Readers, Texts, and Contexts* (Baltimore: Johns Hopkins University Press, 1986), pp. 234–66.

——, *Subjective Criticism* (Baltimore: Johns Hopkins University Press, 1978).

——, "The Determination of Literary Value", *Literature and Psychology*, 17 (1967), pp. 19–30.

Brake, Laurel and Anne Humphreys, "Critical Theory and Periodical Research", *Victorian Periodicals Review*, XXII, 3 (Fall 1989), pp. 94–5.

Brick, Allan R. ,"Lewes's Review of *Wuthering Heights*", *Nineteenth-Century Fiction*, 14 (1960), pp. 355–9.

Brophy, Brigid, Michael Levey, and Charles Osborne. *"The Warden"*, in *Fifty Years of English and American Literature We Could Do Without* (London: Stein and Day, 1968).

Brownell, David, "The Two Worlds of Charlotte Yonge", in *The Worlds of Victorian Fiction*, ed. Jerome H. Buckley (Cambridge, Mass.: Harvard University Press, 1975).

Burns, Wayne, *Charles Reade: A Study in Victorian Authorship* (New York: Bookman Associates, 1961).

Burstyn, Joan N., *Victorian Education and the Ideal of Womanhood* (London: Croom Helm, 1980).

Butler, Judith, *Gender Trouble: Feminism and the Subversion of Identity* (New York: Routledge, 1989).

Byatt, A. S. and Nicholas Warren (eds), *Selected Essays, Poems and Other Writings* (London: Penguin, 1990).

Byers, David Milner, "An Annotated Bibliography of the Criticism on Emily Brontë's *Wuthering Heights*, 1847–1947", diss., University of Minnesota, 1973).

Cadogan, Mary, " 'Sweet, If Somewhat Tomboyish:' The British Response to Louisa May Alcott", *Critical Essays on Louisa May Alcott*, ed. Madeleine B. Stern (Boston: G. K. Hall, 1984), pp. 275–8.

Casey, Ellen Miller, "Weekly Reviews of Fiction: The *Athenaeum* vs. the *Spectator* and the *Saturday Review*", *Victorian Periodicals Review*, XXIII, 1 (Spring 1990), pp. 8–12.

Cecil, David, *Early Victorian Novelists* (London: Constable, 1934).

Chitham, Edward, *A Life of Emily Brontë* (Oxford: Blackwell, 1987).

Coleman, John, *Charles Reade as I Knew Him* (London: Anthony Treherne, 1904).

Coleridge, Christabel, *Charlotte Mary Yonge* (London: Macmillan, 1903).

Coleridge, Sara, *Memoirs and Letters of Sara Coleridge*, edited by her daughter (New York: Harper, 1874).

Collins, Philip, "Business and Bosoms: Some Trollopian Concerns" *Nineteenth-Century Fiction*, 37, 3 (December 1982), pp. 293–315.

Collister, Peter, "After 'Half a Century': Mrs Humphrey Ward on Charlotte and Emily Brontë", *English Studies: A Journal of English Language and Literature*, 66 (1985), pp. 410–31.

Courtney, William Leonard. "Charles Reade's Novels", in *Studies Old and New* (London: Chapman and Hall, 1889), pp. 150–71.

Craig, Edith and Christopher St John (eds), *Ellen Terry's Memoirs* (New York: G. P. Putnam's Sons, 1932).

Crawford, Mary and Roger Chaffin, "The Reader's Construction of Meaning: Cognitive Research on Gender and Comprehension", in E. Flynn and P. Schweickart (eds), *Gender and Reading: Essays on Readers, Texts and Contexts* (Baltimore: Johns Hopkins University Press, 1986), pp. 234–66.

Crump, R. W., *Charlotte and Emily Brontë: A Reference Guide* (Boston: G. K. Hall, 1982).

Cruse, Amy, *The Victorians and their Books* (London: George Allen & Unwin, 1935).

Culler, Jonathan, *On Deconstruction: Theory and Criticism after Structuralism* (Ithaca: Cornell University Press, 1982).

David, Deirdre, *Intellectual Women and Victorian Patriarchy* (London: Macmillan, 1987).

Dawson, Carl, *Victorian Noon: English Literature in 1850* (Baltimore: Johns Hopkins University Press, 1979).

Don Vann, J. and Rosemary T. Van Arsdel (eds), *Victorian Periodicals.*

A Guide to Research (New York: Modern Language Association of America, 1978).

Ellegard, Allvar, *The Readership of the Periodical Press in Mid-Victorian Britain* (Goteborg: Acta Universitatis Goteburgensis, 1957).

Ellmann, Richard, *Oscar Wilde* (New York: Alfred A. Knopf, 1988).

Elwin, Malcolm, *Charles Reade* (London: Jonathan Cape, 1931).

Escott, T. H. S., *Anthony Trollope: His Public Services, Private Friends, and Literary Originals* (London: John Lane, Bodley Head, 1884).

Escott, T. H. S., *Anthony Trollope* (London: John Lane, Bodley Head, 1913).

Everett, Edwin Mallard, *The Party of Humanity: The Fortnightly Review and its Contributors, 1865–1874* (Chapel Hill: University of North Carolina Press, 1939).

Ewbank, Inga-Stina, *Their Proper Sphere: A Study of the Brontë Sisters as Early Victorian Female Novelists* (London: Edward Arnold, 1966).

Fahnestock, Jeanne Rosenmayer, "Geraldine Jewsbury: The Power of the Publisher's Reader", *Nineteenth-Century Fiction*, 28, 3 (December 1973), pp. 253–72.

Fielding, K. J., "Trollope and the *Saturday Review*", *Nineteenth-Century Fiction*, 37, 3 (December 1982), pp. 430–42.

Fish, Stanley, "Literature in the Reader", in J. Tompkins (ed.), *Reader-Response Criticism: From Formalism to Post-Structuralism* (Baltimore: John Hopkins University Press, 1980), pp. 70–133.

Flynn, Elizabeth A., "Gender and Reading" in E. Flynn and P. Schweickart (eds), *Gender and Reading: Essays on Readers, Texts, and Contexts* (Baltimore: Johns Hopkins University Press, 1986), pp. 267–88.

Flynn, Elizabeth A. and Patrocinio P. Schweickart (eds), *Gender and Reading: Essays on Readers, Texts, and Contexts* (Baltimore, Maryland: The Johns Hopkins University Press, 1986).

Frank, Katherine, *A Chainless Soul: A Life of Emily Brontë* (Boston: Houghton Mifflin, 1990).

Fryckstedt, Monica Correa, "Geraldine Jewsbury's *Athenaeum* Reviews: A Mirror of Mid–Victorian Attitudes to Fiction", *Victorian Periodicals Review*, xxiii, 1 (Spring 1990), pp. 13–24.

Fuss, Diana, *Essentially Speaking: Feminism, Nature and Difference* (New York: Routledge, 1989).

Gaskell, Elizabeth, *The Letters of Mrs Gaskell*, ed. J. A. V. Chapple and Arthur Pollard (Manchester: Manchester University Press, 1966).

——, Gaskell, Elizabeth, *The Life of Charlotte Brontë* (London: Smith & Elder, 1892).

Gérin, Winifred, *Emily Brontë* (Oxford: Oxford University Press, 1971).

Gettmann, Royal, *A Victorian Publisher: A Study of the Bentley Papers* (Cambridge: Cambridge University Press, 1965).

Graham, Walter, *English Literary Periodicals* (New York: Thomas Nelson, 1930).

Gregor, Ian (ed.), *Reading the Victorian Novel: Detail into Form* (New York: Barnes & Noble, 1980).

Griest, Guinevere, *Mudie's Circulating Library and the Victorian Novel* (Bloomington: Indiana University Press, 1970).

Haight, Gordon, *George Eliot* (New York and Oxford: Oxford University Press, 1968).

—— (ed.), *The George Eliot Letters*, vol. II (New Haven: Yale University Press, 1954).

—— (ed.), *The George Eliot Letters*, vol. IV (New Haven: Yale University Press, 1955).

—— (ed.), *The George Eliot Letters*, vol. IX (New Haven: Yale University Press, 1978).

Haldane, Charlotte, Preface, *The Heir of Redclyffe*, by Charlotte Yonge (1853; London: Gerald Duckworth, 1964).

Hall, John N., *The Trollope Critics* (Totowa, NJ: Barnes & Noble, 1981).

Halperin, John (ed.), *Trollope Centenary Essays* (New York: St Martin's Press, 1983).

Harrison, Frederic, "Anthony Trollope's Place in Literature", in *Studies in Early Victorian Literature* (London: Edward Arnold, 1895).

Hawthorne, Nathaniel, *The English Note-Books*, ed. Randall Stewart (New York, 1941).

Helling, Rafael, *A Century of Trollope Criticism* (1956; Port Washington, NY: Kennikat Press, 1967).

Helsinger, Elizabeth K., Robin Lauterbach Sheets, and William Veeder (eds), *The Woman Question: Society and Literature in Britain and America, 1837–1883*, vol. 1: *Defining Voices*; vol. 2: *Social Issues*; vol. 3: *Literary Issues* (Chicago: University of Chicago Press, 1983).

Herrnstein Smith, Barbara, "Contingencies of Value" in *Canons*, ed. Robert von Hallberg (Chicago: University of Chicago Press, 1983). pp. 5–40.

Hewish, John, *Emily Brontë* (London: Macmillan, 1969).

Holland, Norman, "Unity, Identity, Text, Self", in *Reader–Response Criticism*, ed. Jane Tompkins (Baltimore and London: Johns Hopkins University Press, 1980), pp. 118–33.

Hollingshead, John, *Gaiety Chronicles* (London: Archibald Constable, 1898).

Honan, Park, "Trollope after a Century", *Contemporary Review*, December 1982, pp. 318–23.

Houghton, Walter E., "Periodical Literature and the Articulate Classes", in J. Shattock and M. Wolff (eds), *The Victorian Periodical Press: Samplings and Soundings* (Leicester University Press, 1982), pp. 3–28.

———, *The Victorian Frame of Mind* (New Haven: Yale University Press, 1957).

Houghton, Walter E. and G. Robert Stange (eds), *Victorian Poetry and Poetics* (1959; Boston: Houghton Mifflin, 1968).

Howells, W. D., *My Literary Passions: Criticism and Fiction* (New York and London: Harper and Brothers, 1895).

Hutton, Richard Holt, "Anthony Trollope's *Autobiography*", *Spectator*, 56, 2887 (27 October 1883), pp. 1377–9.

Irwin, Mary Leslie, *Anthony Trollope: A Bibliography* (New York: H. W. Wilson, 1926).

Iser, Wolfgang, *The Act of Reading: A Theory of Aesthetic Response* (Baltimore: Johns Hopkins University Press, 1978).

———, "Interaction between Text and Reader", in *The Reader in the Text*, ed. Susan Suleiman and Inge Crossman (Princeton, NJ: Princeton University Press, 1980), pp. 106–119.

Jacobs, Naomi, "Gender and Layered Narrative in *Wuthering Heights* and *The Tenant of Wildfell Hall*", *Journal of Narrative Technique*, 16 (1986), pp. 204–19.

James, Henry, "Anthony Trollope", in *Partial Portraits* (London: Macmillan, 1886), pp. 97–133.

James, Louis, "'The Trouble with Betsy': Periodicals and the Common Reader in Mid-Nineteenth-Century England", in J. Shattock and M. Wolff (eds), *The Victorian Periodical Press: Samplings and Soundings* (Leicester: Leicester University Press, 1982), pp. 349–66.

Jardine, Alice and Paul Smith (eds), *Men in Feminism* (New York and London: Methuen, 1987).

Jauss, Hans Robert, "Literary History", in H. Adams and L. Searle (eds), *Critical Theory Since 1965* (Tallahassee: Univeristy Presses of Florida, 1986), pp. 163–183.

———, *Toward an Aesthetic of Reception* (Minneapolis: University of Minnesota Press, 1982).

Jeaffreson, J. Cordy, "Miss Yonge", *Novels and Novelists from Elizabeth to Victoria* (London: Hurst and Blackett, 1858), pp. 406–7.

Kellett, E. E. , "The Press.", in G. M. Young, *Early Victorian England: 1830–1865* (London: Oxford University Press, 1934), vol. 2, pp. 1–98.

Kendrick, Walter M., T*he Novel-Machine: The Theory and Fiction of Anthony Trollope* (Baltimore: Johns Hopkins University Press, 1980).

Lauter, Paul, *Canons and Contexts* (Oxford, New York: Oxford University Press, 1991).

Law, Alice, *Patrick Branwell Brontë* (London: A. M. Philpot, 1923; New York: Richard West, 1974).

Leavis, Q. D., *Fiction and the Reading Public* (London: Chatto and Windus, 1965).

Leenhardt, Jacques, "Toward a Sociology of Reading", in S. Suleiman and I. Crosman (eds), *The Reader in the Text* (Princeton, NJ: Princeton University Press, 1980), pp. 205–23.

Lovett, Robert Morss, *The History of the Novel in England* (Boston: Houghton Mifflin, 1932).

Lyons, Anne K., *Anthony Trollope: An Annotated Bibliography of Periodical Works By and About Him in the United States and Great Britain to 1900* (Greenwood, Fla: Penkevill, 1985).

Macdonald, Susan Peck, *Anthony Trollope* (Boston: Twayne, 1987).

Macovski, Michael S., "*Wuthering Heights* and the Rhetoric of Interpretation", *English Literary History*, 54 (1987), pp. 363–84.

Madden, Lionel and Diana Dixon, *The Nineteenth-Century Periodical Press in Britain: A Bibliography of Modern Studies, 1901–1971* (Toronto: Victorian Periodicals Newsletter, 1975).

Marchand, Leslie A., *The Athenaeum: A Mirror of Victorian Culture* (Chapel Hill: University of North Carolina Press, 1941).

Mare, Margaret and Alicia C. Percival, *Victorian Best-Seller: The World of Charlotte Yonge* (London: George G. Harrap, 1948).

Maugham, Somerset, *Great Novelists and their Novels* (Philadelphia: John C. Winston, 1948).

McCarthy, Justin, *Reminiscences* (New York and London: Harper and Brothers, 1900).

McMaster, Juliet, "Anthony Trollope", in Ira Nadel and William Fredeman (eds), *Dictionary of Literary Biography*, vol. 21: *Victorian Novelists before 1885* (Detroit, Michigan: Gale Research Company, 1983).

Miles, Peter, *Wuthering Heights* (London: Macmillan, 1990).

Mitchell, Sally, "Sentiment and Suffering: Women's Recreational Reading in the 1860s" *Victorian Studies*, 21, 1 (Autumn 1977), pp. 29–45.

Moberly, C. A. E., *Dulce Domum* (London: John Murray, 1911).

Modleski, Tania, "Feminism and the Power of Interpretation: Some Critical Readings", in Teresa De Lauretis (ed), *Feminist*

Studies/Critical Studies (Bloomington: Indiana University Press, 1986), pp. 121–38.

Monk, Wendy (ed)., *The Journals of Caroline Fox, 1835–71* (London: Elek, 1972).

More, Paul Elmer, "My Debt to Trollope", in *The Demon of the Absolute* (Princeton: Princeton University Press, 1928).

Nadel, Ira Bruce (ed.), *Victorian Fiction: A Collection of Essays from the Period* (New York: Barnes & Noble, 1980).

Nadel, Ira and William E. Fredeman (eds), *Dictionary of Literary Biography*, vol. 21: *Victorian Novelists before 1885* (Detroit, Mich: Gale Research Company, 1983).

Nardin, Jane, "Conservative Comedy and the Women of *Barchester Towers*", *Studies in the Novel*, XVIII, 4 (Winter 1986), pp. 381–94.

———, *He Knew She Was Right: The Independent Woman in the Novels of Anthony Trollope* (Carbondale: University of Illinois Press, 1989).

Nineteenth-Century Literature Criticism, 6: "Anthony Trollope", pp. 450–520.

North, John, "The Rationale: Why Read Victorian Periodicals", in *Victorian Periodicals: A Guide to Research*, ed. J. Don Vann and Rosemary T. VanArsdel (New York: Modern Language Association, 1978).

Ohmann, Carol, "*Emily Brontë in the Hands of Male Critics*", *College English*, 32 (1971) pp. 906–13.

Oliphant, Margaret, *The Victorian Age of English Literature* (Philadelphia: David Mckay, 1892).

——— et al., *Women Novelists of Queen Victoria's Reign: An Appreciation* (London: Hurst & Blackett, 1897).

Oliphant, Margaret and Mrs Porter, *Annals of a Publishing House* (Edinburgh and London: William Blackwood, 1888).

Olmsted, John Charles and Jeffrey Egan Welch, *The Reputation of Trollope: An Annotated Bibliography, 1925–1975* (New York: Garland, 1978).

Orwell, George, "Charles Reade", *The Collected Essays, Journals and Letters of George Orwell: My Country Right or Left, 1940–1943*, vol. II, ed. Sonia Orwell and Ian Angus (London: Secker and Warburg, 1968), pp. 34–7.

Palmegiano, E. M., *Women and British Periodicals 1832–1867: A Bibliography* (New York: Garland Publishing, 1976).

Parrish, Morris L. (ed.), "On English Prose Fiction as a Rational Amusement", in *Four Lectures*, by Anthony Trollope (Constable, 1938; rpt. Norwood Editions, 1977), pp. 94–124.

Passel, Anne, *Charlotte and Emily Brontë: An Annotated Bibliography* (New York: Garland Publishing, 1979).

Payn, James, *Some Literary Recollections* (New York: Harper & Brothers, 1884).

Poovey, Mary, *Uneven Developments: The Ideological Work of Gender in Mid-Victorian England* (Chicago: University of Chicago Press, 1988).

Poulet, Georges, "Criticism and the Experience of Interiority", in J. Tompkins (ed.), *Reader–Response Criticism: From Formalism to Post-Structuralism* (Baltimore: John Hopkins University Press, 1980), pp. 41–9.

Prentis, Barbara, *The Brontë Sisters and George Eliot* (London: Macmillan, 1988).

Pykett, Lyn, *Emily Brontë* (London: Macmillan, 1989).

Radway, Janice A., *Reading the Romance: Women, Patriarchy, and Popular Literature* (Chapel Hill: University of North Carolina Press, 1984).

Read, Sir Herbert, "Charlotte and Emily Brontë", *Yale Review*, 1903, rpt. in *Reason and Romanticism* (1926).

Reade, Charles and Reverend Compton Reade, *Charles Reade* (New York: Harper and Brothers, 1887).

Ritchie, Anne Thackeray, *Chapters from some Unwritten Memoirs* (New York: Harper, 1895).

Rives, Leone, *Charles Reade. Sa vie, ses romans* (Toulouse: Lion, 1940).

Robertson Scott, J. W., *The Story of the Pall Mall Gazette* (London: Oxford University Press, 1950).

Robinson, A. Mary F., *Emily Brontë* (Boston: Roberts, 1883).

Romanes, Ethel, *Charlotte Mary Yonge* (London: A. W. Mowbray, 1908).

Rowbotham, Judith, *Good Girls make Good Wives: Guidance for Girls in Victorian Fiction* (Oxford: Basil Blackwell, 1989).

Sadleir, Michael, *Trollope: A Commentary* (Farrar, Strauss, and Giroux, 1927, rpt. New York, 1947).

Sala, George Augustus, *Things I Have Seen and People I Have Known* (London: Cassell, 1894).

Sanger, C. P., *The Structure of Wuthering Heights* (London: Leonard and Virginia Woolf, 1926).

Scheuerle, William H., "Biographical Resources", in J. Don Vann and R. VanArsdel (eds), *Victorian Periodicals: A Guide to Research* (New York: Modern Language Association, 1978), pp. 64–80.

Schweickart, Patrocinio, "Reading Ourselves: Toward a Feminist Theory of Reading", in E. Flynn and P. Schweickart, *Gender and Reading: Essays on Readers, Texts and Contexts* (Baltimore: Johns Hopkins University Press, 1986), pp. 31–62.

Scholes, Robert, "Reading Like a Man", in Alice Jardine and Paul Smith (eds), *Men in Feminism* (New York and London: 1987), pp. 204–18.

Shattock, Joanne and Michael Wolff (eds), *The Victorian Periodical Press: Samplings and Soundings* (Leicester: Leicester University Press, 1982).

Showalter, Elaine, *A Literature of their Own: British Women Novelists from Brontë to Lessing* (Princeton, NJ: Princeton University Press, 1977).

—— (ed.), *Speaking of Gender* (New York: Routledge, 1989).

Simpson, Charles, *Emily Brontë* (London: Country Life, 1929).

Skilton, A., *Anthony Trollope and his Contemporaries: A Study in the Theory and Conventions of mid-Victorian Fiction* (London: Longman, 1972).

Smalley, Donald, *Trollope: The Critical Heritage* (London: Routledge & Kegan Paul, 1969).

Smith, Elton E., *Charles Reade* (Boston: Twayne, 1976).

Spark, Muriel and Derek Stanford, *Emily Brontë* (London: Owen, 1953).

Stang, Richard, *The Theory of the Novel in England, 1850–1870* (New York: Columbia University Press, 1959).

Steig, Michael, *Stories of Reading. Subjectivity and Literary Understanding* (Baltimore: Johns Hopkins University Press, 1989).

Stephen, Leslie, "Anthony Trollope", in *Studies of a Biographer*, vol. IV (London: G. P. Putnam, 1907), pp. 156–60.

Stevenson, Lionel, *Victorian Fiction: A Guide to Research* (Cambridge, Mass.: Harvard University Press, 1964).

Suleiman, Susan and Inge Crosman, *The Reader in the Text* (Princeton, NJ: Princeton University Press, 1980).

Super, R. H., *The Chronicler of Barsetshire: A Life of Anthony Trollope* (Ann Arbor: University of Michigan Press, 1988).

Sutherland, John, "Publishing History: A Hole at the Centre of Literary Sociology", in *Literature and Social Practice*, ed. Philippe Desan, Priscilla Parkhurst Ferguson and Wendy Griswold (Chicago: University of Chicago Press, 1989), pp. 267–82.

——, "Charlotte Mary Yonge", *The Longman Companion to Victorian Fiction* (London: Longman, 1988).

——, *Victorian Novelists and Publishers* (Chicago: University of Chicago Press, 1976).

Tayler, Irene, *Holy Ghosts: The Male Muses of Emily Brontë* (New York: Columbia University Press, 1990).

Thrall, Miriam M. H., *Rebellious Fraser's: Nol Yorke's Magazine in the Days of Maginn, Thackeray, and Carlyle* (New York: Columbia University Press, 1934).

Tillotson, Geoffrey and Kathleen Tillotson, *Mid-Victorian Studies* (London: Athlone Press, 1965).

Tillotson, K., "*The Heir of Redclyffe*", in Geoffrey and Kathleen Tillotson, *Mid-Victorian Studies* (London: Athlone Press, 1965), pp. 49–55.

——, *Novels of the Eighteen-Forties* (Oxford: Clarendon Press, 1954).

Tompkins, Jane (ed.), *Reader-Response Criticism: From Formalism to Post-Structuralism* (Baltimore: Johns Hopkins University Press, 1980).

——, *Sensational Designs: The Cultural Work of American Fiction 1790–1860* (Oxford: Oxford University Press, 1985).

Tuchman, Gaye and Nina E. Fortin, *Edging Women Out: Victorian Novelists, Publishers, and Social Change* (New Haven: Yale University Press, 1989).

——, "When the Prevalent Don't Prevail: Male Hegemony and the Victorian Novel", in *Conflict and Consensus: A Festschrift in Honor of Lewis A. Coser*, ed. Walter W. Powell and Richard Robbins (New York: Free Press, 1984), pp. 139–60.

Warhol, Robyn R., *Gendered Interventions: Narrative Discourse in The Victorian Novel* (New Jersey: Rutgers University Press, 1989).

Watson, Melvin R., "Wuthering Heights and the Critics", *Trollopian* (1949), pp. 243–63.

Watt, Ian (ed.), *The Victorian Novel: Modern Essays in Criticism* (London: Oxford University Press, 1971).

Weir, Edith M., "Contemporary Reviews of the First Brontë Novels", *Brontë Society Transactions* (1947).

Weldon, Fay, *Growing Rich* (London: Harper Collins, 1992.)

White, Cynthia L., *Women's Magazines 1693–1968* (London: Michael Joseph, 1979).

Willis, Irene Cooper, *The Authorship of Wuthering Heights* (London: Hogarth Press, 1936).

Wilson, Romer, *All Alone: The Life and Private History of Emily Jane Brontë* (London: Chatto & Windus, 1928).

Winnifrith, T. J., *The Brontës and their Background: Romance and Reality* (London: Macmillan, 1973).

Wolff, Robert Lee, *Gains and Losses: Novels of Faith and Doubt in Victorian England* (London: Garland Publishing, 1977).

Women in Publishing, *Reviewing the Reviews: A Woman's Place on the Book Page* (London: Journeyman, 1987).

Woolf, Virginia, *A Room of One's Own* (1929; San Diego, New York and London: Harcourt Brace Jovanovich, 1989).

Woolford, John, "Periodicals and the Practice of Literary Criticism, 1855–64", in J. Shattock and M. Wolff (eds), *The Victorian Periodical Press: Samplings and Soundings* (Leicester: Leicester University Press, 1982), pp. 109–44.

Yaeger, Patricia, "Violence in the Sitting Room: *Wuthering Heights* and the Woman's Novel", *Genre*, 21 (1988), pp. 203–29.

Yates, Gayle Graham (ed.), *Harriet Martineau on Women* (New Brunswick, NJ: Rutgers University Press, 1985).

Young, G. M. (ed.) *Early Victorian England: 1830–1865*, 2 vols (London: Oxford University Press, 1934).

Index